FAR AWAY, I LAND

Far Away, I Land

....life's intertwining
journeys have come
full circle

a novel by

Viki Ales-Crouch

PORTLAND • OREGON
INKWATERPRESS.COM

Scan to find more information about this book.

Publisher: Inkwater Press | www.inkwaterpress.com

Paperback   ISBN-13 978-1-62901-025-0 | ISBN-10 1-62901-025-1
Hardback   ISBN-13 978-1-62901-026-7 | ISBN-10 1-62901-026-X
Kindle   ISBN-13 978-1-62901-027-4 | ISBN-10 1-62901-027-8
ePub   ISBN-13 978-1-62901-028-1 | ISBN-10 1-62901-028-6

Printed in the U.S.A.
All paper is acid free and meets all ANSI standards for archival quality paper.

3 5 7 9 10 8 6 4

If love equates to sacrifice, then I have been its lamb
For I know not how to breathe without its grasp around my heart ...
                                          Viki Alles-Crouch

The greatest joy in life is to be able to give your heart away to those you love and adore.

This book is my heart and I give it freely to

MY DEAREST MOTHER, whose character and strength will always be my inspiration ... I have been blessed to be your daughter.

MY FATHER, whose memory remains a silent beacon in my life.

MY HUSBAND, who is all that is rare in this world; you are an enigma, whose unyielding tenacity, magnanimous personality, and deep rooted faith changed my world forever. You taught me to see and experience the luscious taste of mango and the bitter taste of gourd and treat both with the same reverence.

AND FINALLY, MY TWO CHILDREN, my greatest source of joy and laughter. Should these words be my legacy, I want you to always remember how loved you both are and for you to never forget your beginnings; hold fast to the end, hand in hand ... as loyalty and family will always remain the most important things in life.

CONTENTS

Chapter 1: The Dresser...1

Chapter 2: Nameless...11

Chapter 3: Circle of Life 21

Chapter 4: The Implications of War............................31

Chapter 5: Edes Csillagom..37

Chapter 6: The Difference 45

Chapter 7: Ceasefire 53

Chapter 8: A Timely Exchange 61

Chapter 9: The Shackles of Circumstance.................. 69

Chapter 10: Aftershock... 85

Chapter 11: Five Rupee Rogue 107

Chapter 12: The Butterfly Effect...............................121

Chapter 13: London Fog... 137

Chapter 14: All Aboard 153

Chapter 15: On the Other Side of the Mountain 173

Chapter 16: As Fate Would Have It 195

Chapter 17: Maverick...219

Chapter 18: St. Anthony 237

Chapter 19: Freedom 259

Chapter 20: Pede Claudo 281

Chapter 21: The Key 287

Chapter 22: Mum's the Word 295

Chapter 23: Myopia 303

Chapter 24: Brownian Motion 317

Chapter 25: Yesterday's Tomorrow 327

Chapter 26: Our Destiny Awaits 335

Chapter 27: Faraway Island 347

FAR AWAY, I LAND

CHAPTER ONE
THE DRESSER

We must tie a knot to the foundation of our
life, so whenever comfort need be, we can
return without ever getting lost.

I T WAS A COZY SUMMER'S NIGHT, AND THE COOL NIGHT AIR caressed her whole body like it was baby oil against the skin, filling her soul with peaceful thoughts of home-baked bread and loving arms that comfort. It was in this state of bliss that her eyes grew heavy, swinging open and shut in rhythm with the creaking gate, while the drum of crickets and the sweet smell of fresh cut grass rocked her to sleep.

In a sea of down-filled blankets, her mind ventured into a dream world that was filled with cascading flower gardens, frolicking puppies, and round-bottomed ground hogs wiggling along the grass, guiding her to the secret forts tucked deep within her vivid imagination. Her dreams served only to mimic and embellish a world that she was already familiar with, as she was incapable of seeing the bad in anything or anyone.

༺☉༻

HER ANGELIC DEMEANOR WAS apparent from the time she was born, which made both her parents fiercely protective of her. They often would sit in the parlor listening to classical music, reminiscent of their lives in Europe. This ultimately conducted the mood in the house, with either passionate crescendos that made one's heart burst with joy or diminuendos that sent the heart into sadness, depending on the stanza.

On one such night, Robert gazed adoringly at his little baby girl swaddled in a blanket in a crib near his chair. As the music resonated in the background, something curious caught his eye. He neared his head in order to get a closer look, only to realize that his baby was quietly sobbing. *How could this be? She's only a baby!* he thought. The music's tempo became lively and the child's whole face then blossomed into an adorable smile, and she kicked her tiny feet in keeping with the beat.

"This is incredible!" Robert exclaimed, making known his discovery to his wife. He gently picked the baby up and rocked her in his arms, a sight Elizabeth never tired of.

"What is it, Robert?" Elizabeth smiled, gently patting her baby's brow.

"Watch her expression; she's being swayed by the music!" he said.

They put her back into the crib and quietly observed as "Wotan's Farewell," from Richard Wagner's *Die Walküre* played on. The cry of the violins reached a heart wrenching pitch and soon the baby began to sob once more.

"Turn off that damn music!" Robert exclaimed, not wanting to ever expose his baby princess to anything that would upset her.

Elizabeth quietly conceded, knowing all too well that her daughter had inherited the emotional heart of her Hungarian ancestry. *She will have to be strong*, Elizabeth thought to herself, quietly praying that her daughter's emotions would become her strength rather than her weakness.

This rather pleasant arrangement of evening cocktails and relaxing to the sound of music had become a very nice and civilized routine, Elizabeth had thought. It was something her father had done in the old country. With the czardas playing somewhere in the village, he would sit on the woodpile at the side of the house, singing whilst enjoying his evening glass of Palinka. **"Egészségedre!"** he would toast to his little Erzsike. Elizabeth smiled at the memory, knowing that it was in complete contrast to the luxury she was now accustomed, still able to derive pride from it nonetheless. Life was good, her children were well taken care of, there was always lots of food on the table; she was contented being the homemaker of her family.

The walls in this seemingly strong foundation began to crack when memories began to surface; memories too painful to describe and infra dig if one ever uttered the mention of a problem. The erosion began when Elizabeth began hiding the problems society was too quick to judge, and Robert's life went from sweet to sour depending on the day, the pressure or the mood. There was nothing any of them could do, not even his precious little princess could help in the end.

BEYA WAS A HAPPY child, appeased by the small pleasures in life, like making mud pies in the back yard and using the buds off the cedar hedge as her spices. Her mother fully understood her little girl, eternally giving into her childish ways by supplying her with old pots, aprons, wooden spoons, and a small table. A fresh pot of tea and cinnamon toast would be part of Beya's daily routine throughout summer, up to the first snow fall, for her to serve to her friends, who ranged from birds to squirrels and to the occasional rabbit.

The willow tree was her best friend. It stood in the center of the backyard, swaying melodically in the wind and tickling her as she played in the garden. She imagined it coming to life with tentacles that could both amuse and protect her. Her greatest pleasure was sleeping on a lawn chair under the willow, falling asleep dreaming about the millions of magical fairies that lived within the tree, who would only sneak out when the night sky appeared. She imagined the fairies watering her mother's garden and sprinkling magic dust all over it, which explained why every morning there was always a thick layer of dew surrounding the garden and every flower seemed to be smiling. It also explained why the neighbor's gardens never looked quite as good, as they didn't have a willow tree, and therefore, could never know the honor of such a friend as this.

Every morning when the family gathered at the breakfast table, her mother would make huge portions of bacon and eggs, pancakes, and oatmeal, as if they were all lumberjacks and would have to eat enough to get them through to dinner. This, however, was not the case, but Elizabeth believed food was love, so portions were always huge. Beya, therefore, learnt from a very young age the importance of cooking a good meal, as it was a chance for the whole family to sit together, laugh, and enjoy the food and the company.

She used to watch her father closely as he meticulously laid his sunny-side up egg on a slice of toast, cut a small wedge of fried tomato with a rasher of bacon, and layered it piece by piece on top of the egg. He told her this made each morsel he put in his mouth a harmoniously balanced taste of savory. He would then sip on his glass of freshly squeezed orange juice and read the morning paper.

"Would you like some, dear?" he would lovingly ask his daughter, who seemed to be mesmerized by this routine.

"No, Daddy, you go ahead." Whereupon she would smile and help in the kitchen to supply her two brothers, who seemed too caught up in their own world, with food.

"Daddy, you should see my fort behind the hedge. I even have a stray cat as a tenant! So I've piled some old tires and filled them with cozy blankets. He likes it!" Beya said one morning, smiling sweetly.

"What did you name the cat, Beya?" asked her father, an ardent animal lover.

"Boots! Cause that's where I found him; in the garage in your old pair of boots!"

"Those were my boots, by the way!" Rudi exclaimed, angrily.

"So, what harm could a cat do?" shouted his mother from the kitchen.

"Cat shit!" said Rudi. At which point young Alan began to giggle and Beya began tickling him.

"Hey, none of that language!" said Robert with a twinkle in his eye.

"Sorry, Dad, have to go!" said Rudi, anxious to get to his friends.

"Look, it's snowing!" exclaimed young Alan, excited to go out.

"Oh, Boots, he'll need more protection now! Quick, Alan, find that old umbrella; we've got some work to do!" said Beya.

The two little ones were quick to put on their winter jackets and run out to the backyard, which was speckled with white. Robert watched from the kitchen window as Beya gathered old sheets from the shed and motherly directed her little brother to help her gently wrap each bush, as if they were human. "What sweet children," Robert said adoringly. "I hope they will have happy lives; they deserve nothing but the best."

"Yes, Robert, Beya, Alan, Rudi, we all do; I hope you remember that tonight," she uttered and sadly left the room, leaving Robert to stand pensive and guilt ridden.

WITH A WISTFUL SMILE on her face, Beya had slept peacefully until the sound of voices resonated through the ventilation of the house, arousing her curiosity. As she gazed up at the ceiling, trying to distinguish between sleep and distraction, the distinctive smell of peonies filtered through her bedroom window, filling her senses and luring her back to sleep; until her half-conscious state realized she, in fact, heard someone crying. She gazed through the ivy-covered sill upon the balcony, through the railing that overlooked the front lawn. The moonlight created a silhouette around the single evergreen, which looked like a sleeping giant in the night. It was a sight that made her feel protected as a very small child, as she would picture it coming to life with personified ferocity; ready, willing, and able to defend their castle, no matter the cost. She still felt that protection as she grew up and always felt her home was her castle.

She wandered downstairs, her bare feet sinking into the lush pile of the carpet with every step. Although the sound was crying, Beya was not particularly worried, as her mother was known for staying up until all hours of the night, ironing while watching emotional old movies or baking her tart apple pies, perhaps thinking about old times or past love.

Many times Beya would quietly creep down to the family room just to curl up on the couch next to her on the premise of having an earache or not being able to sleep. Just the sound of her mother's voice meant love, as it permeated her speech, her smile, and her touch, filling Beya with the absolute certainty that she was very much loved and adored. This time the sound was coming from the garage. *Bang, bang, bang...*

"Who could possibly be working in the garage at this hour?" she wondered. It wouldn't be surprising if her mother were hosing down the garage after gardening late into to the night, but at two in the morning?

As she neared the door, the muffled noise became clear.

An all too familiar occurrence, coupled with her mother's will to carry on, filled the girl with anguish. *What had he done now?* she thought.

"Mother, Mother, what's wrong? What are you doing?"

"Oh hello darling, did I *vake* you?" she said, trying to hide her tears.

"No, Mamma, I couldn't sleep," she said.

"*Vell,* let's go in and I'll make us some tea."

"What are you doing, Mamma?"

"I'm painting furniture. You *veren't* supposed to see this until tomorrow; it's your birthday present. ... Hey, it's already past midnight, HAPPY BIRTHDAY, MY DARLING LITTLE GIRL!"

She gazed into her mother's eyes and was filled with an overwhelming love, one that stemmed from genuine adoration and empathy, for she resented her father for all that he could have been to them but was not.

Notwithstanding the fact that it was her birthday, like all birthdays and special occasions before, this one was no different; her father had come home drunk, leaving her mother in a state of utter vulnerability and disillusionment.

God, what sadness he would evoke. ... Not that they were soul mates or that they were well suited, but he was her husband and with it came expectation, Beya thought.

"What has he done, Mamma?" the young girl said, trying to suppress her own disappointment.

"Oh, vell," she said in her strong Zsa Zsa Gabor accent, "I just vanted your room to be complete with a beautiful princess svuite of furniture, but of course, just the mention of spending money sent him to the bottle. I managed to collect enough from his valet! I found this shop vhich sold unfinished replicas. All I had to do vas paint it vhite and then I got this gold paint for the trim. ..."

"Oh, Mamma," she said, no longer able to hold back the tears, "I love you."

"Do you like it?" her mother asked.

"Oh, Mamma, I love it and will cherish it for the rest of my life. ..."

NO TRUER WORDS WERE *ever spoken*, she thought as she gazed at the old white dresser placed perfectly in an alcove in the bathroom of their new mountain retreat. If it could only speak, what a story it would tell; so many homes, so many beginnings, and so many endings. This, however, would be, no doubt, its final landing place and perhaps hers.

CHAPTER TWO

NAMELESS

"...Who has seen the wind? Neither you
nor I. But when the trees bows down their
heads, the wind is passing by."

-"Who Has Seen the Wind" by Christina
Georgina Rossetti

Nothing ever goes unnoticed.

THE BABY SPRANG TO LIFE WITH THE USUAL COAXING SPANK on the bottom by the village midwife. The hut filled with cries from both mother and child, with the father proudly exclaiming *"Heri-lassanai-Aney!"*

He was the youngest of six, five of whom were girls. So much expectation lay on his youthful shoulders to become a breadwinner from the time he could walk. Already the girls were being taught to gather vegetables, cook, and collect water from the stream and sticks from the forest floor. It was the boy, however, who had to chase cars, offering freshly picked avocados, flowers, and rampe, or offering to wash the cars, anything to earn a few rupees.

They were Buddhists, like their forefathers going back to their three-thousand-year-old ancestry, in both belief and lifestyle.

Foreigners passed through the villages with their flashy, brightly colored automobiles, and soon the boy learnt what to expect from people. He realized that not all people gave readily; some with strange accents and cameras would give rupees and not take the fruit that he offered, and others who spoke Sinhalese took more than they gave.

The ones who were very *sudu* wanted him to say *"pleeze"* and *"tank ... U,"* which seemed to make them smile and always resulted in a rupee or two. ...

As the hot sun would begin to set at dusk, the village boys would gather on the dirt roads and begin to play cricket. This was the greatest love of their lives, a chance to let their spirits soar. The cricket bats were usually second or third hand, donated by local teams to the villages, or in some cases, the boys would patiently carve out their own bats. Owning a ball was a great luxury, as they were either found with the greatest of luck, otherwise, they used coconuts to hit.

After many hours the boy would wonder into his hut where *Ama* had made a tasty curry out of jackfruit, plucked from the same tree that caused him to scrape his knee earlier that day when he climbed the tall tree to use as a look out for oncoming traffic.

He sat on the mud floor, holding the banana leaf plate, and began to eat his evening meal of rice, curry, and seeni sambol with his hands. He was hungry and this was the first real meal he had had all day.

His *Ama* used to say, "Hunger is good because it makes you appreciate your food and not waste,"... but she knew why there was only one meal a day. She wistfully looked on, as there was nothing she could do to change this situation; this was their life. Maybe in the next life, life would be more kind.

Spiritually, the son knew by the look in his *Ama's* eyes that it was the look of longing. *Someday, someday, Ama will have her own well and a garden in the back with all the vegetables and fruit we need to never go hungry,* thought the boy with naive optimism.

Really, he was not *that* hungry. Foreigners always gave enough so that he could buy his sisters treats from the village kade, or they handed him their leftovers through the car windows.

It always struck him how wasteful *they* were. Sometimes their leftovers could fill his stomach and that of his siblings. Nonetheless, he was thankful for their wastefulness and for his good fortune.

"Palayan de," the clerk shouted, but this time the boy had rupees to flash before his eyes, and as if mesmerized by greed, the clerk said, *"Ender, ender Putha."* This time it would be pleasant. He quickly chose small packets of milk toffee for his sisters, and when the clerk was not looking, he popped one into his mouth.

"Bohoma esthutaie," the boy said, with the toffee safely tucked under his tongue, quickly leaving the premises.

He was now considered a man. His sisters were given in marriage to some locals with their dowry of a bull each. One had taken her life when, after she gave herself to her husband, he vanished. The shame was too great, as rumors quickly spread that he had reunited with an old love and could not be apart from her. She, feeling disgraced and humiliated, in her ignorance, drank a bottle of poison to end her sorrow.

Life was simple, but it was not easy, and as for fair, the young man knew all too well that it was not fair. His *Ama* was ill with diabetes, his father drunk with illicit *Kaseepu* every night, and all the boy could do was live life instinctively, like a leopard in the wild, *survival of the fittest.*

It was an unusually busy day in the village, as there was talk that some local businessmen were investing in the area, setting up a clothing manufacturing facility. He knew he would have to be there volunteering, begging, anything to get an opportunity for a stable income.

After countless days he managed to charm his way into a job by working without pay until they noticed him on the construction site.

After hot milky tea and a piece of bread, he would start off his day at 5:30 a.m., digging the earth. One day he counted 250 buckets by 10:00 a.m.; after that, he lost count, or maybe he just didn't know the numbers past that point.

His bronze skin caramelized under the midday sun, and he would grow nauseous as his stomach churned with hunger. How he longed for a sip of water, but no one seemed to notice. He feared that if he dared leave the site, he would lose his job, so there he remained for 12 hours, sometimes 14, until the whistle was blown for the next shift of workers.

When he came home, his staple diet of rice and dhal would be handed to him. The nausea would leave and sleep would overwhelm him like a gas mask on a patient in an operating theatre.

The factory's foundation had been laid and needed to set for the next month. Hopefully, the monsoon would not come early that year. The lorry backed into the lot and unloaded the container. Curiosity led him to climb up the side of the container and try to peer inside. To no avail; whatever was inside would remain a mystery.

THERE WAS A PARTY atmosphere amongst the workers, as that afternoon, Sri Lanka and Australia were playing in the Cricket Semi-final. The boy had never seen them play. He could only imagine. For years he had heard stories of the great Muttiah Muralitharan, how he could spin the ball and deceive the batsman. There were posters of this cricket hero pasted all around his village.

Once he came across an old t-shirt with his faded picture on it. He wore it like a trophy, and when Amma could not repair it anymore, he cut the picture of his hero from the shirt and pinned it on the clay wall of his hut, above his mat, at night and carried it with him in his pocket by day.

The driver of the truck noticed that after unloading the

container, the screws of the hitch became loose. Without hesitation, he sprang to his feet to see if he could repair it. No tools were available. The driver had to be in Colombo by afternoon to reload, and everyone was getting ready for the much anticipated match.

Without thinking, the boy volunteered to ride in the back of the trailer. He would physically hold the screws in place. This would be his chance, a first in his lifetime. He would travel out of the village by truck to the big city of Colombo! Maybe, if Lord Buddha was on his side, he could somehow see the match, just a glimpse. He would try to climb the walls of the stadium or find a tall tree, anything just to be close to the one thing that brought him joy in his short lifetime.

The road to Colombo was bumpy and the fumes from the diesel engine revolted him. The dizziness dulled his mind as thoughts of cricket gave him the strength to endure. The screws were increasingly hot and his fingers grew red and burnt. He needed to use his Muralitharan shirt to ease the pain.

Tall buildings appeared and then huge signs, street lights, people, Victoria Park. The wheels screeched to a halt.

He lay on the ground holding the tattered shirt in his hand. His eyes were wide open, as if dreaming of the match, but strikingly motionless.

He would remain forever … *nameless*.

☙❦❧

BEYA PULLED UP TO the lights, programmed to stop whenever red appeared. The traffic was denser than usual, but that day was the big match; perhaps that was why the police were everywhere.

A lorry remained in a half-turn by the corner. She wondered why he did not move ahead. After all, they usually were so reckless that whenever they had a chance, they etched there way forward no matter how little the space was.

A foreign man gingerly walked across the street, towards the back of the truck. A look of horror crossed his face as his hands clasped over his mouth. Her eyes followed his as his head looked down, and there on the ground was a young man, clenching something in his hand. His face was like a deflated mask, staring off towards the stadium.

"Oh my God!" Her body began to tremble, almost electrocuted by shock; her tears began to flow. The traffic police signaled them to move forward, and her foot touched the pedal as if it had ears. For her mind, her thoughts, and her sight were glued to the scene, unable to register what she had just witnessed.

Her children stood outside the international school waiting for their mother to pick them up. Pale and shattered, she muttered in panicked murmurs what she had just seen. She opened the car door and vomited over and over. With each descriptive sentence came the gruesome reality of what she had just witnessed.

Why didn't anyone else react the way she did? Were they all immune to this? Was it the boy's bad Karma? Were they thinking it was his fate? Why did only the foreign man react like her?

The boy was a son of somebody, but no one seemed to care. He would remain nameless to most, but for her, he would be remembered forever, haunting her and beckoning the question, what if?

ↀↀ

THE CROWDS CHEERED AND danced as Sri Lanka won convincingly by 112 runs. Beya looked at the big screen and all she could see was his face.

Life was not fair.

CHAPTER THREE

CIRCLE OF LIFE

To live your life fully meant a willingness to change.

LATELY, SHE FOUND HERSELF FEELING RATHER DAZED, WALKING around in a dream world. Was she just going through the motions on this foreign isle? How did she end up there, and if there was such a thing as fate, what would be her role?

Back home, if someone died on the street like that, it would have been front-page news. His body would be covered, police would clear the scene, and anyone who was directly involved would be taken to the hospital. It was the least one would do in a civilized society. But this was a civilized society. Civilized long before any other country in the world, and yet there remained an enormous gulf between them.

When she first came there, she used to feel so violated. The staring and the difficulty communicating drove her insane. It toughened her, made her a different person, a stronger woman. ... She had truly changed.

Slowly she began to accept the differences as cultural and taught those lessons to her children to aid in their transition. The longer she stayed, the easier it became to identify with the people. After all, her husband was of this land and his blood ran through their children's veins, and in time, it too would run through hers. She resigned herself to this fate. This was their heritage, and they had been blessed with the opportunity to experience all of it, the good and the bad.

In her reminiscent thoughts, she would go back in time. What a journey it had been; exhilarating, exciting, traumatic, happy, and sad; a roller coaster ride, of sorts.

The friends she had back home, the culture she came from, may not have tolerated all that she had witnessed in this place, and yet, thousands of miles from home and decades later, she remained quite content in a marriage that began too quickly and withstood tests, especially that of time.

They say people are a product of their environment. If so, maybe her childhood had to do with why she could tolerate the ups and downs of her current life, and why her husband's childhood made him all of who he was.

Her first thoughts went to her father, who in life taught her how *not* to end up, and in death taught her that life was full circle. All that she had witnessed in her childhood was not his whole life, and therefore, only a small part of who he actually was. It was perhaps all the good he did in his life that made way for his most loving departure from this world in the end, surrounded by the family who stood by him through thick and thin. The circle was now complete.

HE WAS BORN ROBERT Edmund Cross, six pounds, five ounces, in a private hospital in London, England on September 18, 1922. He was the son of Brigadier General Rupert Bland Cross and Olive Houchin of Hampton.

He was an adorable little one who loved his mother dearly and feared his father dearly. He had a younger sister, Pauline, who was vastly different from him, both in looks and character.

Young Robert grew up under the strict supervision and iron fist of his father, Rupert. His mother, a figurehead of the Victorian era, sat finely dressed and powdered, never raising her voice above a peep and never laying a hand on her son, affectionately or otherwise.

Her hands occupied the piano, and at most times during the day, it was this that she played with, not the cherubic cheeks of her children, who seemed oblivious to this and just looked on. It was not that they were equally unaffectionate, but rather that they were expected to be. Many times young Robert sat gazing in adoration at his mother, admiring her genteel ways and sweet round smile. He loved the wind and would sit by the window hoping it would stir so he could breathe in the lovely smell of rose perfume from his mother's hair. She was, in Robert's eyes, an English Rose, to be admired from afar and never handled. He was happy to have one such as this for a mother and amiably sat on the periphery, pretending to occupy himself.

Many admired her, as she often played by special request for the London Philharmonic Orchestra. On those occasions the house took on a certain grandeur, as she would enter the drawing room in her finest evening gown, made of ivory lace and mother of pearl, with her hair gently twisted under an ancestral diamond tiara, and she would be escorted by a dashing young Rupert, who would be clad in a formal stiff tux and tails, moustache waxed, and an arrogant glint in his eye. Once again, a feather-light peck would be the most allotted per child upon her exit, and even this would have a stern overshadow from their father.

Some say the opportunities presented to her were due to her Uncle Houchin, Lord Mayor of London, playing favors for his much loved Olive, but all the same, she was a talent, understated though she was.

The limelight for Olive was short-lived, as the demands on Rupert increased over time, due to the war, and soon they were transferred to Canada, a proud member of the Commonwealth of England, *"Long Live the King."*

The transition was difficult. Few knew the couple, and their upper-crust traditions, spawned from England, simply were not present in Canada. Their evenings out together became less and less, and Rupert's evenings at the Mess became more and more. There were occasional celebrations like Victoria Day and Canada Day, which were, to Olive, reminiscent of the life that once was. But the change was drastic, so drastic change had to be made, at least in attitude.

Olive traded her life in the limelight and high society for a quiet life in London, Ontario, taking up crocheting over concertos, baking over Beethoven, and listening to the strums on the radio over Mozart. Olive didn't seem to mind; in fact, she didn't seem to react to anything, good or bad, and remained indifferent in everything she did or said. She was a true diplomat, and as the years went on, young Robert would learn to resent her ability to sit on the fence for most anything.

The move to Canada came at a time when the children were just four and six, so her hands would be full, or at least the nanny's would be, while Rupert moved on to the post of Brigadier General of the Canadian Armed Forces.

Although young Robert crossed the Atlantic at four, it would not be his last crossing, as the demands of war would beckon his presence overseas when war reared its ugly head once again.

Until then, Robert grew up in that sleepy little town in one of the few Tudor-style mansions that sat imposingly at the corner of Lawrence and Queen Street. Its grand height stood out for all to see and had almost as much presence as the brigadier had on the neighborhood. He and Olive led a seemingly exemplary life, a pillar of the Protestant Church, where Olive could put her talents to use playing for the local choir. All who attended would tip their hats at the Cross family with the utmost sincerity, or perhaps fear, and quietly take their seats. The family would walk from church to the house, as it was just one block away, and in that stretch would be approached by the local butcher, the pastor, and, on one particular occasion, the school master.

The school master was, himself, from England and was a tall, lanky fellow who carried himself with shear arrogance. In fact, his body was composed of more arrogance than brawn, which seemed to exaggerate his mouth whenever he spoke, for that was all he was talented at, talking loudly and gossiping. The brigadier, upon meeting Mr. Winch, spoke to him as if he was an officer and expected a full report on his children. With little or no expectation, both men did a quick rundown on Pauline's school report, as if seemingly unimportant, and then Mr. Winch hastily made way for his report on young Robert.

"Unfortunately, Brigadier, sir, your son Robert's behavior is most wanting, for when he does show up to school, he is, more often than not, late, coming unprepared for class, without having done his homework. ... Then he begins to rabble-rouse amongst his peers. It is most disturbing to me as the headmaster and to the rest of the class," said Mr. Winch in an all-too-satisfied manner.

"I see, thank you for your most thorough report, Winch. ... That will be all," commanded the brigadier.

Upon arrival at the house, all gathered around the dining table awaiting the serving of the Sunday lamb. Mashed potatoes, creamed peas, and mint sauce were carefully presented, and the roast was placed before the brigadier. There was always tension at the table. At least young Robert felt the tension, for his mother was expressionless and his sister followed suit. His father radiated control over all in the room, and all awaited his initial gestures to begin before any would dare. The room took on an unusual silence, for the brigadier was most somber that day, and once again, no one dared initiate conversation for fear it would be the wrong subject matter.

As he carved the roast, plates were carefully passed around the table, no one moving too anxiously or too slowly. There was even a certain speed at which to do things. All who sat there were scrutinized to the point where young Robert felt he was wearing a strait jacket most of the time. How he longed to tell his father of his friend Joey's discovery, of the fishing hole nearby, or that the latest Model T was being unveiled in London, but to no avail. He could only daydream about life outside this shell and that someday he would be free from this suffocating surrounding. It was in a state of daydream that young Robert felt the hard shaft of the barrel of a gun press against his skull; this bolted him back into reality, along with the loud shouting from his father.

"You were told to eat everything you are given on your plate and not to play with your food. Eat it now or you'll eat this bullet!" commanded the brigadier. Young Robert, too shocked for words or lamb, proceeded to do as his father said, fearful of the consequences lest he did not obey.

He glanced at his mother and sister after the meal, searching for some ounce of concern, but all he could see was fear in his mother's eyes and his sister cowering. He knew from that moment on that they would need him as a safe harbor forever.

Life became a vicious circle of oppression and rebellion. Finally, young Robert, who was by then a young man, turned to stealing cars as a form of mischief, but really, if truth was known, it was done to disgrace his father, who had been immortalized by King George the VI with the Order of the British Empire. Soon, museums and libraries were named after him and there was no escaping the command and control of the brigadier.

Overseas, the winds of change unfolded. World War II began, and like all great leaders, the brigadier's son was used to exemplify all that was right and good in the name of the king. Robert, left with little choice, was put on a ship and sent to war; he was just 18.

He kissed his mother on the cheek for more than the allotted time, feeling a deepened sense of sadness for her coupled with an excited enthusiasm for change, for *to live your life fully meant a willingness to change*, and change was definitely upon him. ...

CHAPTER FOUR

THE IMPLICATIONS OF WAR

Is the ability to adapt to horrific situations and treat them as normal in order to survive.

HUNGARY 1939

TIGHTLY WRAPPED IN SWADDLING cloth and tucked deep within the guise of a hay stack, the little baby girl and mother lay huddled and shivering against the frosty night air, fearing *they* would be entering the Magyar land. The sound of bombing overhead was the beginning of World War II. The German fighter jets circled above and around, but their target that night was Poland. Fear ignited into flames of tension and hate; the whole of Europe knew what this implied, and no one would sleep well that night or for years to come. Although she was far too young to understand the implications of that night, she would grow up in the knowledge much sooner than ever imagined.

࿐

ITALY 1939

DEEP WITHIN THE FOREST on the outskirt of Sienna, Major Robert Cross ordered his troops to dig their trenches. The next day would be a long day, as the British and Canadian troops planned a sneak attack on the enemy. That night they needed to rest.

"And take your mosquito nets and nail them on top of the trench; we don't want you dying of some incurable disease." Bob smirked. *But as for me*, he thought, *I'm too damn tired to dig.*

Once his men were down for the night, Bob fell to the ground with a thud; all six-foot eight inches of his tall frame lay exhausted upon the ground. *Those trenches are too similar to graves*, he thought, haphazardly assembling the net just inches above his head so as not to be irritated by mosquitoes.

Dawn came with the swift fire of guns and exploding grenades. "What the hell is going on!" exclaimed Bob, who was jerked awake by battle cries. "Yes, sir, Major."

"UP PRONTO. GET TO YOUR POSITIONS. ... THE ENEMY HAS BEEN ALERTED. ... GOD DAMN IT, THEY TOLD ME SNEAK ATTACK. ... THERE'S BEEN A LEAK!" shouted Bob, who rose to his feet with rocket speed.

He seemed oblivious to the seven gunshots holes that now appeared on his mosquito net.

It was typical of Robert to remain unaffected by danger. The past year overseas had truly hardened him. The torment of his father's iron fist was no comparison to the harsh reality of war. Maggot-eaten flesh and the nauseating smell of decomposing bodies had surrounded him over this time, turning the once mischievous prankster into a tough, *say it as it is* man amongst the men. The leader in him was running through his veins, just as his father had suspected, and he needed the war to bring that out.

If one actually needs a war to bring about something positive.

Letters home were candy-coated for his mother's sake, with requests for peanut butter and candy bars. She never knew how her boy was being affected by the terrors of war, as she would proudly read the letters aloud, with Rupert sitting within earshot wearing an all-knowing expression of both pride and relief. The relief was not that his son was still safe, but rather, that he was made a major and was moving up in the ranks. That was Rupert's sole concern, for he didn't want his reputation to ever again be tarnished by the likes of his destructive adolescent.

A package from London, Ontario came amongst several packages from Canada. Major Cross took his package with a silent tinge of sadness that he could not be home during that time. It was Christmas 1940, and the troops set up camp in Padua, where although all were enemies, all recognized the occasion, and a silent cease fire appeared to be in order.

Spirits were down. Bob's infantry needed some moral boosting, so moral boosting it would be. Out came the staple rum, the canned corned beef, the cigarettes, all to the sounds of Bing Crosby's White Christmas playing in the background. The men began to laugh, and they sang along with the music.

"I'm dreaming... of a White Christmas. Just like the one I used to know."

"I'm dreaming of my sweet, Lucy, just like the girl I had before!" sang the men, grinning from ear to ear, some dancing with each other.

"You'd look a whole lot better in a dress, Jerry!" joked the men.

The dinner bell rang out and the men happily gathered around the table, where the newly promoted Major Cross raised his glass of rum.

"Men, as head of the King's Infantry Regiment, I want to tell you all how proud I am of all of you and your achievements. It hasn't been easy; we've lost a lot of good men along the way, some of whom I want to remember with two minutes of silence."

The men somberly removed their caps and bowed their heads, for most had lost either their best friend from home or from the war. The fact was, they were all brothers, sharing in an experience that would seal the bonds of friendship forever.

"Men, Merry Christmas! Now let's eat!" exclaimed Bob,

and the men raised their glasses and, in unison, shouted, "Merry Christmas, Major!"

As the leader, the major had to be an example throughout his tenure. That evening would be no different. He was a humble man, refusing to be waited upon, opting rather to help his fellow men. So alongside Tom the chef, Bob "The Cat" Cross, as he was affectionately nicknamed for escaping death so often, began to dole out the mashed potatoes and pot roast. "Tonight, men, I managed to pull a few strings. Tonight I'm Santa Claus bringing you all chocolate pudding for dessert!" Happiness reigned supreme as if they all had won the lottery. "Me first!" shouted Shorty.

"No, me, you had first's nibs on the roast," teased Bill.

"There's enough for all of you," grinned the major as he ladled out the pudding. ...

Smiles and laughter turned to shock and confusion. "*White Christmas, White Christmas, White Christmas,*" skipped the record player, replaying it over and over again. As the heady tinge of a bullet pierced through the major's ear, soaring blood into the pudding bowl, which seemed to float in the air in timeless motion. The ladle was halved and fell sputtering to the floor, as if to coincide with the crashing of Tom's lifeless body onto the table. Everyone scattered erratically, with the taste of chocolate still on their tongues, now turning bittersweet. ...

Another loss, another horrific nightmare; the major would never eat chocolate pudding again. ...

CHAPTER FIVE

EDES CSILLAGOM

"Édes Csillagom" is an endearing Hungarian
expression meaning "My Sweet Star."

HUNGARY 1942

ERZSIKE HOPPED, SKIPPED, AND JUMPED ABOUT ON THE STONY grass, singing gleefully, as it was the first chance she had had all week to leave the safety of her small little house.

"Not so loud, Erzsikem, you'll disturb the guards," her mother said sternly, while chopping cabbage in the kitchen.

"*Istenem*, cabbage soup again. I cannot wait for the taste of csirke paprikás on my lips," Erzsike complained.

"Don't be sad, darling; it will be over soon. The professor predicted it this morning," consoled her father.

"Shhh, don't even mention his name; no one must know," scolded Rozali to her husband, expecting him to be more discreet.

Although Erzsike could hear the conversation, she chose not to speak, for she wanted to be a child then, and she feared that she would once again be ordered back to the attic to hide.

For six months of the war, they had harbored Lenny Malkovitz, a Jewish professor, in their attic, away from the German wrath. Many a night they would hold their breath, praying not to be found out as the army would march past their small village of Szoc.

"I can't stand this," uttered Rozali, Erzsike's mother, crying from the pains of war and the pains of circumstance.

"You must not complain; they will see it in your eyes.

Besides, he is a good man. Jesus will love us more and protect us from them and their guns." Karoly tried to comfort her.

"*Istenem,*" Rozali sighed, crossing herself.

"Come, Erzsike, dinner is ready!" Hot cabbage soup adorned with a prize piece of Debreceni was placed before the family.

"*Finom!*" Erzsike exclaimed.

"Here, my *édes csillagom,* you eat mine. I am not that hungry," said her father, Karoly, who had a special love for his darling wildflower.

"You spoil her!" preached her mother.

"No, I just love her." Her father smiled.

It saddened him to know that his darling daughter, the only survivor after six stillbirths, had arrived in a world so bleak and full of fear, but such were the thoughts of most parents during the war. There were many who committed suicide as a family in order to escape its painful grasp. But this was a man of courage and great pride. He refused to give into fear and taught all he could to his daughter, for she would be the son he never had. As for Rozali, Erzsike stood as a reminder of all that she once was, healthy, happy, and young, and reminded her of all that she would have to submit too in order to survive.

For those reasons, Rozali never caressed her daughter; instead, she chose to criticize her. "Why must you smile so much? People will think you are arrogant!" and if her father ever complimented her intelligence, her mother would say, "*It is pointless for a woman to be too intelligent; it only gets her in trouble.*"

So the battle of wills continued in the household, but it was her father who was the boss, and therefore, when the decision came to protect the Jewish professor from the Germans, he took little time in gathering his belongings and opening the secret passage to the attic. *He can teach Erzsike*, he thought, which was exactly what he did.

Erzsike was four years old when the professor arrived at their front door. During the six months he was there, she was put next to the professor, who happily taught her what would normally be taught in two years in the time they were given. He used dried beans in the attic storage room for counting, then as the numbers increased and her vocabulary grew, so did the array of props he used to teach her as much as he possibly could.

"She is like a blotting paper, Karoly; you should be very proud of her. Why does her mother bother her so with so much work? She is only a child; let her be a child," the professor would plead.

"My wife is in great pain, and I am only home for a few hours a day. She needs help feeding the chickens, rolling the dough, and cleaning, for she has terrible arthritis and the pain is excruciating. I am sure you understand," Karoly defended his wife.

"Ah, but I do. If only I could come down for a few hours a day to help. How I would so enjoy it," pined the professor.

"No, you must not even think this way. You are not safe, nor will my family be should the authorities find out," cried Karoly.

"Yes, yes, I know, but still, the desire to wish is there," said the professor.

Soon, the war was over, and life returned to an altered state of normal, but for Erzsike, war was all she knew, and it had taught her to be strong, courageous, and defiant. It was this strength that saved her father's life when, just days after the Jewish professor made his way out of the attic and to freedom at the border of Austria, a rumor spread that another Jew had been caught. Many believed that Karoly and his family were harboring a Jew, but no one had any proof. Six months was a long time, but somehow they'd managed to keep it a secret by covering their tracks.

The danger unbeknown to young Erzsike, an older German soldier, who was leaving the town, asked what her name was and how old she was, and she answered. Shocked at hearing that she was a mere five years old, he questioned her about her teaching. Having been privy to prior reports of a stowaway in their midst, he grilled young Erzsike over and over again, whereupon she proudly recited her alphabet and multiplication tables with true perfection. When Karoly came home, he asked Rozali. "Where is Erzsikem?"

"I sent her to buy bread," said Rozali, unconcerned that her daughter had still not returned. "Why did you do that? You knew I would be home soon; why didn't you wait?" Karoly exclaimed.

"Why are you so upset? It is only around the corner."

"The Germans are vacating the area today; do you not know anything woman!" he shouted, slamming the tiny wooden door behind him.

His face grew pale when he saw his daughter face to face with the enemy. *Istenem, please, God, please protect her*, he prayed.

"Erzsikem, come quickly; it is dinner time," said her father, trying to conceal his fear.

"Coming, Papa," Erzsike said happily. The soldier held the small girl by the shoulder.

"Wait, little one, we need to ask your father some questions." The German smirked.

Immediately sensing that something was wrong, Erzsike put her hand upon her shoulder and pushed the soldiers hand off it.

"NO, I must leave now. My father is calling!" But this just served to aggravate and amuse the soldier.

"Come here, man!" the soldier ordered.

Karoly sheepishly cowered toward the men. *They must know about the professor. It doesn't matter; as long as Erzsike is freed, nothing else matters*, he thought.

As if resigning himself to his fate, Karoly began what sounded like a confession, then Erzsike stomped her father's foot and began to cry.

"I'm so sorry, Papa, I didn't mean to hurt you."

"Don't worry, Erzsike, you didn't hurt me," he said, once again proceeding with his confession. Again, she stomped his foot.

"Oh, Papa, I don't feel well. Please, Papa, take me home. I think I am sick!" She cried, shouted, and wailed so much that all those around her became increasingly agitated, especially the guard, who, at that point, forgot what he was wanting and told the father to get rid of the little nuisance.

"What is wrong, Erzsike?" Karoly asked.

But she continued to cry and cried until she entered their home.

"What is this, Erzsike?" questioned her papa.

"Nothing, Papa, I am fine now," she said, secure in the knowledge that they were safe.

"And you say nothing is gained with intelligence, Rozalia! You can certainly learn from your daughter! I believe she just saved my life!"

"Oh, Papa, , *szeretlek tégedet*."

"*Szeretlek tégedet*, Erzsikem. You are my *édes csillagom*." Her father smiled with pride and enveloped her in the warmth of his loving arms.

CHAPTER SIX

THE DIFFERENCE

A determining point or factor that
distinguishes one thing from another.

SHE ENTERED LIFE IN THE USUAL WAY, WITH THE CARESS OF her mother's breast, wrapped in love, and surrounded by the warmth of broad smiles and chuckling laughter. She was raised in an atmosphere of close family ties, in a mansion filled with toys and plenty of food on the table. She grew as if by osmosis, absorbing the abounding air around her, which seemingly had a high caloric value, for she grew up despite the fact that in the first few years of life, she rarely ate. This, however, went unnoticed, for one doesn't miss what one doesn't have, or in this case, never had.

The fact was that she grew up during the war, which meant most were subjected to curfew and strife, at poverty's door step. The resonance of laughter was often against the backdrop of tears and bombs, but this was overshadowed by her youthful naivety. She was unaware of the differences between happy and sad, rich and poor, war and peace. But as she grew up and began on her journey of life, where mansions suddenly became shacks and toys became stones, the differences became painfully clear.

Perhaps it was because of the war that circumstances helped her gain the advantage. It was like she was an angel sent by God, restoring hope within a family of despair, giving her mother the love she longed for after so many attempts at motherhood.

She felt her mother's pain each day as they made their way to the cemetery to lay fresh flowers on all seven graves. Six were babies who died at birth and the other was her older brother, Sanyi, who sadly died at the age of seven in a construction accident where he was crushed beneath a boulder at a building site. His death, more than the others, sent Rozali into a perpetual state of depression and anger, for she blamed anyone and everyone for the death of her *edes* Sanyi. Erzsike was too young to understand what death was, but whatever it was, she certainly didn't like it or what it had done to her mother.

It was on those occasions that Erzsike would wander through the gates of the cemetery to the field beyond, where the ivy covered boulder in the middle became her mansion and the stones beneath were her possessions. It was there that she would dream. Dream of what lay beyond the mountains. As she grew older, her pondering became an urgent need to find the answer to what the differences were that spawned from the war and why they existed. Those questions occupied her every thought and soon became what sustained her in the darkest moments of the war.

THE WAR HAD BEEN relatively kind to Bob "The Cat" Cross. Now a brigadier, he had seen it all, the deaths of dear and close friends and the breakdown of others. He discovered the differences within himself that occurred because of the war; the need to be responsible when the desire to be remiss was ever present, the urge to gamble when the urge to be respected stood in the way. The love of women never changed, and so some behaviors just persisted, and in this case, became accentuated.

"One in every port," the soldiers would laugh, often comparing entries to their infamous black books.

"The nurses in England were especially attendant, didn't you think, Brigadier, sir?" they would say with a smirk, but Bob remained his debonair self.

"I don't kiss and tell men," he would say with a stern voice, sending cold shivers of regret down the officers' backs, "'cause if I did, I'd lose my voice from the amount of talking I'd have to do!" He'd grin, sending sighs of relief and laughter amongst the barracks.

The fact was, Bob and his Clark Gable facade could have any woman, and most of the time he did, taking little time for the conquest and almost no time for the follow up!

Such was the case with the Head of Nurses in London. Her name was Susan Dorsey and she was a beauty. She and Bob spent many a day and night together, sharing both passion and companionship, for both were isolated and both needed the other. As time passed, their needs grew deeper and their desire hungrier.

It was nearing the end of 1943 and the last of the regiment was to be cleared out of Italy. His mission in London had been to get more supplies for his regiment, and it was time to rejoin to his men.

"Please, Bob, don't go; I need you," Susan pleaded, but Bob was not apt to chafe that easily.

"Look, Sue, let's cut this out. Don't get hysterical on me. I said this was just going to be the weekend and now I have my duty to fulfill," he said sternly.

Her eyes welled up with tears, and she turned to ice as she buttoned her uniform and walked out, slamming the door behind her.

"Jesus Christ!" Bob exclaimed, running out into the hall after her. "What the hell is wrong with you?"

FAR AWAY, I LAND

"Absolutely nothing, Bob, absolutely nothing," she said in her cool North London accent.

"Good, then. ... I'll be in Italy for the next month and expect to have all matters complete by month's end, alright?"

"Everything is just fine, Bob; don't hurry back. I won't be waiting for you," she declared, which made his shirt collar feel suddenly like a noose.

"Fine, then, have it your way!" he mumbled, fitting his jacket and marching down the hall. "Bloody woman!" he stammered, secretly pining for her scent the moment he hit the staircase.

Susan turned to watch the man she loved walk down the hallway and out of her life. ...

I now know where my loyalties must lie, she thought and began to cry, asking her colleague to take over her shift.

On the plane back to Italy, the brigadier had little else to reflect on except Sue. He wondered how their relationship deteriorated so fast and why she had been so emotional. *So unlike her,* he thought. *I'll patch things up when I return ... I have a war to fight,* he said to himself, trying to redirect his mind, unaware of the dangers that lay ahead.

The Canadian Armed Forces jet landed at Ciampino Airport in Rome; his men were still camped in Venafro. *Tommy will appreciate these,* he grimaced as he unpacked the arsenal, *and Jack will get a kick out of these magazines. Poor bugger lost his girl last month and can't get over the guilt of putting her in harm's way. Such a bonita lass, she was,* he thought flippantly. *Well, can't take too much time mourning; we just have to move on ...,* he reminded himself.

The men cheered when they saw his jeep come near their tents. "Brigadier, sir, welcome back!"

"Thank you men. Bill, give me an update."

"All quiet, sir. The past few days have had very little gun fire. We were waiting for you to assess the situation, sir. I think we have this section covered; maybe our troops can advance."

"No, men, this is a ploy. I'll have to radio dispatch to get the go-ahead before we make any moves."

But the radio signal was lost deep in the valley of the extremely rocky terrain, and the men had already been apprehensive about what to do. "Men, tomorrow we'll make haste, advancing at the break of dawn. You all get some shut-eye, and we'll move into the city by 0400 hours," Bob ordered his troops.

"Right, sir," they said as they prepared for their eternal sleep.

The night seemed oblivious to the tensions below. The moon still shone and the stars sparkled, but the earth grew angry and its soul began to tremor. By morn, the earth had opened its hungry mouth and devoured the salty skin of its prey. All that remained was the numbed body of a single man, drenched in the sweat of her angry landscape, covered with shrapnel, and left for dead.

The light shone intermittently between bouts of consciousness, the weight of his pain deepened the mud beneath him, slowly, slowly pulling him into its anxious throat, ready to devour one more victim.

But somehow, the gods of fate shone on him, and when he awoke, it appeared that heaven was in India and the holy water was Chai.

What a difference the war made.

CHAPTER SEVEN

CEASEFIRE

The war was over, but peace was yet to come.

ITALY-SWITZERLAND BORDER 1943–1944

THE ROAD TO RECOVERY WAS INTERMITTENTLY FILLED WITH lingering images of blood, the dying faces of friends, and the frightening look of foe, which had him reeling between delusion and confusion. This kept the brigadier in a constant cold sweat. Dozing to the memory of concertos and being jerked awake by Italian folk music and chanting, he grew bewildered, and his recollections faded with the daily setting of the sun. *Who were these men who adorned themselves with white cloth around their heads? And why were they helping him?* he thought as he fell back into deep slumber.

It had been three weeks since that fateful night when his entire regiment was so brutally murdered. *Why the hell did they attack?* he pondered. *We were all so close to going home and leaving the horror behind us.*

"You are up, Brigadier, sir; how do you feel? Would you like some more tea perhaps?" asked a young Indian soldier.

"Where am I, and who the hell are you?" Bob asked in a most intimidating voice.

"I am Reddy, Colonel Reddy, army doctor for Seik Regiment 345, and you are in a British hospital on the border of Italy and Switzerland, which is under the jurisdiction of the British. It's a safe hold, now that the war is officially over," Reddy answered.

But the war was not over for the brigadier, who felt as if the war had just started that fateful night.

With utmost caution, he murmured, "The others?" To which the doctor, with downcast eyes, proceeded to answer the brigadier with reciprocated caution.

"I'm very sorry, sir," he said, and left Bob to his own devices.

I'm sorry. … I'm so sorry, men. … I really let you down, he repeated to himself, sobbing for the first time in his life. He sighed a weighty sigh of deep sorrow and regret, which drilled a hole right down to his very marrow that would fester in him for the rest of his life.

ENGLAND 1945

HE CONSCIENTIOUSLY SAT AT his desk typing the last of the transfer documents out for the captain.

"Cyril, what are you still doing here? The men are all down at the pub celebrating; remember, the war is over!"

"Yes, sir, I know. Just wanted to finish the letters of condolences to the families of Infantry 436. Their remains are being flown back home. Just one survivor, the Canadian, Brigadier Cross. He'll be ready for transfer by the week's end."

"Sad that was. ... Thank God it's all over," muttered the captain.

"Yes, thank God," Cyril reiterated with utmost reverence.

Such a professional man that young Alvis is. Wish I could have had more like him. Now he's returning home to some island in the sun. Don't blame him, not for a second, the captain thought, motioning for him to go to the pub.

Cyril smiled, undistracted, and continued to type.

☙◉☚

"Brigadier Cross, you're back. How are you doing, old chap?" uttered the captain.

"Everyone I can and the sucker's twice!" laughed Bob.

"Good to see you're the same as usual! Cyril, I want to meet one of the great soldiers you've been writing reports about. Brigadier Cross, meet one of our finest private secretaries, Cyril Alvis"

The two men shook hands for an inordinate amount of time, as if destiny predicated they should take that moment in time.

"I'm so sorry to hear about your regiment, sir; it must be very painful for you," Cyril said earnestly.

"Thank you, it is and, I predict, always will be," said Bob mournfully.

"Oh no, let's not go there. You're coming with me, Bob. Too many tears; it's time to celebrate. Cyril, join us?"

"Oh no, sir, but thank you," he said as he pointed to his work.

"Understand you set sail tomorrow, Cyril."

"Yes, I do," Cyril replied almost regretfully.

"Where is home?" asked Bob.

"Ceylon, sir."

"Ah, one of my former men, a brave, brave man, has just been declared a war hero by Winston Churchill himself: Colonel Leonard Birchall. They call him *The Savior of Ceylon*; he was able to forewarn the British base in Colombo that the Japanese were coming. Don't know whether he's dead or alive at this point. Some say he died and other's think he's still a prisoner of war."

"Yes sir. My country and I, of course, are most grateful to that very great Canadian," Cyril declared most patriotically.

"As for this Canadian, I merely enjoyed a good cup of tea at the GFH in the breezy capital of Colombo. Ceylon is beautiful island I am told, as I'm afraid I only had a few hours before we boarded," recollected Bob.

"Thank you for reminding me. I'm looking forward to seeing that beauty once again. I'll have a cup of tea at the Galle Face Hotel on my return in your honor, sir," Cyril replied, as if to convince himself that this was what he longed for.

"Thank you kindly," said the brigadier.

"You're an officer and gentlemen," said the captain.

"Thank you, sir," uttered Cyril.

"Good work, Brigadier Cross; an honor to have met you."

"The same." Bob smiled as he left the room, anxious to reunite with his long lost love, Sue, who was waiting for him in the hallway. It had been their first time seeing each other since Bob's near death experience in the final days of the war and word of his whereabouts and convalescence only came months later.

Cyril sat at his desk and completed the final death notice. *What a shame; so many lives lost. I will add these poor souls to my prayers of the faithfully departed,* he sighed, as if that was his calling in life.

He collected his trusty notebooks and his Waterman Signature Series Fountain Pen, which was a treasured gift from his father. It was given to his father in 1907 when he returned to Ceylon after taking silk to Lincoln's Inn.

Cyril patiently took all his personal items and a few mementos he had gathered during his stay and put them into his briefcase. He waited in the dark, reflecting on all that had transpired. He waited for the sweet caress of one last goodbye ... but only a memory met him in the shadows of darkness.

The sounds of jubilation permeated the corridors, in sharp contrast to the grey atmosphere and hush-filled rooms that occupied the building for so many sorrowful years. *The noise, although joyful, is inappropriate,* he thought, as too few returned, especially those innocently caught in the crossfire.

He pushed in his chair for the final time.

The war was over, but at what cost?

CHAPTER EIGHT

A TIMELY EXCHANGE

Good in theory, but not in practice.

CEYLON 1945

THE JETTY WAS FRENZIED WITH ACTIVITY AS THE TRADERS gathered near the barge to load and unload their fares. Tea, spices, and coffee being loaded, and specialty items from England being unloaded, all orders from Cargill's for expatriates living on the island.

A naval band was playing on the dock, whilst crewmen played cards on overturned trunks. The venders were selling their local specialties, and the priest, Father Fernando, stood outside the congregation as the **Missions to Seamen** sign was being painted above the Church of St. Christopher, an appropriate saint to look over the travelers who wandered in and out of its gates.

The tall, rather pious looking man walked down the gangway looking highly distracted. He carried his brown leather briefcase, with the initials C. E. A. engraved into the fine Connolly leather. Despite the chaos surrounding the port, Cyril was deep in thought as he clutched his little black book in his hands. The book was marked with a single burgundy ribbon that waved in the wind. As he continued to walk, the ribbon hooked onto the railing, which pulled it farther and farther out of the book, until he felt a tug at his arm and turned to see a young dockhand holding the ribbon.

"Hey, what are you doing?" Cyril said. "Keep your hands away from that!" But the boy seemed oblivious to what he was saying and merely shrugged his shoulders and disappeared into the crowd.

Exacerbated, Cyril carefully untwined the ribbon, methodically folded it, and lovingly inserted it into his wallet, which he tucked deep within his breast coat pocket.

This scene was observed from the shore by a very young and very impressionable Harriet Meedeniya, who gazed at him, wondering why he held on so dearly to a burgundy ribbon.

"Oh, Father, I wasn't looking!" She blushed.

"Oh yes you were, my dear, and it is not becoming of a lady!" Harriet looked down indignantly. "Don't worry, dear, I won't say anything to your mother," he reassured her. *After all, it was only human,* he thought.

Secretly, the young girl knew her father was right. She had noticed the tall man at the jetty and felt smitten for the first time in her life. Perhaps this was what Mummy had meant when she spoke of fate and love at first site, an idea that was highly debated amongst her lady friends.

If God really loves you, He finds the person you will love forever and somehow chances a meeting, Harriet thought, as if playing it out, scene by scene in her head. She suddenly grew sad, as instinctively she knew this would not be the case for herself. She was wise enough to realize that this handsome stranger was coming back from England. She felt that someone as handsome as he would not go unnoticed while abroad and had heard that women in the West were far more direct than any lady of the East. She wondered what history he had. *Did he have a wife? Would she ever see him again?* she thought, and the thoughts made her desperate with emotional curiosity.

"Child, get to this side. Do I have to put a leash on you!" grumbled her father, who loved her dearly.

What Harriet hadn't realized was that this tall handsome

stranger was returning from England after the war, which had marred most men to some extent or form.

She continued to watch him as he disembarked the ship. As he tucked the wallet into his pocket, he discovered his pocket watch was missing. Not knowing what to do, he ran back onto the ship, only to glance back at the port to see the boy who had knocked into him on the gangway exiting the scene at a very hurried pace.

"Stop him! Thief!" Cyril shouted, which captured the attention of many on the land side, including the thunder-struck Harriet and her father, Aloysius Meedeniya, businessman extraordinaire, who took it upon himself to instigate officers to capture the thief.

By the time Cyril made it down the gangway once again, Meedeniya had remanded the youth and stood authoritatively in his brown Chester Barrie suit and monocle.

"I say, kind sir, what is this you say? Thief? What on earth has this poor bloke stolen from you?"

Out of breath, filled with rage, and affected by the fact that he still had his sea legs on, Cyril uttered, "He has my father's Patek Philippe pocket watch; it's engraved with our family crest and initial P.R. Alvis!"

"Not Philip Alvis, the famed Galle Court judge?" inquired Meedeniya.

"One in the same, sir. Philip Alvis is my father," said Cyril.

"Officers, look into his pants, his pockets, search him thoroughly," commanded Meedeniya, and without further ado, the watch was found.

"All right, is this your watch sir?" said the officer.

"Yes, it is; there is only one of a kind. Now arrest him!" ordered Cyril, gaining back his power after feeling slighted earlier on.

"I understand you're angry, young man, but it is the times in which we live in. What harm is he to you now? Let the poor scavenger go. He probably needed it to feed his family," implored Meedeniya.

"What harm? What harm you ask? Injustice has occurred; he must be punished in accordance with the law," sneered Cyril in utter self-righteousness.

"*Anay, Sali nes, Sali nes,*" the thief cried, clinging to Cyril's arm for compassion. "Unhand me, you barbarian; doesn't even speak the King's English!" And with that show of utter contempt, the youth was cuffed and taken away.

"I see, like father, like son, no doubt you too follow the legal profession, judging by your briefcase?" inquired Meedeniya.

"I would hope judging by my principle's, sir!" And with that, he tipped his hat to Meedeniya and smiled at the beautiful young girl, who was now completely mesmerized. He made his exit, following the police to file the charges.

"Stop staring, Harriet. My word, what has become of you!" uttered her father, quite perturbed and alarmed at the same time, to which she blushed even more and tried to pretend disinterest by redirecting her attention to the men unloading the ship.

On the way back into town, both remained silent, quietly reviewing the events that had unfolded.

His briefcase is made of the finest Connolly leather, thought Meedeniya. *It looks much the same as those made at Holland and Holland in Barclay Square. He knows good things in life; ... perhaps that smile Harri's way was proof of that.* However, upon second glance at his daughter, his fatherly sense of responsibility towards his innocent daughter loomed a protective shadow.

The Alvis name was notorious for justice, but to what end? Philip Alvis was renowned as the *Hanging Judge*.

As the coach moved forward, he drifted off to sleep, which turned his worried thoughts into a nightmare.

"No!" shouted Meedeniya.

"Why, Papa! What happened?" cried the startled girl.

The elderly man leaned forward to expose his daughter's neck. ...

"What, Papa, what do you want?"

"Oh, oh. ... nothing my dear," he said, looking extremely disturbed. "Just a bad dream."

"Don't worry, Papa, I will say a rosary for you," Harriet comforted him in utter innocence.

But as the man gazed at the rosary beads, all he could see was a noose.

"Pray with me." Harriet smiled sweetly, unaware of the thoughts that crossed her father's mind.

Harriet was the second eldest of five daughters and one brother. She was the most beautiful and also one of the smartest, but at the time, beautiful meant marriage proposals very early in life to protect a girl's honor.

Harriet became quiet and secretive over the next few weeks, and was often caught daydreaming and forgetting the world to verse. Not her usual giggling self.

"Whatever is wrong with this girl?" complained her mother, but her father knew she was love struck. Smitten from the moment she laid eyes on the stoic and handsome young Alvis. He didn't dare tell his wife; he wanted to avoid being chastised for bringing their daughter to ill-suited areas of town. He had just recently received a note in the post thanking him for apprehending the thief at the port. The note was written on a letterhead:

MR. CYRIL BERTRAND ALVIS ESQ.
PRIVATE SECRETARY TO THE
INSPECTOR OF POLICE, SIR PETER RANDOLPH

Impressive young man, right age, good Catholic family; no sooner had the idea formed in his mind than the doorbell rang, and the mail was delivered, carrying once again a note from Cyril Alvis.

"Who is writing, Aloy?" Maude, his wife of twenty years, inquired. She was doing needlepoint in the grand room, whose ceiling reined supremely, thirty feet above the antique furnishings of ebony and teak.

"It is an invitation for tea to the both of us and our daughter Harri," said Aloy Meedeniya to his wife. "I surmise it is moreover a pre-proposal, if you want to know what I think." Aloy grinned guardedly.

It was the rare occasion that she dropped her needles and became firmly entrenched in all that he had to say. As this enthusiasm for hearing as well as talking was an unusual event indeed, the conversation and all its details lasted for hours into the night.

CHAPTER NINE

THE SHACKLES OF CIRCUMSTANCE

"What lies behind us and what lies before us are tiny matters compared to what lies within us."

-Ralph Waldo Emerson

HUNGARY 1944

AS THE CSÁRDÁS REVERBERATED AGAINST THE CLAY TILED roofs of the little village, a child's tears were muffled by the shouts and laughter of people celebrating the church feast in the small village. She sat alone, in a woodpile near the shed, sadly wiping away the tears from her disillusioned brown eyes.

"My daddy is a murderer," she kept muttering to herself, not realizing the full implications of her words.

"Why do you cry, little one?" said her neighbor, old Pista Bacsi, who appeared out of nowhere in the shadow of the moonlight.

Startled, Erzsike sprung to her feet, frightened by Old Bacsi, who only had one leg, wore an eye patch, and eternally smelled of alcohol. "Nothing," said Erzsike, but the old man had heard her.

"Why is your father a murderer, little one?" he said, knowing all too well that he couldn't possibly be.

But with that, Erzsike ran inside, only to be met by her mother, who sternly told her to wash her face. "*Istenem*, she is always crying for no reason. Now it is the goose feathers, yesterday the pig! She is a silly child!" and with that, she wiped her hands on her apron and swung the gate closed.

Erzsike's mother was not a happy woman, always cursing things, working too hard, and constantly in eternal pain. Every day she became more and more riddled in arthritic pain, which would eventually lead to her eventually being unable to walk, so seeing the old man in his crippled state was only a reminder of things to come.

"Why are you so rude to our neighbor; he only asked a question?" said Karoly, just home after celebrating in the streets.

"He asks why you are a murderer. Should I invite him in for tea, or perhaps I should make him some palacsinta!"

To which, with a twinkle in his eye, he walked into his sweet Erzsike's room.

"Erzsike, why do you cry so? You know when your mother plucks the goose feathers they feel better"

"No, Papa, they are crying. I can hear them; they are in pain, and I think they will die," cried the little girl.

"Yes, at first they are in pain, but when it is over with, they are happy! They can walk freely, and they are not so hot! It's like when you have a sore tooth. It is hurting so much so we have to pull it out, and this hurts so much too, but when it's over, you feel better, don't you?" asked her loving father.

"Oh yes, Papa, I feel better only because you give me chocolate and then I feel better."

"So you see," Karoly told Rozali, "I think we must give them some chocolate. What do you think?" Karoly smiled.

"Are you crazy, man; do you think we have money like that to waste? Perhaps you should give them a kick!" sneered Rozali.

"Mamma!" Erzsike cried.

"Roza, please, you are upsetting Erzsike, *Istenem*." pleaded Karoly. "Don't worry, Erzsike, after you all go to bed, I will sneak out and feed them some chocolate, then they will feel better and so will you," he lovingly whispered into Erzsike's ear.

"Oh yes, Papa, *köszönöm szépen*." To which she happily

curled up in the freshly cleaned white linen her mother had painstakingly made, washed, and ironed.

"Now sleep, my little one," and with one blow, the candle was out and Erzsike was lulled to sleep on a wave of new-found happiness coupled with the melodic strums of joy set against the night sky.

The village of Szőc consisted of a small crescent street, a church, an extremely small schoolhouse, and paths that led to both the *Szőlőhegy*, or vineyard, and the cemetery, which together kept the village men both pleasantly intoxicated and ever mindful of their mortality. It was a hard life, but no one in the village lacked for anything.

On that occasion, the goose feathers were collected to use as down fill for pillows and duvet covers. This usually happened in the spring in preparation for winter and, of course, for dowries for the young women of the town whose goals were to get married as soon as possible. Usually a group of women and Nagy Leányok, the most senior and well-respected lady from the village, would gather to prepare these things for the home. It was at gatherings like this that the older women taught the younger women how to sew, crochet, and do needlepoint. On these occasions there was always a storyteller by the name of Lina Néni who used to go into great detail and derive much pleasure from scaring the impressionable youths with ghost stories and old wives' tales.

Erzsike wished to be older so she could enjoy the few pleasures in life that she felt she could only experience with age, or so her mother kept telling her; however, Erzsike was a determined little girl and got herself into a lot of mischief, only to have it covered up by her dear father.

On that night there was a church feast, and the town gathered to dance and to celebrate the Feast of St. Anthony, the miracle worker who would bless the town with money and success if they prayed hard enough. But Rozali was skeptical of St. Anthony's effectiveness, as she always was, and her pain just led her down the path of disbelief in everything, including a cure for her pain, let alone a miracle.

Erzsike, on the other hand, was an eternal optimist, strong willed, and determined.

It happened that one morning, after eating her breakfast of bread and cured bacon with lots of paprika sprinkled on it—*"Tejjel ettem a kását attól nőttem ekkorát,"* Erzsike sang while eating her *regeli* breakfast—she wandered outside near the garden and watched the neighbor boys throwing stones like marbles, and she quickly ran over to play.

"What do you want? You're not a boy, and you can't play with us!" But Erzsike was not going to take no for an answer.

"Why do you say this to me? I know how to play better than all of you!" So, like a tomboy, Erzsike showed them how to throw stones by throwing them at the boys, so they ran home to their mothers, like wimpy noodles, she thought!

Erzsike continued this mindset throughout her life, never to be afraid of anyone or anything, as challenges remained steadfast in her path.

One boy said, "I'll play with you if you show me your panties."

"What do you mean show you?" So with that, Erzsike was quick and said to him, knowing that her father was not too far from the scene. "Sure, I'll show you mine if you show me yours first."

So, like a fool, the boy lowered his trousers, exposing himself.

"Ha, Ha, ha!" exclaimed Erzsike. "Mine is so much more interesting than yours!" And with that, she hopped over, picked up the stones, and ran off into the garden near her father, whose eyes turned in the direction of the boy.

"Hey, what the hell are you doing! *Shiks, shiks*, get out of here before I tell your parents!" hollered Karoly, attempting to be fierce.

Erzsike roared with laughter in the bushes and caught the disapproving but mischievous glint of pride in her father's eyes. But those times were far and few between. Usually, her childhood consisted of helping her mother gather vegetables, fetch water from the town's well, wash laundry, roll dough, iron, cook, feed the barn animals, and milk the cows. It was constant harassment, and it was neither the life she wanted nor was destined to have.

Erzsike was born when World War II began. It was a time of great unrest as news of Hitler's invasion of Poland spread across Hungary and most Hungarians braced themselves against what would be the inevitable.

In March 1944, Germany invaded Hungary to install a pro-Nazi puppet government. The invasion was in response to Hungary's attempt to get out of the war by withdrawing its troops from the Eastern Front.

Erzsike was only four, very inquisitive, and filled with a patriotism unseen in children of such a young age. This stemmed from watching her father sing songs of love for Hungary in the woodshed, sometimes alone and often in the company of other men from the village. She would hear her mother complain about them always being drunk and that there was so much work to be done, but Erzsike could not understand what was so wrong with what her father was doing. He was a hardworking man, and to Erzsike, he was her hero, always strong, always happy, and constantly protecting with so much love.

"Why do you sing those songs, Erzsike. It is not for a girl to do. Come, help me with my hair; I cannot hold this brush anymore!" shouted her very frustrated mother. Erzsike obediently came and brushed her mother's hair, and she massaged her mother's hands every night. She knew she was in pain, but sometimes would have loved to be loved back. For her mother, life was about bitterness, burden, and hardship. She had suffered the loss of six stillborn births, and her dear son had just been killed in a construction accident.

"My Sanyi, what a good boy he was," she quietly moaned, but every time Erzsike tried to get close to her apron, she was shunned. "Go, go and brush your hair!" Rozali would spurt.

"Stop screaming at her, woman! She will grow to hate you one day!" Karoly would often shout.

"Come , my *édes csillagom,* I will brush your hair," he said as he gently patted her small head, and he proceeded to brush and braid her hair as best he could, for his hands were big, stiff, and awkward with such gentle hair in his hands.

"I worry about her, Rozalia. What will happen when the Germans come? I will have to fight and you will be here alone; you are in pain, but you cannot ask this little girl to work so hard!" But relaxing was not an option. What began as purgatory for the young girl soon became a daily routine of constant chores.

Erzsike was very good with her hands; she was a good student and could learn anything with one lesson. She was burdened with getting all the work done, whether in the house or in the garden, as her mother became more and more helpless, crippled both physically and mentally.

Tension was everywhere, and although the small child had no idea of war, there was talk, and her father soon began sporting military uniforms and then left home for weeks on end. It was during this separation that a kind stranger knocked at their door. It was a bearded gentleman in a suit. "Hello, Madame, may I come in?"

"What do you want?" she asked suspiciously.

"I come begging you for your kind assistance; here, I brought you some bread and jam," said the kind stranger, handing over the gifts.

It had been months since she had seen jam and she quickly tucked it into her apron.

"What do you want, sir?" Rozali said in a defrosted tone, but noise from the street sent out shock waves and the man pushed his way into the door. As he took off his hat out of respect and desperation, he went on his knees.

"Please hide me, perhaps in your attic or in the shed; I am fleeing from the Nazi's." A loud noise rang out, causing Rozali to instinctively protect the desperate stranger. She hated the Nazi's and what they had done to her Magyar land. She pulled his arm exposing a tattooed number on his forearm.

"Quick, through this door and up the ladder. I will remove it once you are up there, and then you must close the floor board. I will send you food later, after they leave. Be still, the floor creaks!" she appealed to him.

Realizing that she had exposed her daughter to this deadly secret, she quickly ordered Erzsike to peel onions for soup and not say a word. "But, Mamma," Erzsike questioned.

"Say nothing, Erzsike; do you hear me?" Rozali warned in a frightened tone.

So Erzsike began peeling as her mother instructed, one after the other. "How many more, Mamma?" asked Erzsike.

"Many, Erzsike, I am making lecsó; keep peeling" she urged.

And with that, the door bolted open. "Where is he?" ordered a soldier.

"Who are you talking about?" asked Rozali, trying to camouflage her fear with unconcern.

"I know you are lying; there is an escaped Jew wondering around this area. Where is he?" the Nazi soldier ordered.

"I don't know, but my husband will be home shortly" Rozali said, fearing the worst from the soldiers, who were known to take advantage of women.

"Why is the child crying? You are lying!" shouted the soldier, trying to intimidate them.

"No, she is crying because she is peeling onions; can't you see? Everyone cries for this!" Instinctively, Erzsike sunk her face downward and continued peeling the onions, secretly wondering how many more before they would leave.

The soldiers savagely walked through the small house, knocking over bags of flour and breaking open cupboards; then Karoly entered the house like a godsend.

"What are you doing? I mean, can I help you sir?" said Karoly, trying to be as diplomatic as possible.

"What did you say to me, you disrespectful Jew-lover!" and without hesitation, they grabbed him by his shirt and dragged him out to the street. As he was brutally thrown to the ground and told to kneel, he felt the earth cushion his fall as if his Magyar soil was attempting to protect him. The neighbors secretly peered from their homes, stricken with fear. Some of the men looked as if they were trying to find a solution. He feared more would die, as he saw Gaza go to his shed, where he knew the guns were hidden. He could see the geraniums in his kitchen window and could smell the lecsó cooking. There were muffled cries and distant shouting. Like so many others, he'd known this day would come, but was caught off guard by the suddenness. *If only I had time to protect my family*, he thought, and he did the only thing he could do, he prayed. *Jesus Christ, Saint Elizabeth, pray for us, protect us. Dearest Blessed Mother, pray for us, protect us from evil, dear Virgin Maria, help us!*

But Erzsike could not wait inside; against her mother's pleas, she ran outside and shielded her father from the soldiers who were aiming their pistols at him.

"*Istenem*, do not kill my papa; he is my papa; I would die without him," she screamed from her heart, nonstop. The neighbors in the village cried and the tension grew as now a child stood in the way of the rifle and death.

The soldiers started to laugh. "The girl is braver than you are! Go then, go polish our boots and have your wife prepare food for all of us!"

The salty onions simmered in a pot while Karoly went into the shed to get some bacon and sausage to be fried in paprikás and served, ironically, with the bread the Jewish refugee had brought earlier. When he saw the bread, he knew it was not from the village and wondered if what the soldiers were accusing him of was actually true.

They sat crudely on the finely embroidered sheets, slopping their food on themselves, the sheets, and the tablecloth. All Rozali could think of were the hours it took her to get those things clean. They smoked cigars and puffed smoke in Erzsike and her parents' faces, laughing and singing and slowly falling into a state of complete intoxication.

Karoly remained vigilant and on guard, for he was painfully aware of their power over his family and feared the worst for them all, secretly praying that somehow they would survive.

In the attic the Jewish refugee sat on pins, not knowing what second the attic would be opened, not daring to breath the entire time the Nazi's were there.

As the night progressed, the soldier's heads began to nod

off and they finally made their way out, after many hours of being served food and drink. They consumed all the wine the family had in the barrel, and in return, they thanked Karoly by shoving him into the woodshed and breaking the door. "Tomorrow we'll be back for dessert," they said as they luridly smiled to themselves.

Karoly took a bottle in his hand and menacingly held it behind his back, ready to kill if they continued to disrespect his wife. Erzsike hid under the bed, and as she gazed at the little room in which they had been held hostage for so many hours, she witnessed for the first time the love between her parents. The two held each other for what seemed to be forever, and in that moment, Erzsike began to understand what war really was and to what end people would go to survive its toll.

HER INQUISITIVE MIND WAS her blessing and her curse, for she always wanted to know more, and the more she knew, the more she questioned why. *Why didn't things get better? Why couldn't her mother ever be happy? Why didn't she make her happy, and why was war necessary?*

Her presence in her tiny school was intimidating for everyone in the class, for she was clearly different, and the teacher would stop at nothing to emphasize that amongst her peers.

"You see class, Erzsike knows, and she is half your age; shame on all of you!"

But the shame and the guilt lay on Erzsike's shoulders, for she hated to be singled out. She loved her teacher, nonetheless, for she did so enjoy reading and learning as much as she could.

"You have already read that book, Erzsikem? Then read this one!" said the teacher, who had a fondness for wearing baggy pants and playing the accordion. One day, before school began, Erzsike entered the classroom early to help the teacher set up the class, but instead of seeing her normally charming teacher singing and writing on the board, she found him sitting slouched over his desk with his head sunk into his large hands.

"*Hogy vagy*, sir? What is the matter?" inquired Erzsike.

"Oh, Erzsike, you are the only reason I continue to teach," admitted the teacher.

"Why do you say such a thing, sir?" asked Erzsike, but at that moment, a Russian guard slammed open the door, entered, throwing a book on his desk, and in a threatening voice said, "And next time, if I should see another Hungarian history book, it will not be the book that gets torched, it will be you!."

The teacher was filled with a fear and revulsion that permeated his very skin and made him shake. It took every bit of control in him not to take the book and throw it at the guard's head. Instead, for the sake of Erzsike, he bit his tongue and waited for the guard to leave.

"Sir, what was he talking about?" Erzsike fearfully asked.

"Let me explain, my dear Erzsike," the teacher said while caressing her beautiful hands. "War is an ugly thing; it makes people act in terrible ways." At which point he explained why the Russians were trying to hide the true history of their beloved Hungary.

Erzsike, of course, knew this all too well; for even at her young age of six, she had seen more in her life than most would ever see in a lifetime. She had been victim to the stares of German soldiers, the victim of all that ailed her mother, and the victim of attempted molestation by a distant relative. She was a survivor and strong and very stubborn.

Mr. Varga turned to Erzsike and cried, "Erzsike, I cannot do this any longer ... I cannot teach, for they want me to teach their lies, and I refuse. I'd rather leave this country proudly as a *büszke Magyar* than to continue this charade!" he cried.

"No, sir, you still have so much to teach me," cried Erzsike.

"I know and I will, I will teach you the truth, all the truth about our proud Hungarian history. One day the Russians will leave and you will be left behind to teach the truth. You must become a teacher, Erzsike; you must teach every child the truth. This will be your destiny!"

So her path was set; the differences within her set her apart from her peers, her family, and her countrymen. Her ambition drove her forward, and her commitment to this promise guided her through the years of hardship and isolation, knowing the truth when all the others did not. Teachers college would be imminent.

To the Russians, she appeared to be a rising star in the Communist regime, but burning beneath her skin's surface was the truth, the truth that would guide her through life with passion.

She had lived through the worst part of war; she had seen the prejudice and hatred between races, comforted her mother through the pain of loss, and helped save her father on numerous occasions from the Germans. Then the Russians took over where the Germans left off. She would have to remain steadfast; no matter what, she would survive.

ॐ

AS THE SPRING GAVE way to hope, lily of the valley broke

through the earth's crust, and the lakes and rivers began to flow in the direction of freedom. Dogs barked at the site of a man lying in the swamp. His dead body lay frozen in time, with a picture frozen within the palm of his hand.

Lutzi jumped off his horse and ran towards the figure. "Who is it?" said the boy's father.

"I don't know, Papa, but he's holding a picture of Erzsike in his hand!

LENNY MALKOVITZ—*1922-1944*—WAS FOUND FACE down, shot in the back. He had one hand clinging onto his Torah and the other holding a picture of Erzsike. No one ever knew who shot him, but it was suspected that he had been caught in a crossfire, as an escaped prisoner also lay dead just 10 feet away from him.

CHAPTER TEN
AFTERSHOCK

There was no after, just shock.

CEYLON 1946

With the clarity of a *Starry Night* canvass, the Poya moon shone brightly above, overseeing the resident dwellers below.

Young Harriet sat on the verandah of her father's home in Kandy, allowing herself to feel the safety of her parental abode one last night. She looked at things with such hope, determined to make her family proud by accepting Cyril's proposal. Her father seemed so proud of the proposal, she thought, "*Finally, a daughter who marries well!*" she heard him say.

He is so dashing, smart, and well to do; who am I compared to him? she thought with sudden pangs of insecurity. *His eyes were kind*, she thought, *and he was so devout, he didn't drink or smoke, that nothing could possibly go wrong, as long as the love of God remained between them*, she pondered naively.

My sisters did not choose well; that is why Papa is so upset. One married a criminal and the other a foreigner, of all things! How terrible, she thought smugly, *but I am blessed; our marriage will be wonderful, according to our horoscopes, and I will become an Alvis!*

As the auspicious time passed, the minutes on the clock ticked their way into the holy aisles of All Saint's Church. Flowers adorned the altar, wedding saris in a myriad of colors reflected the light of candles, and there was the clicking of the cameras of all the who's who present. A very well-connected Meedeniya sat proudly in the front pew as he watched the British Governor of Ceylon, Sir Andrew Caldecott, sign as witness to the exchanging of vows. Only religious script passed between their lips, for neither revealed to the other what they truly felt.

There had been no emotional or spiritual preparation for the bride, whose interaction with her mother and sisters focused entirely on the wedding ensemble, the jewelry, shoes, hair, and makeup, and, of course, the homecoming outfit, whatever that meant. Expectations upon young Harriet to become a dutiful wife without so much as an in-depth talk to guide her was standard practice at the time, and no one knew that better than Maude, who kept her lips sealed and her eyes focused on the ceremony, as if unable to breath until the goal of marriage had been accomplished. Once that was done, she would not have to worry about her motherly duties; Harriet's hand, soul, and body would become the sole possession of Cyril Alvis. *God be with them. God be with Harri.*

THE WEDDING NIGHT MIGHT well have been traumatic for the naive bride, but Cyril was very gentle and quite experienced, or so it seemed, with women. He knew she was frightened and gently spoke to her throughout, but the nature of what he spoke was not in keeping with the act itself, which for Harriet, made the entire encounter more confusing than it ought to have been. It had seemed to last forever, but in actual fact was completed in mere minutes. He promptly went through all the physical motions without explanation or encouragement, leaving Harriet painfully aware of what she was not briefed about and shocked that this would become one of the many expectations from her husband.

When she awoke the next morning, fully expecting to be

showered in flowers and given her morning tea, she was politely pushed off the bed, for the sheets had to be scrutinized.

Thus began the shock therapy that would rise and fall like the waves in the ocean; only from that time forward, the safety of the shoreline would not be assured.

During what was supposed to the honeymoon period, Harri, as Cyril would call her, began her training period for a "happy marriage." The ritual began with morning tea that included hot fresh milk, to be made in accordance to the finest tea houses in London, for which he provided her a manual. Heat the silver tea pot, rinse, add one teaspoon of loose leaf FBOP Special Blend for him and one for the pot. Tea always had to be fresh from the nearest plantations and kept in a sealed container, never exposed to oxygen. The sugar had to be brown demerara sugar, in squares so that he could place precisely the right amount into his cup each and every time.

This had to be brought to the room immediately upon preparation and with the morning paper. It so happened that on a few such occasions, the tea was not hot enough, and then the entire procedure had to be done again, from the heating of the tea pot to the heating of the milk, lest it coagulate or form skin on the top.

He calmed himself with the knowledge that she was not accustomed to his needs, but strained at the thought of a prolonged training period. If tea was this difficult, what would breakfast be like, and to his horror, the girl could not cook. Boiling water was difficult enough for her, *What on earth did her mother teach this poor wretch?* he thought.

The disappointment for Cyril was overwhelming and the shame for Harriet was unimaginable; however, she was not without solution. For a young lady coming from such a wealthy background, the idea of a cook seemed to be the obvious solution, but this was insolence to Cyril, for which she was awarded her inaugural slap.

The marriage had begun. The honeymoon was over. The much anticipated *Home Coming* was followed by Harriet trying to explain to her guests why her lip was swollen and her eyes red. On a happier note, the in-laws were very pleased and sent glances of approval to the Meedeniya family when presented with the honeymoon sheets studded in the blood of a virgin, like a sacrificial lamb. Maude gave back a most indignant acknowledgement, as if to say, *Of course my Harri was a virgin!* and her father just cringed at the thought.

Pure unadulterated shock reverberated through Harriet; wifely duties, the traditions of the East, and cultural expectations gave way to a mind-numbing acceptance that became her only ally, "*In the valley of death, I fear no evil,*" had only to be replaced by, "*I shall not want. ...*"

Each day was regimented with "how to" instructions: how to make tea, how to reply, on which side of the bed to sleep, when to retire, when to get up, when to serve the meals, and what to make for the meals. The menu was considerably supplied the night prior, and of course, Cyril was a happy man, except when Harri failed to follow the "when to think" instructions, which were never very clear in the first place.

After the disappointment of a very dark and slightly disfigured baby number one, Harri realized that this, too, would be her cross to bear. As if God in Heaven was determined to right the wrong, a fair prince was born. He was healthy, active, alert, and, as was soon to be discovered, a highly intelligent little boy whom they called Premalal. When old Meedeniya first held the infant, he knew immediately he would be the rising star in the family and quietly lulled him, calling him his *Sudu Kumara*, which meant White Prince.

It seemed that this, too, was a mistake in Cyril's warped vision, for, by comparison, baby number two outdid baby number one all the time, which infuriated him, for this was not fair, and justice would have to be served. After all, Cyril Alvis was a just man; in his eyes anyway.

With each passing year, along came a baby, each, supposedly, to outdo the other, but in fact, none did, for it was Premalal who was the fairest of them all, and much like Cinderella, he would have to pay the price for this. As, too, would Harriet, who no longer was young, no longer felt beautiful, and who didn't have an opinion. That had left her years before, when any effort to right her wrong choice in husband resulted in her father essentially saying, *You made your bed, now sleep in it.*

The timing was everything; she once thought it had been her fate, the right timing that led her to the port that afternoon when Cyril had just landed in Ceylon. It was curious timing to have been privy to the look of pain, caused by a lost love, on Cyril's face when he was carefully tucking a certain burgundy ribbon into his wallet and then breast coat pocket. It was bad timing for her to have inquired about it after a dispute in which Harriet accused him of loving someone else. Was it then ironic timing to have been savagely made love to upon mere mention of the incident? Timing was both a curse and a gift, for to all onlookers, she was the one Meedeniya sister who had a successful marriage in a society that seemed to scrutinize everything and everyone.

At least she took solace in the fact that Cyril did not drink or cheat, and that he was controlling only because he cared and wanted his family to be perfect. It was a perfect storm of abuse that would haunt and shape the lives of his family for the rest of their living years.

None more than her son Premalal; it became so bad at times that Harriet would often say to her son, *"Prema, I can't sacrifice the lives of seven others for you!"* and despite his young age, he never held that against her. As time went on, Harriet resigned herself to her fate and actually felt grateful that Cyril only chose one child of eight to abuse.

In the morning, after the father had eaten breakfast, the children, and then only three of them, gathered at the table to eat. Hands had to be scrubbed clean, prayers recited, and manners impeccable; however, at age three, manners were post-toddler stage, unrefined, and, as expected, childish. The eldest, Stephen, would not be able to cut his meat properly due to his club hand, so his younger brother, Prema, would take it upon himself to do so. He quietly helped him in efforts to cover for his brother's inability to hold a fork and a knife at the same time.

Almost 90% of the time, this would be seen by the father as Prema's attempt to keep his brother down, for which he would be ordered from the table, with no food, and told to kneel in the corner.

It became so intense that the mere association to mealtime set Prema into panic mode. The hitting and the fear of being hit caused him to hide in cupboards; it was the only way in which he could feel safe, in the tight seclusion of four walls.

"Prema!" he would scream, to which he had to respond, "Coming, Daddy," and if he did not, he would have to leave the room and repeat "coming, Daddy" over and over again, to the point of utter humiliation, exhaustion, and tears. All the older boys suffered this abusive character assassination, but none were beaten like Prema.

When the child was just three, the beatings became so frequent that he could not sleep in his own bed, and the only solution for him was to hide under his bed for refuge. When that was discovered, he had to resort to trunks, closets, and, on one particular night, kitchen cabinets.

They searched high and low for Premalal. First it was to beat him because Cyril found Prema's shoe not properly lined up with the other shoes in the house; but then it became an urgent need to beat him because he had inconvenienced his father by not being at his beck and call, even at 2:00 a.m. The police were called; search parties were alerted to scan the neighborhood, shouting, "Prema!" which roused the mere toddler but further frightened him. So there he remained, steadfast in the confines of the miniature cabinet that surrounded him. The next morning, he was found, coiled so tightly in the cupboard he gained the nickname Houdini. His fever raged at 103°. When the doctor examined the child, he knew he was the victim of severe child abuse. *"Harriet, I beg you, keep this child away from his father!"* said the doctor, but in her mind there was nothing she could do.

While the other children played happily in the garden with their father, Prema would retreat to Pappy's trunk in the attic and breathe through a straw and rubber pipe, imagining all the while he was on some adventure that required espionage and intrigue. Like the James Bond character he had heard so much about.

Every time Harriet stepped in to defend her son, she was beaten, and the fear of the other children knowing this killed her. So she accepted the father's treatment as being justified and soon realized, if she could not beat him, she could join him.

"Shut your mouth and go to the corner!" she uttered to her son's surprise, but he was still hoping that she was only kidding.

Something had changed in her after she had been severely beaten and left for dead, begging Cyril to let their son eat. The servants found her bruised and in a pool of her own urine. They carefully tended to her wounds and applied makeup over the bruises, as per her request, while all the while secretly hating the master and wanting him dead. The more junior maids left the room crying, "*Anay*, Madame!" and a cloak of silence was put on the rest. Some even said a curse had been put on him from that day forward.

The next time Meedeniya came into to town to dote on his Harri, the servant boy revealed the truth to him and begged him not to reveal the source. His suspicions and perhaps his premonition upon first sight of Alvis had been correct. He wandered into the house stunned, attempting to bring happiness to the children, and he left soon after, only to return a couple hours later with a box of three gold bangles, something he had been going to give at Christmas.

"Why, Papa?" Harri smiled, trying not to reveal the scar above her eye, "It's not my birthday."

"No, it is not your birthday, but I am reminded what joy you have brought to my life because of your birthday, my child," at which he earnestly hugged his daughter and sobbed slightly into her shoulder. Nothing more was ever said, but old Meedeniya knew from that day forward that his visits had to become more frequent, for her sake and the sake of the children.

Nothing changed, so she had to. A light went off in her head and soon her son became her enemy.

"Ah, can't behave, can you? ... Go ahead, apply some *goo*!" she would say with disgust. She seemed to build herself up to an anger point, always to impress her husband. She found nothing appeased him more. It was on those nights of alienating her son that she would be treated the best; their love life improved, and soon, evenings out became more frequent.

Servants were supplied, care of her father, and she ordered them around like a spoiled child. She felt power she hadn't felt in years.

The servants began to sympathize with Prema, forewarning him of either parents' arrival, "*Yunda*, Prema, the Beast of Belston is coming!"

Although the relationship deteriorated to utter resentment, Prema almost preferred it that way, for the pain he felt whenever his father hit his mother was more painful than his beatings. This way, he could just hate, and that fueled him on to the next day and the next.

As Prema grew older, the occupants in the house became more. Meals were strictly monitored and rationed. Regularly being sent from the table during meals, combined with never being allowed to come to the table in the first place, Prema found himself constantly hungry, which eventually fueled a most creative side to the young survivor.

The sound of crows shouting fiendish laughter from the custard apple tree signaled young Prema to leap out of bed. With that, he pulled up his shorts, buttoned his shirt, making sure it was neatly tucked into the shorts, and combed his hair to the side. This was a bizarre ritual for rushing out to the lane to do a chore before his father woke up, but it was necessary and he had been well trained.

It was unusually cool out, and Prema was still very tired and hungry, as he had not eaten since the day before at lunch. His stomach churned as he went to get the shovel to start filling the hole that formed in the laneway every night after tropical showers.

Edison, the servant boy, unwillingly handed Young Master the shovel. "*Mali*, I will do it. Go back to bed; I will say that you did it."

"No, Edison, he'll find out. I'm up now." The boy painstakingly did his chore of penance and stood at attention until he heard the sound of his father's footsteps.

"Prema," shouted his father from the house.

"Coming, Father," Prema instantly replied.

"Your room is a mess!" shouted his father.

"Yes, Father, I know; I was busy filling the laneway for you," Prema explained.

"Insolence! How dare you talk back!" Cyril shouted and slapped his son with the leather of his very large hand. The little boy fell to the ground and quickly gathered himself up and stood at attention. He knew not to say a word.

"When I get home, I expect your room to be clean as a pin! Do you understand?"

"Yes, Father," Prema said and moved aside.

He watched his father get served by his mother and a crew of maids. String Hoppers, seeni sambol, beef curry. Cyril ate with the righteousness of a leader and did not converse with anyone, least of all his wife.

"Harri, don't bother me with your trivial needs; your allowance is in the jar. You go with Sedaris. He will take you food shopping. Otherwise, let the driver go himself; you need not worry yourself." With that, he hollered for a finger bowl and towel. He patiently sipped on his tea, as if analyzing every sip, and then pushed his chair back in a slow but firm fashion and rose from the table, as if expecting applause of some sort for eating his entire breakfast without any help.

"Prema!" he shouted again.

"What can I get you, Cyril? Prema is getting ready for school," said his wife. As swiftly as one swats a fly, she too fell victim to the razor of his slap.

"Was I speaking to you!" her husband said with absolute

venom. Prema had heard the shout and came immediately. Seeing his mother cower in the corner kitchen chair made him fill with anger and resentment.

"Yes, Father?" Prema said.

"Where were you? Didn't I tell you to say, *coming, Daddy* immediately?" he drilled.

"Yes, Father, but I was cleaning my room," Prema pleaded.

It was no use, *putt, putt, putt* in succession across the head and face, only stopping when he heard the sound of the engine on the laneway.

The other children gathered around him, "Goodbye, Father," they said in unison, each dutifully kissing his cheek, except Prema who stood nearer his mother, as if his small frame could shield her in some small measure. He went unnoticed. This was the routine. Every morning, day in and day out, the children were called to the kitchen table, all eight, smallest to biggest, and the food was dished out as if in boot camp.

"Did you hear about the match today?" said Prema in an excited pitch to his brothers, Stephen and Manjula. "I'm going!" Prema declared.

"What do you mean, you're going? Does Daddy know?" the two questioned with heightened curiosity.

"He doesn't have to know; the three of us can go. We'll say we're at Perry's and go," Prema strategized.

"No, Prema, if Daddy finds out ..."

"He won't. Besides, I found five rupees; what about that! I'll buy you ice cream!" And with that promise, it was sealed; cricket and ice cream, who could resist? So after being dropped off at school by Sedaris the driver, the boys planned in the school yard where and when they would meet.

"Where's the five rupees, Prema? Let me see it," said Manjula.

Prema proudly revealed it to him and said, "Here, now let's get some ice cream! So off they went to the local milk bar and immediately ordered three double scoops for themselves, much to the barmaid's surprise. "Are you sure, *Putha*; it will be one rupee?" she asked rather motherly.

"Oh yes, we're sure!" they said, as if exposing a secret to which only the three of them now held. The sticky suds of the ice cream dripped on their uniforms as they hurriedly ran down the street to the cricket stadium. ... It was already the middle of the match and St. Benedict's was catching up with the Royalists score of 225, all out.

The crowd was full of children and parents alike, heavily immersed in the game, joyous that the rains ceased and the match could be played in its entirety.

Life was wonderful, or at least it had the potential to be, and young Prema had the innate ability to suck the marrow out of life, no matter how difficult that seemed to be. He found the good in most everything, whether it was appreciating the taste of a strewn, half-eaten mango, or being able to find enough thread in which to repair his own pants. He felt happiness, but most of all, he felt hope. Hope that one day he would be able to save his mother from her fate of becoming just like his father and be able to buy anything his brothers and sisters ever wanted.

This was one such occasion where he found hope: seeing his brother Stephen simply watching cricket instead of crying because God had not blessed him with a good memory for studies. This made the risk of getting caught all the more worthwhile.

He knew to whom he owed thanks, and while sitting in the stadium at St. Benedict's, his eyes wondered to the left side of the church, which stood beyond the gates of the stadium. It was where the picture of Our Lady of Perpetual Help hung adorned with jasmine and roses all the days of the year.

Our Lady and Prema had a very special relationship, for only she knew of his pain, she and, of course, Jesus, whom the boy would cry for and find solace in whenever he was being unmercifully beaten.

"Yeah, Prasanna hit a six! St. Benedict's won!" shouted Manjula. The boys hugged, oblivious of the time and the ice cream smudges upon their uniforms.

"Oh my God, its five o'clock! Daddy will be home in 20 minutes!" screeched Stephen.

"Don't worry," said Prema, "I know a shortcut." So the boys hightailed it out of the stadium, past the milk bar, around the corner from Perera & Sons Bakery, across the backyard of old Mr. Wickramasinghe, and even having enough time to whip a stone at the backside of a cat before making their way through a loosened plank of their fence.

Edison saw the boys muddle through the tight gap and hurried them into the house, knowing all too well that there would be hell to pay should they look like they did when their father arrived.

"Quick, sandals in the bucket, strip down, give me your clothes, wash up, and your shorts are on the bed!" Stephen and Manjula quickly obliged, but Prema took his time, knowing that nothing he did pleased his father anyway, so he would clean up, but only once he knew his brothers were in the clear.

The boys just managed to get fully clean and dressed. They positioned themselves at the table with school books open when their father walked in.

There were rules even for their father's grand arrival each

night. First the servant boy had to stand at attention, ready to take his coat, his briefcase, and his stick, which he used to whack unsuspecting people out of the way and to help him to stand even more erect. Then the servant could only speak when spoken to, "Good evening, *Putha*."

"Good evening, sir," which would be followed by, "Tea, sir?"

"No, *Putha*, ginger beer. It is a very hot and sticky day, indeed."

Harriet would then line up with the little ones, in order of preference it seemed, for the older one was in the house, the more peripheral one was made to feel.

"Hello, darling *Putha*," the father adoringly said to small Danuka, who clung to his father's pant leg. The girls, Manori, Manisha, and Pavani, all curtsied, and then upon the delightful exclamation of the father, "What's this?" proceeded to bend down to give a warm embrace to his daughters.

"The girls have been practicing their curtsey for the piano recital at St. Theresa's, one week from today," said their mother, grateful for a happy smile.

The two boys just stood at attention by their school books, still sweating profusely from the run home. "Boys?" said their father sternly.

"Coming, sir," they both said, slowly walking towards their father.

"What have you been up to?" He sensed guilt in their eyes.

"Nothing, sir, I mean, we've been studying, sir," mumbled Manjula, the quicker of the two, but Stephen remained silent with his eyes downward.

"What have you been studying?"

"Math," said Manjula.

"I wasn't asking you, Manjula, I was asking Stephen."

"Math, sir," said Stephen unconvincingly.

"Oh really, then why is your English book open?" he cross-examined.

"Uh, uh," he began to stutter, "because …" And without so much as a bat of the eye, the father slapped him across the face.

"You're lying to your father? Where is that useless culprit; where is Prema?" said their father, now getting haughtier by the second.

Prema, having heard the questions, walked fearlessly into the room, ready to take anything that came his way. "Good evening, Father" said Prema.

"Don't be insolent; what were you doing?" he shouted.

"We were studying, sir," he innocently replied.

"Then where are your books?"

"I just put them away; I was helping Stephen with …"

"With what, English?" he uttered victoriously.

But, fortunately, Prema had ears like tuning forks. "No, math, sir. Isn't that right, Stephen?" Stephen was now crying from the pain and the shock of the slap.

"Why can't you do better in math? You're a disgrace; your younger brother has to teach you!" His arms started to swing, *putt, putt, putt* across the head and face. But Prema could not stand for it; he could endure anything but see his siblings victimized by his father.

"Sir, he's doing well in math; he got 100%. I was just double checking his work!" Prema uttered quickly.

"Is that so?" simmered the father, catching his breath.

"Yes, sir," cried Prema.

"Go then, go finish your studies!"

The entire household stood at attention, mortified at what he might do. "You heard your father; go do your studies," Harriet interjected with a shaky voice, not daring to look up. "Come, children, time to get ready for dinner," she said protectively, and with that, they all seized the opportunity to scramble to various rooms of the house to avoid conflict.

What seemed to be a stare off contest between Prema and Cyril soon lost its luster, and Cyril retired to his study. "Where's my ginger beer?"

The three older boys gathered in their room. "My God, that was close; I feel sick!" said Stephen.

"Don't be silly. Everything will be fine; you'll see," said Prema and he proceeded to recite a funny poem to cheer up his very red-faced brother.

"The dogs they held a meeting;
Some travelled by rail and some by motor car.
Once inside the meeting place all instructions took
That each were to take his asshole out and hang it on a hook.
Scarcely were they seated down when someone shouted 'fire!'
All in a bunch they ran and had their asshole's mixed up,
Which is why a dog you know will leave a juicy bone
And sniff another's ass, hoping to find his own!"

The boys were sitting on the bed, laughing in delight, when their father shot into their room like a bat out of hell. "Who taught that disgraceful rubbish to you? he shouted.

"Tony Offen told me," said Prema proudly, thinking it was quite a good verse.

"No dinner for you, young man. Now get yourself to confession!"

Quite prepared for this, Prema said, quite unaffected, "Righto, sir;, I'm off then," and quickly exited the room before his father's shoe reached his backside.

Harriet stood in the background, wondering how much more of this abuse could her family endure. But life took hold, routines were followed, and, seemingly, all had been forgotten the moment Prema left the house, at least for the moment.

Prema, a mere eight years old, wandered to church, instinctively knowing that if he did not, the priest would rat him out, so he went, only, in his time. He had other things to do first.

Along the way, he stopped at the house of his friend, Brian Obeysekera, where Brian's mother was often baking lovely short eats for snacks before dinner. At first, it was the smell of karapincha frying in seeni sambol that led him down the pathway, but then it was the hope that Mrs. Obeysekera would see him and take pity upon the small underdeveloped child.

"Prema, is that you?" called Mrs. Obeysekera.

"Yes, Madame, is Brian home?"

"Oh no, they were stopping at Fountain Café at Elephant House after the game—it's a hot one today." She smiled, sensing there was more to his visit.

"Oh," Prema said, unable to hide his disappointment.

"Prema, come, child, come here. I've just baked some nice fish cutlets, and now the boys won't be here to enjoy them," she spoke coaxingly. "Come."

In an instant the boy ravenously ran across the lawn and joyously ate the delicious treats.

"My goodness, you were really hungry; here, take some more," she said, coyly looking away so that he could fill his pockets. "And here is a nice glass of cold milk to wash it down." She smiled angelically.

"Thank you, Madame, thank you so much," said Prema, saddened by the fact that he did not have a container in which to store the gigantic glass of milk set before him.

"What's wrong, Prema, don't you like milk?" she asked, concerned.

"Oh yes, of course, thank you, Madame, sorry to be a bother," at which point he obligingly drank the entire glass, approximately one week's worth in one go.

He savored the rich creaminess of the milk as it coated his tongue and cooled his soul. As it filled his tiny stomach, he could actually feel it expand in effort to accommodate the savory meal set before him.

She watched the child in his ragged shorts and hand-me-down shirt, and she gazed at his hands, which were far older than his years, and at the yellowish color to certain parts of his body. Then it struck her, he was an abused child. The most obvious mark of abuse resided on the palette of who he was and was reflected through his very sad brown eyes.

"It's a pleasure to watch you eat; it's nice to have my baking appreciated, Prema." She smiled.

"Brian is very lucky, Madame, *bohoma esthutaie*." Prema smiled and said his goodbyes.

"Remember, you are always welcome here, no matter what time of day or night," she said to him firmly, gazing into his eyes. He wanted to hug and kiss her, but instead, returned the invite to her, out of fear of being discovered, not realizing his answer revealed the depth of his abuse that much more.

Prema, feeling loved and full, happily skipped to church. After all, he could speak to Our Lady again, and he always had time for His Blessed Mother.

"Forgive me, Father, for I have sinned," said the boy, kneeling in the confessional.

"What have you done, child," uttered the priest.

"Father Thomas?" inquired Prema.

"No, no, Father O'Hare. I've only just arrived at your parish in Colombo. Now tell me, young lad, why aren't you home eating your dinner with your family, or studying, for that matter. What terrible sin have you committed to bring you out at his late hour?" the priest inquired curiously.

"Well, Father, I recited a verse I just learnt from a friend at school and was telling it to my brothers, when my father overheard. ..."

"Oh heavens, a bit of a poet, are we? So go ahead, tell us the verse, and let me be the judge. I'll be your literary agent, as it were!" the priest encouraged.

At which point, unable to make out whether he was only kidding and desirous of saying it once again out loud, Prema began again. "*The dogs ...*"

At first, there was silence, and then the entire confessional began to rattle at a thunderous rate. Prema, alarmed and thinking that he had killed the priest with his wicked words, began praying for forgiveness, and then he jumped out of the confessional and ran to the other side in efforts to save the priest, who was now in such a deep state of hysteria that his face went from bright red to almost blue!

"Father, Father, are you alright? I'm so sorry, Father!" he cried.

"Go, child, don't worry; you won't be going to hell any-time soon. Bless you, now go and do what boys do at this hour; go home to bed!" He smiled broadly and gave him a blessing, still laughing as he made his way past the altar.

The encounter served to confuse more than comfort Prema. "Who was that priest and what will I tell my father? If I tell him the truth, he will get infuriated, perhaps even chastise this nice new priest."

On his way home, Prema discovered that he could see clearly into Sonia Agrawal's bedroom in the night and qui-etly watched her brush her long black hair. He soon forgot his fear and began to discover the power of a beautiful woman.

"What did the priest say? I trust he was thoroughly disappointed in you," conveyed his father, who was waiting to be vindicated.

"Yes, Father, I have to pray the rosary for one hour every day."

"Damn good, now get to bed," he roared.

Harriet had kept a plate out for him, but his father put it away. "You see, I was right!" he gloated. "He deserves nothing!"

She sat quietly at the kitchen table, watching a fly land in and around her hand. Such a small insect and even it was audacious in her presence. The weight of her depression felt like a boulder around her neck. She felt no bigger than the fly and far less significant. *I'm no better than he is; I am worthless*, she thought as she rose to her feet out of duty and then slowly dragged her feet to bed.

CHAPTER ELEVEN
FIVE RUPEE ROGUE

A thorn defends the rose, harming only
those who would steal the blossom.

FLASH FORWARD 2010

THE JEEP WEAVED IN AND OUT OF THE CHAOTIC TRAFFIC SO typical of Sri Lanka. Cars, HiAce vans, buses, three-wheelers, cows, dogs, and people jumped in front of the jeep, which was slowing so the driver could fixate upon the various fare for sale in the small village they were now in. The jeep stopped. As the elegant man with salt and pepper hair gingerly walked to the curb nearer the *kade,* he heard the shop keeper shouting at a small boy. *"Palayan de, thief!"* The small child ran out of the shop and caught the eye of the man who walked inside the shop.

"How *Putha?* What happened?" inquired the man. But the boy was too sad and scared to speak. The clerk continued to scream abuse when the elderly man gave him a stern look of disapproval.

"Yes, Mahathaya?" The clerk smiled coyly, realizing the caliber of the customer who had just set foot in his humble shop.

"Suduru Samba thiyanawada? Do you have it or not?" asked the man, irritated by the clerk's whole demeanor.

"Why yes, *Mahathaya,* over here, come look," said the clerk, shoving his sarong between his legs. As the man made his way to the gunnysacks filled with spices, Maldive fish, rice, coconuts, and dhal, a thick sheet of black lifted from it as the clerk gyrated with exaggerated enthusiasm. It was the type of hand gesture suitable for shooing a cat, but did the trick for the flies that rose up for him to identify the rice from the dhal.

Perhaps he would have caught the look of disgust on the gentleman's face if he wasn't so distracted by the boy, who remained at the periphery of the shop, still mesmerized by the look of compassion that the gentleman had given him earlier.

"*Palayan de Putha! Palayan de!*" shouted the barbaric shopkeeper.

"That's quite enough!" exclaimed the gentleman, who was now furious at the unwarranted abuse of the shopkeeper towards the boy.

As the boy began to walk away, dejected, a frail hand was put on his shoulder. The boy turned around and protectively hugged his mother, who could barely stand.

The gentleman watched from within the shop with concern.

"*No, Ammey, No!*" said the boy to his mother, but she insisted and entered the shop from which he had just been chased as the clerk stood defiantly, ready to hurl out more abuse.

Although extremely poor, the woman maintained her dignity by placing a five rupee coin on the counter.

"*Makada?* What's this?" said the clerk.

The woman who was not as old as her withered frame and years of pain reflected on her face, uttered in a whisper of a voice, "I want to buy five-rupees-worth of sugar," she repeated with a clarity and strength of all the angels in heaven.

"I'll take the five rupees for that Five Rupee Rogue of a son of yours!" shouted the clerk.

Suddenly, with the speed of summer lightening, the shrill of a loud and impassioned voice filled the tiny *kade.*

"Five Rupee Rogue, Five Rupee Rogue? You're the rogue! Now get on your knees and apologize to this poor woman, and after you're done, pack five kilos of everything in your shop for this lady!" shouted the compassionate man.

"*Mokada?*" uttered the stunned clerk.

"You heard me!" shouted the man, who was now like a god in the eyes of the onlookers that gathered outside the shop.

"A thousand apologies, Madame, I'm so sorry; please forgive me!" begged the clerk, perplexed as to who she was to this gentleman.

The little boy ran to the feet of the gentleman and worshipped him, but as his mother proceeded to do the same, she dropped to the floor, unable to move.

"*Ammey!*" the little boy cried.

"*Name modada?* What is your name, son?" asked the man.

"*Samiras Mahathaya.* My name is *Samiras.*"

"Don't worry, Samiras, we'll take good care of your mother."

"Tell me, what do you want to be when you grow up, *Putha?*"

"I want to be a medical doctor, so that I can heal my *Ammey,*" cried the boy.

"If you study very hard, Samiras, I will make sure that happens," promised the man with the compassion of a saint.

CEYLON 1954

EVERY SATURDAY THERE WAS a time for chores, and their father had an entire schedule for the eldest boys to follow, while the girls in the family were treated like princesses and taken to Salon Moira.

"Salon MoiiiiiiiiiiiiiiiRA" Manjula said sarcastically. "I want to go! Why only the girls? It's not fair!"

To which Prema exclaimed, "Because the barber with the dull clippers does a much better job!"

The humiliation alone of having to stand on a milk box while the half-blind barber shaved around the ears and clipped around the soup bowl which was placed upon their tiny heads made them feel like they were getting ready for the slaughter!

"How humiliating!" exclaimed Manjula, who was beyond envy, secretly wanting to be in his father's favored-son position once again.

"Just pray for what you want, Manjula; besides, we had ice cream and watched the cricket match yesterday and they didn't, so don't be mad," comforted Prema, but the seeds of jealousy were too deeply rooted in Manjula, and it became his sole desire to get what he wanted, even if it was entirely self-serving.

On that day they had to organize the tools in the garage, having to empty all the jars, separate the various sizes of tools into different containers, and make sure that each nail and screw was clean and shiny. To Prema, it was the most pointless exercise in the world, for his father must have had the biggest collection of unused nails on the planet. For a man who did not even know how to hammer a nail into a wall, this truly was pathetic. Observations like this came to Prema early in life and served to only erode any kernel of respect he ever had for this stranger who was his father. Because they knew of their father's sadistic tendencies, they worked at a snail's pace to ensure no more chores were added to the list. Three hours later, the girls arrived, well fed, well groomed, and well spoilt.

Manjula vanished to the boys' room and drew a chalk line down the middle of the room, thus proceeding to clean his side of the room, in the words of his father, "like a new pin." Determined to gain favor with this father when he was called, he took his time coming, and when asked where he was, he said quite proudly, "Cleaning my room!"

"Cleaning your room!" exclaimed his father in such an excitable tone, one would have thought the lottery had been won. The joy showing on his face was unmistakable. "What a good boy, Manjula, so organized, so meticulous; you remind me of me," he gloated. "Manjula, I truly believe that in the years to come, you will make a fine gentleman planter!" and with that, it was cemented; Manjula would become his new pet and do anything for the honor of his father's praise.

As Stephen and Prema entered the room, their father was embracing Manjula, and he gave them both a look of absolute disgust. "I know what you'll both be doing for the rest of the day."

To which the boys both nodded and replied, "Yes, sir," with downcast eyes.

"What the hell, man? What are you doing, aiming for son of the year?" exclaimed Prema, who was tired and irritated from the day's nail cleaning exercise. "We've already been cleaning all day, now no dinner till this cursed job is over."

"What? He said to do it before he left, don't you remember?" said Manjula defensively, knowing all too well that he had not.

"You forget, Manjula, I'm the one with the memory," Prema said as he raised the broom and began to sweep. "You go ahead, Stephen, I know you're hungry; I'll clean your side as well."

No one noticed he was not at the table for dinner. His mother was just thankful there was no further conflict and allowed herself the luxury of enjoying the rest of the night, conflict free.

❧

EVERY SUNDAY AFTER THE horrible journey of being shoved

into the back seat of the Morris Minor to travel to and from church, the family would exit the car nauseous, over-heated, and thirsty. It was on days like those, that, for once, all Prema wished he to do was lie under the shade of a tree and drift off to sleep, but this was not to be. Cyril would put on his khaki shorts, which always meant they would be de-bugging the mattresses. Prema and the servants were ordered to drag out all nine mattresses from the house and line them up in the garage. Cyril put his glasses on to ensure precision as he dipped the paint brush in the Shelltox and spread it evenly over each and every mattress, as if painting a prize worthy statue. The smell was horrible, so sickening, in fact, that Prema, still queasy from the car ride home, would nearly faint from the fumes. Each time he became uneasy on his feet, the mattress would sway and Cyril would lose his place. "You little bastard, I'm make you drink it if you don't hold it still!"

Edison watched and always insisted upon doing it, but like a sadist, the more kindness extended to Prema, the more viciously Cyril treated him.

Prema was growing up, and he saw clear signs of a maniac in his father, and he knew all too well he would have to get out, somehow, somewhere, but for the time being, his endeavors would have to keep him steady. Cyril had a mania about everything, including making Manjula his little snitch, praising him and petting him whenever he had a chance. Prema would rather have sold his soul to the devil than not remain himself: sloppy, obstinate, defiant, and determined to survive.

Thanks to the alliance with Edison, Prema learnt how to pry open the storage cabinets in the kitchen, which were kept under lock and key, to remove tins of prunes and cream and beans, and to sip ginger beer out of bottles and replace it with soda, and to hide this food supply up on the roof in a bag that he lowered into the chimney stack for safekeeping. Whenever something went missing, the entire house was searched, but nothing was ever found.

One Monday morning, as the boys got ready for school, Sedaris started the engine and waited for Sir to come out. Upon approaching the car, Mr. Jayasuriya greeted Cyril over the gate, unaware of the problems this would cause.

"Mr. Alvis, did you enjoy the match on Friday? Saw the boys in the stand, but didn't see you there."

Cyril looked taken aback. "Friday's match?"

"Yes, St. Benedict's vs. St. Thomas's," Jayasuriya went on.

"Oh, yes, of course," he muttered. "I've been distracted with a case I'm working on. ... Nice to see you." Cyril smiled and got into the car.

The boys came out and climbed into the car. "Let's go, Sedaris."

"Daddy, Prema is not yet in the car," said Stephen.

"Don't worry, the little rat knows how to walk," said the father, locking the doors.

He waited until he saw his son and then instructed Sedaris to proceed. Prema started running after the car, confused as to why they were leaving without him.

"Sedaris, Sedaris!" shouted Prema, but nothing; he kept driving, not at his usual pace, but slow enough to be followed. Prema was already on the street and did not know what to do. Stop chasing the car and walk, or keep chasing the car. He felt like a rabbit being lured by a carrot on a string and thought, *I guess I'll keep chasing.*

As this scene was being created outside the car, Cyril began his own investigation inside the car. "What's this about a cricket match on Friday?" ordered the father. To which Stephen's eyes began to well up in absolute fear. "Don't worry, *Putha*, I know it wasn't your doing. You probably were lied to by your brother, isn't that right, *Putha*?" He gently stroked Manjula's head. "All I want to know is, where did he get the money?"

Stephen began to cry and Manjula smiled coyly, "Well, Daddy, I wanted to tell you, but Prema threatened us. You see, he showed us his five rupee coin, and when I confronted him and asked him from where he stole the five rupees, he said he would buy us ice cream and take us to the cricket match if we kept quiet."

"Is that so?" said the father. "Don't worry, *Putha*, I will take you both for ice cream after school today, and you don't have to worry that the money I use is stolen, Okay, boys?" the father devilishly said.

"Yes, Father," said the boys in unison as they arrived at the school.

"Goodbye, Father," said Manjula, smiling victoriously, with Stephen standing close by unable to speak.

Prema reached the car, sweating and red-faced, with spectators all around. "Hey, Prema, next time, attach yourself to the front of the car and pull it to school. It's obvious you're the workhorse in the family!" they shouted, laughing.

Cyril jumped out of the car and grabbed the collar of Prema's shirt with such ferocity that the boys on the sideline quickly disassembled for fear of getting caught in his chafe. "So you're the Five Rupee Rogue, are you? Just come with me. I'll show you what they do to rogues," he said as he dragged the helpless child into the school's principal's office.

He walked into the office and threw his son into the room, causing him to trip and fall onto the principal's desk. "What's this, Mr. Alvis?" asked Father Stanley.

"It seems my son has learnt nothing from my strict upbringing, nor has he learnt a thing from this school. Either you publically discipline him for stealing or I will!" shouted Cyril.

Feeling rather like Pontius Pilate, Father Stanley tried to plead with him. "Mr. Alvis, I understand that you are mad. I will have him write lines and kneel in the corner," he said, as if plea bargaining for the youth.

"No, that's not good enough!" He proceeded to slap his son's head, whilst kicking his snow white shins till the tar from his boot tattooed his leg.

"Mr. Alvis, please, this is not the place!" But the horror in the child's eyes was too much to bear and the priest quickly agreed so as to spare the child from any more torture, for the moment.

"Do it now!" ordered Cyril, sweating like he had just run a marathon.

"Uh, what do you mean sir?" said Father Stanley.

"Take him to the auditorium, now, and whip him. I'm not leaving until I witness for myself that the right discipline is given for the offence."

"Sir, this is your son!" said Father Stanley, but at that moment, Cyril grabbed the boy's head and began whacking it against the desk.

"No, no, I will do it!" said Father Stanley in a sickened voice.

"What's all the noise about?" said the monsignor, who walked into the room.

"Ah, Monsignor, a pleasure to see you again," Cyril said, and he promptly bent on his knees and kissed his ring.

"I see; more bad behavior, Prema?" the monsignor said contemptuously, glaring at the boy who was barely conscious.

As if both men delighted in punishment, they proceeded down the hall and into the auditorium, where Prema was publically humiliated in front of the entire school, pants down and consecrated over a desk. The monsignor carefully chose his whip of pleasure, which he soaked in water near the desk. He carefully analyzed its texture and whipped it across the table so as to get everyone's attention. "This is to show all you boys that stealing is a sin and that this is a Five Rupee Rogue!" at which point, he began to whip Prema across the flesh of his buttocks, over and over again. "You will not sin! You will not sin!" he climaxed with each passing whip.

The boys in the auditorium began shouting, "Five Rupee Rogue," but soon tired of the display and began to feel sick, none more than Stephen, who fainted in the audience. Prema blacked out on the desk, focusing entirely on the crucifix of Jesus. *Oh, Lord God, I know what you have endured is far worse. I offer this up in your name*, the boy mentally prayed until he finally fainted.

He was put in the nurse's room and tended to medically. They wanted to make him kneel the rest of the day, but if truth were known, he must have suffered internal injuries, a broken rib and a concussion perhaps, but no one really cared to find out.

It was Father O'Hare, visiting the school that day, who first saw the boy. He was barely recognizable, but the small boy's sad eyes were unmistakable. "My God, nurse, what has happened?" to which the nurse just shook her head and whimpered.

After school, Cyril showed up at the school promptly to take Manjula Stephen for ice cream. "Father, where is Prema?" asked Stephen. But all Cyril cared about was his promise.

"You see, children, your father is a man of his word. Do you see that, *Putha?*" He smiled at Manjula, who didn't know whether to cry or smile.

"Daddy, where is Prema," repeated Stephen.

"Ice cream it is!" said their father as they drove away from the school to Fountain Café.

Neither child could eat their ice cream, but they were compelled to in order to please their father. By that time Stephen was convinced that his brother was dead.

Father O'Hare prayed over young Prema, holding his hand, putting ice chips on his swollen lips, and placing cold compresses upon his brow. *"Dear Father in Heaven, protect this child from this horrendous abuse. Please keep him safe in your loving hands and away from all evil. Please shroud him in your love from this day forward, for, my God, I certainly will. ... Amen."*

After a doctor was brought to the school dormitory, the boy's wounds were set in plaster casts and bandages, and he was given some liquid nourishment to keep up his strength. Father O'Hare remained at his bedside till the morning.

Harriet was sick with worry. She knew something horrible had happened, but no one would say. "He was punished and is now staying at the dormitory for the night. Now get to bed," shouted Cyril to his wife.

Later in the night, she tiptoed into the boys' room and asked Stephen, "What has happened to Prema? Stephen, tell me." The boy sobbed in her arms and vomited upon the explanation.

"Dear God, what has he done; what has he done to him this time!" And with that, Manjula awoke and told her quite proudly that he had been righteously punished for stealing five rupees.

Like a dagger in her heart, she knew at that moment that a Judas had been born into the soul of her son.

"I gave him that money. I gave him that money to buy food," she sobbed, and she prayed the rosary till morning.

CHAPTER TWELVE

THE BUTTERFLY EFFECT

The butterfly effect is a theory that encapsulates the concept of sensitive dependence on initial conditions in the chaos theory; namely, a small change at one place in a complex system can have large effects elsewhere.

HUNGARY 1955

As THE OVERWHELMING GRASP OF COMMUNISM CANCEROUSLY seeped into Hungary, conflicts between the cultures, the ideologies, the elderly, the youth, the truth, and the lies smashed heads like two fighters in a ring.

Hungary diminished to hostage status as Russian propaganda forced its way through the gates of parliament, offices, schools, and homes. Russian signs and plaques were erected everywhere honoring the great Premier, Joseph Stalin, and Hungarians were force-fed this propaganda; similar to geese being fattened to make froi grois.

The elderly aged tenfold, wanting to die rather than give in, and the youth tried to develop a taste for this bitter pill, often choking in the attempt. Many Hungarians died, escaped, or were jailed while attempting to revolt against this Soviet powerhouse.

The force and fluidity of the attack was so tactically superior, that many Hungarians wished the Germans would return. No woman was safe from any Russian soldier, and no Hungarian history book escaped the fires of vengeance and hate. This was all done in the hope that somehow the elimination of the written word would obliterate the memory of the people.

Erzsike bore witness to this assault upon her Magyar land. She was given very poignant decisions to make during her formative years, which quite literally shaped the very outcome of her destiny. She listened to the fearful tears of her mother and other women in her small town and saw how this fear emasculated every husband, father, and brother within the country. She heard the intoxicated verses of the Hungarian anthem, which would rise and fall in volume with every shift change of the guards. For thirty minutes the crescendo pitch would reach the greatest heights of all, from the hearts of pride-filled Hungarians who dared take the chance of being heard.

This provided her with a potpourri of emotions, which ranged from pride and joy to anger and shame. It prodded her to learn the truth of the past, but made her wise with the need to survive by excelling in the propaganda of the lies set before her.

She watched her beloved teachers grow bitter and frustrated, and became privy to knowing that beloved Father Varna had left his robes and escaped to Vienna with Sister Maria. These seemingly small events, when combined, demonstrated the impact the war had on the people of Hungary. The turmoil that existed during those tumultuous years caused stirrings, which only could be referred to as the butterfly effect.

With each new idea came the birth of another ideology. Whilst appeals for monolithic unity amongst Communists were made, the force of resistance led to cracks in the foundation of the Soviet propaganda.

The treacherous conquest of Hungary by the Communists caused the autonomy of a people to be destroyed. This sent ripple effects around the world. In the US, when Truman became the 32nd President of the United States, he called on its citizens to lead the democratic world and denounce Communism. The US Senate Committee on Foreign Relations prompted the president to order a complete investigation of war crimes against Hungary, to be reviewed by the United Nations.

In Moscow, editorials in the newspaper *Pravda* began to accuse the US of double-dealing. Allegations flew, creating discord that ultimately led to putting blight on truce hopes between North America and Russia.

In Germany, the Democratic Republic began talks about erecting a wall as a barrier that would completely cut West Berlin off from surrounding East Germany and from East Berlin. In 1961 construction of the Berlin Wall began. The Berlin Wall served to prevent the massive emigration and defection that marked Germany and the Communist Eastern Bloc during the post-World War II period.

The world was changing at an alarming speed. There was a sense of urgency never before seen or experienced. War begot war and hate fueled the pot. People felt the need to take sides and fight for what their instincts dictated was their righteous cause, and Erzsike, too, was forced to decide.

It seemed her path was clear; she was Hungarian, and she would fight for Hungary, but she also knew that she would have to survive. So she decided to do what many others were compelled to do; she camouflaged her true heart and appeared to become a rising star in the Communist regime.

Too young to leave home and too smart to remain, she made her way to Teacher's College, much to the irritation of her mother, who was now crippled with rheumatoid arthritis. It was a promise she had made to her teachers and she would carry it through. Erzsike hid old Hungarian text books in her attic, for she had learnt that if they could conceal the presence of a person within their home, then surely books would be easy to hide. During the day she memorized Communist dogma and approved Communist teachings, and in the night she memorized the truth by candlelight.

Erzsike was blossoming into a beautiful young lady and was admired by all who knew her in her tiny village. There were many suitors, but she'd captured the heart of a certain handsome stranger who would secretly hide in the forest just to see her face as she made her way home each night from college.

It was on one such night, when Erzsike was walking home, that she tripped on a branch and scraped her knee on the underbrush. It did not seem like much of a fall, but Erzsike was brought to tears. She sobbed deeply as she sat on the forest floor, seemingly undaunted by the tear in her stockings, but rather vexed by something within her bag. She pulled out a text, opened it and ripped out the page. "Liars!" she shouted, without knowing that she was being watched.

"Miss, Miss, *hogy vagy*, are you alright?" uttered the very handsome young man.

Startled, she rose to her feet, too proud to be seen that way. "*Igen,* of course I'm alright. What makes you think otherwise?" she said almost arrogantly.

He smiled "I saw you crying; did you hurt yourself?"

"Oh no, I mean, yes, but I'm alright," she said, not knowing who he was or with whom he stood allegiance.

"Forgive me for startling you. My name is Rudi, Rudi Kölcsey; I live in the next town," and as if to exonerate himself of her suspicious glances, "I'm Hungarian." At which point he began to sing the anthem.

"Isten, áldd meg a magyart
Jó kedvvel, bôséggel,
Nyújts feléje védô kart,
Ha küzd ellenséggel;

Balsors, akit régen tép,
Hozz rá víg esztendôt,
Megbûnhôdte már e nép
A múltat s jövendôt!"

The words penetrated her entire being, easing her tension and defrosting her heart. As he sang, initially to charm the striking young lady with the long braided hair and sad brown eyes, Erzsike joined in unison with this handsome young man, needing desperately to feel the love for her country once again. Her shy notes became louder and louder as she felt the beating of her heart dance with joy within her soul. Her tears flowed as he grasped her hands to sing the final verse.

Caught up in the moment, the two embraced. As the seconds passed a gentle breeze carried the sweet smell of *gyöngyvirág* in the air, which served as a reminder of happier days when ignorance was bliss. A safe haven had formed in her mind, sheltering them from all the evil in the world. As their eyes met, he gazed deeply into her soul and knew his heart had found a new home.

"You are so very, very beautiful." He smiled. "Forgive me, your name?"

Still mesmerized by his gaze, Erzsike became uncharacteristically lost for words and fumbled in her reply, "Mmm … Erzsike, Erzsike Puha."

"*Csókolom*, Erzsike," he leaned forward to kiss her cheek, which was customary.

"*Csókolom*," she replied as the ivory of her skin brushed his freshly shaven face.

Rudi helped her assemble her books and offered to carry them home as they made their way out of the thick of the forest. "You are a student at the college?" he inquired.

"Yes, Teacher's College" she said proudly

"So tell me, Teacher's College, is it Hungarian or Soviet teachings?" he asked almost hesitantly.

"I do not wish to talk of this," she said protectively, increasing her pace towards the road.

"I'm sorry, I didn't mean to pry. I am a soldier, a Magyar. So you see, we both, we both are surviving," he spoke passionately.

"I understand," said Erzsike, wanting to feel the light-hearted flutter she had felt for the first time in her life just minutes earlier.

"Hey, look, look over there, it is an Aquila heliaca, an Imperial Eagle. It is so rare, such an honour to see this magnificent national treasure." Rudi's gaze fixated across the puszta.

"Yes, I believe it is a bird of prey. Why is it encircling over top?" questioned Erzsike.

The two stopped, intently watching the bird's direction. "It has landed over there; come let's see what it's caught." He took her hand and began to run across the grasslands of Hortóbagy but as they got closer, a more gruesome scene was unveiled. There, slightly camouflaged in the tall grass, was a dead Russian soldier, whose dishevelled body lay strewn in a deserted part of the area. Only his jacket and helmet remained, he was nude from the waist down, his genitalia, or what remained of it, was a bloody mess, and the Hungarian flag was wrapped around his neck in a mark of absolute defiance.

Erzsike wanted to scream but sunk her head into the Rudi's sleeve, and he immediately put his arms around the frightened girl. Neither said a word, knowing the danger that lay before them. At that moment, a small boy ran into sight towards the body, not realizing that there were witnesses. As he saw the two, he raised a gun towards them in a desperate attempt to survive.

"*Nemszabad!*" Rudi exclaimed. "*Beszélsz magyarul?*" To whichthe boy, no more than eleven, dropped the gun and began to cry. Rudi ran to his side to both prevent the threat of gunfire and to console the youth.

"What has happened?" asked Erzsike.

"My mother, she tried to save us, she tried so hard, and then they took her and beat her and raped her, my mother, my mother ..." He sobbed uncontrollably. "I had to kill the bastard, I had to; Papa would have done the same. I knew I had to before he tried to touch my sisters."

"We understand," cried Rudi, as if now in sync with Erzsike, whose tears of compassion gripped her so overwhelmingly that she too hugged the small child.

"Where is your mother, your sisters?" inquired Rudi.

"They are back at the house. My mother is very badly hurt; my sisters, they are very young, but I couldn't leave him here," cried the boy.

"You're right. I want you to take Miss Erzsike to your house; she will help mend your mother and quell the fears of your sisters. I need you to return here with two shovels, some alcohol, and some matches. "*Érted?*" Rudi instructed.

"*Igen.*" He wiped his tears, deriving strength from Rudi's directive.

At which point Rudi caressed Erzsike, kissed her gingerly on the lips, and said adoringly to her, "Don't worry, I will take care of everything. Can you handle this request?"

"Yes, *igen,* I will do everything to help my sister, don't worry ... and please, please be careful; hide under the tree until he returns. We have scared away the eagle, so no one will see as long as you stay out of sight." She held his hand and then rushed deep into the forest once again, following the boy.

When Erzsike entered the house, three little girls, between the ages of five and nine, sat cowering around the bed where their mother lay, tattered and bleeding. They were crying desperately, the eldest holding the mother's hand and the other two sucking their fingers and twirling their hair into a frenzied state of confusion. The mother attempted to ease their pain by comforting them, but she was so badly beaten that her face was unrecognizable, and blood covered the sheets, the floor, and the walls. Erzsike quickly told the boy to go ahead and do what Rudi had asked and assured him that everything would be fine.

She kissed and hugged the girls and asked them to be her nursemaids, to which they readily obliged. "I would like you to put some water on the fire, and I would like you to get me some towels, some medicines, and some alcohol, if you can find it," instructed Erzsike, who then quietly spoke into the ear of the mother who lay exhausted and traumatized.

"Don't worry," she whispered calmingly, "you have nothing more to fear; he is gone; the man who did this to you is dead, do you hear me? I'm here to help you." Erzsike said, softly caressing her face and slowly cleaning her wounds. "Your children are safe," she whispered. She put compresses upon her head and began to assess her injuries. The girls managed to find some medical supplies, and Erzsike began to dress most of the wounds on her arms, hands, and face. After slowly undressing the woman, Erzsike threw her blood-stained, ripped dress into the fire, knowing all too well that she would not want a reminder of this day. Her breasts were so bruised, it looked as if the soldier had tried to physically rip them off her chest. Her pelvis was tender and it appeared that her ribs were cracked, based on her difficulty breathing.

Erzsike didn't know what to do for the mother, gynaecologically. Sensing this, the mother whispered, "Hot water, towels, alcohol."

Sympathetic to the sensitivity of the moment, Erzsike gave the girls a glass of milk and some cookies she found in the cupboard, and then asked the eldest daughter to read a story to her younger sisters in the next room. Then Erzsike fetched a pail of water and returned to the humble room with more towels. With great care, she slowly unbuttoned the sleeves of the mother's blouse and gently tried to remove it by raising her arms, but the pain was too great. At that moment, Erzsike did the only practical thing, she cut the under-slip and blouse off her back and began disinfecting her wounds. It was a daunting task just for Erzsike to see the poor woman this way. With every groan, Erzsike could feel every pain the woman endured, right down to her core. Every so often, she just held the woman closely in her arms, for the memory would suddenly be fresh in the woman's mind and then panic would cause her to tremble and cry incessantly.

"Don't worry, *csillagom*, everything will be all right," Erzsike said calmly and tenderly, cradling her in her arms. In order to give her mental strength and a goal to focus on, Erzsike suggested, "Now let us get cleaned up for your children, so they will know that you will be all right, okay?

"*Igen, igen, köszönöm szépen,*" she whimpered, trying to get back the emotional strength of a mother.

After she was completely stripped naked, Erzsike slowly put a blanket over her shoulders and threw the rest of her clothes into the fire. Then with a soft sponge, she began squeezing water up and around her pelvis, allowing the warm water to slowly penetrate her violated groin. The woman groaned in agony, for the water was mixed with a mild disinfectant, and as it touched her wounds, they stung. Erzsike continued this process until the water ran clear. It took several minutes for this, and by that time, the poor woman was shivering. Erzsike slowly and gently towel dried the woman, who she later learnt was named Andrea.

"Andrea, where are your clothes?" She pointed to them and Erzsike diligently gathered all that she needed. She patted petroleum jelly on a soft piece of flannel and gently put it onto her groin before putting on her panties. Andrea's eyes closed from the comfort of the warm cloth. A cotton under-slip was gradually put on her, one arm and then the next, and then it was carefully buttoned in the back. This same procedure was followed with a dress, and then an apron was tied on top. Erzsike gently brushed her hair and tied it back and then covered her head injuries with a scarf. Then she went into her own purse and began to cover Andrea's bruises with a bit of makeup so that the children would not have to be as traumatized at the site of their beloved mother.

"*Köszönöm szépen,*" Andrea cried. "*Szivessen, édes csillagom.* I'm here for you; you are surrounded by love, do you understand?"

"*Igen,* yes, thank you," she repeated. She tried to stand, but her injuries were too much.

"Here, you sit on this chair while I clean up this area," said Erzsike.

All the bedding was removed, and all evidence was burnt. Then Erzsike removed the mattress and cleaned the walls and the floor, removing the ghastly signs of the attack. While the floor dried, she put water on for tea and more water on to boil some eggs. She found some salami in the shed, cut it up, mixed it with the eggs and some bread, and began to set the table. Then she made some red current tea with honey and gave it to Andrea, who slipped in and out of consciousness.

Erzsike sprinkled some perfume onto the mattress to remove any unpleasant odours and made the bed with fresh linen, fluffing the pillows and placing them so that Andrea could sit up in a show of strength for her children. Erzsike gingerly walked her to the bed and tucked her in under the covers. Gently putting a towel on her lap, she fed her hot soup to help her keep up her strength and gave her two aspirins to ease the pain.

Then she went into the next room and asked the girls if they were hungry. "What about our mother?" asked the girls, at which point their brother walked through the door, Rudi following close behind.

"Mamma?" he cried and all four ran into the room. To their pleasant surprise, everything was clean and their mother looked so much better, though they didn't realize scars of her wounds would never go away for the rest of her life.

"Children, *draga csillagom*. Mamma is fine!" Andrea assured, kissing their heads as they hugged her tightly, not knowing that the pressure of their tiny bodies were hurting her.

"Children, Mamma just needs to sleep. Let's eat some supper; you all must be so hungry!" Erzsike said, luring them into the next room.

The little boy, named Tibi, clung to Erzsike's waist, thanking her profusely. She bent down and hugged the little boy, saying, "Don't worry, your mamma will be alright; you all will be just fine; you are safe."

Rudi watched Erzsike in absolute admiration. After putting out the food, she gazed in his direction. "What have you done?" she asked worriedly.

"Don't worry, all has been taken care of; no one will ever find that Soviet bastard again." responded Rudi, filled with rage.

As she hugged him, the smell of alcohol and smoke was all over him.

"I think you both better clean yourselves," she urged Rudi and little Tibi, to which they immediately obliged.

"I will stay here tonight. Apparently her husband will return tomorrow," said Erzsike, "but I need you to deliver a message to my parents."

"Of course, I will do so and be back later this evening to stand guard. I'm not leaving any of you alone tonight," and without much objection, they parted company. Rudi over the puszta and Erzsike behind the wooden door, which she shut and locked to keep out all evil.

She added wood to the fire and gave each child some warm cocoa to drink. After giving the mother a shot of very strong cognac, she went back near the fire, knelt down before the crucifix and began to pray with the children. As they sat in silence, each reflecting on the horror of the day's events, Erzsike prayed aloud:

"Dear Saint Michael the Archangel, defend us in the day of battle. Be our safeguard against the wickedness and snares of the devil. May God rebuke him, we humbly pray. And do thou, Prince of the Heavenly Host, by the power of God, thrust into hell Satan and the other wicked spirits who wander the world for the ruin of souls. Amen."

Meanwhile, Rudi walked another half a kilometre to Erzsike's house, which unbeknown to her, was very familiar to him, as he had been admiring her from afar for months on end. After telling her father what had happened, Erzsike's mother sadly shook her head and promptly went to work, putting a basket of bread, salami, eggs, and csirka paprikás together to bring back with him for the family.

As Rudi waited outside Erzsike's house while her mother prepared the basket, he saw the cemetery behind the house and wandered out back in a rather hurried fashion. Karoly, Erzsike's father, came out with a bottle to offer the young man a drink, and he saw him burying something under a newly placed gravestone. He knew instinctively not to ask.

The insidious perversions of one evil act proved to have the potential to taint the lives of each and every person that was witness to its destructive path. Karoly knew this would not be the last of it.

CHAPTER THIRTEEN

LONDON FOG

Sometimes the greatest journey is finding your
way back into the heart of the one you love.

LONDON 1945

THE DENSE FOG ONLY SERVED TO ADD TO BOB'S ALREADY CON-fused state of mind. It seemed it had been unsettled from the days of the war, as he didn't know whether to live life more bombastically, in contrast to the death he had witnessed, or to finally clip his wings and settle down.

The answer appeared to come via a trunk call from Colonel Stewart, a friend and fellow soldier from the war.

"Bob, is that you, ol' boy?" shouted Stewart, "how the hell are you?" However, it was not Bob, but rather his father, Rupert, who expected always to be addressed as sir.

"This is Sir Rupert Bland Cross, and who is this, who?" he said authoritatively.

"Yes, sir, Brigadier, sir!" he said as if standing at attention. "Colonel Stewart, sir"

"What can I help you with, Colonel?" Rupert spoke.

"I am calling from England and am searching for your son, Robert, sir!"

"Oh yes, he is at work now, doing some business on the side. Doesn't seem to be made of the same army genes as I am."

"Yes, sir, not many are, sir!" Colonel Stewart obliged, not wanting to ruffle feathers with one so notorious. For everyone knew his record as an officer, it was impeccable:

Cross, Rupert Bradley, Brigadier General, ED— Officer, Order of the British Empire—Military District Number 1, awarded 6 January 1945. Service in CEF, 11

Jan 1915 to 10 Jan 1919; NAPM Jan 1919 to 1 Feb 1938, including command of the 1st Hussars, from 1 January 1933 to 1 February 1938. In 1940 he organized and commanded No. 1 Coy VG of C (AF). On authorization of 30-day training centres, he was appointed to organize and command No. 11 Training Centre, Woodstock, Ontario. The foregoing duties were most effectively performed. On organization of the Driving and Maintenance School, Woodstock, 1 November 1942, Colonel Cross was again selected to command.

The citation had been practically memorized by his son, and everyone who knew and respected Bob reciprocated the gesture as not to forget. Brigadier General Cross became notorious for driving the type of military vehicles to be taught while organizing the famed Military Training Centre. By his example and leadership, sound judgement, and determination, he developed the first and most outstanding military training centre, unique in its service to the Canadian Army, and a credit to the Department of National Defence.

"Congratulations on being awarded the Order of British Empire, sir; we all solute you!" and again the clicking of his boots could be heard in the background of the call.

"At ease, Colonel, and thank you. I will certainly pass on the message that you called. Is it urgent?" inquired Rupert.

"It is, sir" replied Colonel Stewart, not willing to divulge the nature of the call.

"Then call tomorrow morning, 9:00 a.m. our time. I will make sure Robert is here to accept the call."

"Thank you, sir, goodnight," and then the phone went silent.

Bob, Robert as he was referred to by his parents, visited on occasion, but lived in the city for the benefit of entrepreneurial work and his love life, which continued to be between cities and also between continents. When told of the incoming call, Bob arrived promptly at 8:45 a.m. to be sure to receive the call on time. He, too, had become a stickler for time; the discipline had been drilled into him during the war, and his father was relieved to see this change in his son. Bob was extremely well-respected and well-liked by his fellow officers, so when the war ended, he remained in Europe for a few months, travelling between London and Italy, forming strong alliances, before eventually going back home out of concern for his aged mother.

Although Bob had served for the Canadian Armed Forces in Europe, he could only relate to the army procedures oversees. Canada was where he had been brought up, so when he returned home, the routines of the war no longer existed, the friends he had were either dead or back in Europe, and he found himself feeling quite lost. He began to find solace in rum, the same rum that had been a staple during the war.

Rum rations were a British naval tradition, inherited by the Royal Canadian Navy and Armed Forces, and became a staple of daily life for the soldiers. Upon entering the Royal Canadian Navy and the Canadian Armed Forces, men were given the option of a rum ration or comparable pay. When given their ration of "grog" which was rum tempered with water, the men would have to consume it in front of an officer to prevent the rations from being hoarded. The rum was not given in large quantities, but was thought to help soldiers and sailors get through the cold nights and to ease the many horrors of war.

The horrors remained fresh in Bob's mind and became more vivid as he aged, more so than when it had played out on the ground. For most, the experience of war was surreal and the atrocities so graphic that they would opt not to share their pain with loved ones. The number of casualties spoke volumes: 45,000 Canadian soldiers died in World War II.

By D-Day, June 6, 1944, the landings at Normandy were accomplished by multiple beachheads, two made by the

American forces at Omaha and Utah beaches, two by British forces at Sword and Gold beaches, and a final one at Juno Beach, made by the 3rd Canadian Infantry Division and penetrating farther into France than any other Allied force. After the Normandy landings, a Canadian spearhead drove northeast into the Netherlands, which Canada liberated not long after.

These were the military accomplishments of great soldiers, of which Bob was very much a part, but his need to sway from the fold became evident while he was in Europe, and he became involved in the business end of things, in terms of trading between Canada and England. At the time, half the British Army Transport requirements were supplied by Canadian manufacturers. Bob had formed strong business relations, negotiating the sale of armored tanks and the very popular soft-skinned CMP trucks to England, which Britain maintained was the most important military contribution to Allied victory. Canada had sent over 800,000 trucks to Europe, which equaled the total production of Germany, England, France, and Italy combined.

Bob's amiable personality and formidable look took him to places around Europe that, for most, were excluded to members only. His personality and his reputation preceded him, and where being able to hold his liquor was the true measure of a man, Bob's manhood stood resolute.

His allure as a man also stood resolute, for he suspected he had fathered many a child along the coast of Italy, into France, and, as confirmed by his friend Colonel Stewart, in England. Sue, however, remained the love of Bob's life. Although his relationship with her was the most turbulent, it was also the most passionate, and the two shared the commonality of language, culture, and humor. So when news of her pregnancy came along, Bob was eager to sail back to England.

The information was from a very reliable source, as Sue's

best friend was dating Colonel Stewart and shared all the intimate details Sue chose not to share with him.

Ready to settle down and have a family, Bob sailed back to England, but swore his friend to secrecy. In the weeks that followed, Bob resigned himself to his monogamic fate, and smiled at the thought of being a father.

When he arrived in London, Bob went to the hospital where Sue had been working and was told that she was on leave in the small town of Essex, living at home with her parents. When he rang the doorbell, an unfamiliar young man opened the door, unaware of who Bob was.

"Hello," said Bob as he took off his fedora hat and smiled with the charm of Cary Grant.

"Hello," the man said, puzzled.

"I'm Brigadier Robert Cross, here to visit Sue, Susan Dorsey." To which the man grew very insecure and asked that Bob wait at the door.

When Sue appeared, she was clearly well into her seventh or eighth month of pregnancy and looked very uncomfortable at the sight of Bob. "Bob, what are you doing here?"

To which Bob smiled and said, "I know about the baby," at which point he flung open the door and gently picked up Sue in his arms.

"Oh my, Bob, I, uh ... I ..." she stumbled.

The gentleman caller, infuriated, grabbed his jacket and stormed out the door.

"Who was that jackass?" asked Bob humorously.

"He's Jacob Flynn, a very nice pilot. He's been calling on me," Sue answered protectively.

"Well," said Bob, "I can't blame the poor bastard, but he need not worry himself now!."

"What is this, a military bombardment? You haven't the

decency to reply to my letters for months, and then you suddenly show up at my door?" Sue exclaimed.

Bob may have been a cad, but a liar he was not. "What letters?" he asked, shocked.

"How else would you know about the baby?" Sue debated.

"I know because of my friend, Colonel Stewart; he's been dating Jenny. I've never received so much as a postcard from you," exclaimed Bob.

"Do you expect me to believe that?" she cried.

"Yes ... yes, I do," he said as he took her in his strong arms and kissed her tenderly.

After many awkward minutes alone, the two were interrupted by Sue's parents. "Mr. and Mrs. Dorsey, Brigadier Robert Cross, it's a pleasure to finally meet you." Bob extended his hand with a most genuine smile.

The Dorsey's looked taken aback by his stature, but Mr. Dorsey could only see red and attempted to punch Bob in the face. Immediately, military training switch into gear and Bob blocked the punch so as not to reciprocate.

"No, Daddy, no. Please, he didn't know," Sue pleaded, forming a barricade between the two men.

"What do you mean he didn't know; all those letters?" Mr. Dorsey shouted.

"Sir, I'm here only because I received word from my friend, Colonel Stewart. I sailed to England immediately upon hearing the news. I'm most delighted and desirous of asking your daughter's hand in marriage, if you would agree." Bob, who was holding Sue's hand protectively, smiled.

"Oh, Sue!" exclaimed her mother. "This is wonderful news; how very romantic!"

Upon seeing the reactions around the room, Mr. Dorsey eventually smiled and shook the hand of his now intended son-in-law. "Drinks everyone?" exclaimed Mr. Dorsey.

"I'll get out the glasses," said the most ecstatic mother of the bride.

What followed were many anxious days and nights spent between Essex and London, during which the two discussed their feelings, their goals, and their future. During this time, Bob was quick to learn, much to his amazement, that not only was Sue unwilling to move to Canada to start a new life with him, she was not even willing to move to London, where the start of their relationship first began.

She was once such a progressive young woman, determined, strong, and funny, and for some reason the pregnancy made her quite girly and insecure. She had claimed that the months of not hearing from Bob had left a gap that needed to be filled, and so her only escape to prevent public humiliation was to start a relationship with Jacob Flynn, who was now hopelessly in love with her, wanting her hand in marriage, and quite willing to live anywhere she opted, which meant Essex.

Bob tried to convince her, and he tried to understand that perhaps this vulnerability would pass, but the fact was, they really did not know each other. The war had created a world in which all things fun and recreational were heightened when put against a backdrop of fear and death. Relationships were entered into without inhibition, and passion reached orgasmic climax without much effort. Those were the times, and now a baby's future rested in the balance.

After a meal of fish and chips at The Clarence Pub, Bob escorted Sue back to the hotel to rest. They were walking past the Horse Guards sentry posts just off Trafalgar Square and down the courtyard when a little spat began. Sensitive to the fact that Sue was with child, he suggested they take a break and told her he would see her in the morning.

He called upon his friends Colonel Stewart, Staff Sergeant Milford, and Lieutenant Brody to meet him at The

Freemasons Arms. "You know, where the Football Association was founded, mate!" Bob shouted over the phone.

"That's debatable, Ducky! We'll be there at 9:00 p.m., my friend. It'll be good to catch up!" said Milford, excitedly.

The four met up and proceeded on a pub crawl that spanned from Convent Garden to Nell of Old Drury, to The Dog and Duck on Bateman Street, to the George Inn on High Street, where each began to quote Dickens after reading the plaque on the wall commemorating it as being Charles Dickens' watering hole. Intrigued by this, each man took on their favorite parts of the book *Tale of Two Cities*, in which Milford pretended to be Charles Darnay, Lieutenant Brody acted like Sydney Carton, and Colonel Stewart played a very flirtatious Lucie Manette. Bob watched, highly entertained by seeing such lighthearted blokes making fun. The drama became extended to real life when Stewart, who had too much to drink and clearly could not hold his liquor like Bob, began imitating Sue.

"That's enough, Stewart," Bob said sternly, "that's enough," but the more he heard the dialogue, the more true the words became.

"Oh, Bob, I can't leave me mumsy; have to live in Essex me whole life, and you can become a gardener or something. Certainly no travelling for you, m'dear; no, I'm going to snip off your family jewels and hang them on the mantle, I will!" laughed Lieutenant Brody.

Bob felt trapped for the first time in his life, he felt trapped and just wanted to escape.

"C'mon, boys, one more pub before they close. Let's go to The Star Pub at Belgrave Mews. Maybe the four of us can plan another Great Train Robbery like the others!"

"Now there's a plan, my boy; lead on, lead us on!" shouted the trio in unison.

When Bob awoke the next morning, he was in bed with two bountiful women, who lay strewn across the sheets, half-naked. His two buddies lay on the floor wearing bras tied around their heads like flags on a flag pole. One sat halfcocked on a chair with the latest imported issue of the controversial Playboy magazine opened at the centerfold, as if trying to convert it to a blow up doll while sporting a woman's panties like a hat! *Well that was one hell of a pub crawl*, Bob thought, smirking to himself whilst trying to extricate himself from a most delicate situation.

He carefully lifted the sheets, exhumed his underwear, and managed to find almost all of his clothes, half of which were dangling from the chandelier in the room. He showered and shaved and tried to dress himself as well as the situation permitted. In the lobby he took a tomato juice with a swig of Winchester sauce and washed it down with strong black coffee, an old army trick that never failed him.

Where the hell am I, he thought to himself, too proud to ask. "Can I see your menu," asked Bob, in efforts to place himself.

"Yes, sir, one moment." The menu was delivered, at which point the famed Claridge's insignia was presented to him.

"Not bad for sloshed!" Bob remarked under his breath.

"I'm sorry, sir? What can I get for you?" asked the waiter.

"I'll have two eggs, fried, four rashes of bacon, crisp, and toast, burnt," Bob ordered authoritatively, "and bring me freshly squeezed orange juice and a bowl of oatmeal with cream to start, and the paper. Brown sugar on the oatmeal, brown!" Bob ordered.

"Thank you, sir," the waiter said and then vanished, astonished at the amount ordered.

Bob started to read the paper, but couldn't help but reflect on his situation and the trapped way he felt. He was a man who lived off his instincts, and nothing was right about this situation. It was a matter of honor. He couldn't leave Sue for love of all the freedom in the world; it wouldn't be right.

He was eating pensively and carefully when he glanced at his watch and realized it was close to noon. "Oh God, what am I thinking!" Bob exclaimed, and hurriedly threw some bills on the table and made a quick exit.

"Taxi!" A new Austin FX3, built by Carbodies of Coventry, promptly pulled up at the curb.

"Where to, sir?"

Bob stepped in, impressed with the spaciousness of the vehicle, and said, "The Dorchester Hotel, and please, I'm in a hurry."

When Bob arrived, he ran through the lobby, up the stairs to the junior suite he and Sue were sharing, only to see the maid cleaning the room.

"Sorry, sir, the lady left early morning, about three hours ago, bags and everything. She seemed awfully upset; two of you have luv spat?" the nosy maid inquired.

"I don't believe that's your place, now is it?" Bob snapped and ran back down the stairs to the concierge. "Sue Dorsey, has she checked out?"

"Not officially, Mr. Cross, although we saw her leave by taxi this morning, fairly early. The bill, I assume, will be covered by you?" inquired the desk clerk.

"Yes, of course," Bob replied, glancing through the bill and hurriedly paying it.

"Oh, and sir, this was left for you." The desk clerk handed him a note.

Dear Bob, it's over. The baby is not yours, so you don't have to worry, and we're not your responsibility. I'll be fine. I'm accepting Jack's proposal. Go back to Canada where you will be happy. I will

*always love you, but not enough to follow you and
your ways. All the very best. Love, Sue, xoxox.*

It was official. Over, just like that. He sat in the hotel
lobby chair for one hour, stunned. He wondered why his feet
didn't leap for the door, why grief had not overtaken him,
or why he didn't inquire where she might have gone. He
knew and he knew he didn't want to follow. He wasn't sure if
what she said was true about the baby, but it was convenient
for both of them to let sleeping dogs lie. *What was the truth
anyway? We're born, we live, we die; hopefully we have some good
memories in between*, he comforted himself.

Already he had brooded too much; it was time to move
on. He decided to take a train to Genoa, Italy, on the spur
of the moment, to meet his good friend Giovanni. *He will be
happy to see me and perhaps we can discuss this new business in the
textiles he talks so much about.* It was a seemingly short journey
by train, and Bob's mind was occupied the entire journey
with what had transpired and all the emotions attached. He
needed change and was desperate for a new direction.

Giovanni embraced Bob warmly upon his arrival. "Bob,
my good friend, you sava my life. I'll always remember you
sava my life!"

"Hey, I knew I could look forward to some great meals if
I did!" laughed Bob.

"Come, my mother, she's waiting, cooked enough for the
entire year 'cause I tell her you a big guy!"

"Sounds great, Giovanni. Lead the way; I could eat like
a horse!" replied Bob, happy he had made the journey. It
would soon become the first in a series of business trips to
Italy over the years as Bob made the transition from army to
business and formed alliances between continents, merging
his contacts of the past to a foundation for the future.

Every trip he made in the years that followed they

discussed life, love, disappointments whilst building a strong business together. "Bobby, it's a must to visit the Cerruti shop. The father, Fratelli, he's not saying much to many, but his son, Nino, is his pride and joy; kid's got talent! Next year, they launch their first readymade men's suit line, called 'Hitman.' They're now thinking of a launch in '57, so I'm saying get in with them now and you can be first to hold the collection in North America!"

In the week that followed, they travelled the length and breadth of Italy. "Here we are, Via Forcella Milan, you see, the Cerruti shop. Probably will call it Cerruti & Son very soon." As they entered the shop, Bob was waited on, with attention from head to foot, by the tailors, who were so happy to have a tall model to suit.

"*Prego*, you will look *bellisimo!*" the tailors cheered, as if suiting the president.

"What's with all the enthusiasm?" asked Bob, shocked by the overwhelming joy they were showering upon him.

"Bob, you have to know something; Italians will show joy for three things: food, women, and money!" They laughed.

"Okay, so as not to kill the joy, we'll talk about a deal. Gentlemen, how many suits can we get by October? How much, and when?" After many espressos and several shots of amaretto, the deal was signed.

"Congratulations, Bob. Consider yourself a maverick in the field of men's fashion!" Giovanni said with great pride.

"What maverick? I'm only buying the suits; Cerruti is the maverick!" Bob smiled.

"Okay, then a farseeing businessman; you're quite the entrepreneur, Bob. I just knew you had it in you!" exclaimed Giovanni, who looked like a dwarf in Bob's presence.

The two boarded the train to Biella. It was only 104 kilometers from Milan, so they were able to get there by nightfall. The beautiful women Bob tipped his hat to out of respect became the topic of conversation.

"I'm telling you, Bobby, with textile business for you, I'll be your pimp! You're like Casanova; the women, they go wild!"

"I can see that, Giovanni, but I'm sure it's you!" said Bob with a twinkle in his eye. When they landed, they went to a small trattoria to eat.

"I'll have one of everything" said Bob, tempted by everything and unable to decide, "and a bottle of Chianti!"

The representatives from the Ermenegildo Zegna factory met them for drinks after dinner. "Tonight we laugh, we drink, we love some women. Tomorrow is another day; we work then!" The men toasted glasses and soon the "London Fog" of yesteryear became the "Italian Blur" of Bob's daily constitutional.

What a life, Bob thought to himself as he woke the next morning feeling more contented than he had been for years. The fabrics were absolutely incredible.

"My God, what quality wool and cashmere, wool and silk blends, Super 140's; this is fantastic!" exclaimed Bob. "Send me 10 dozen of each cloth length and three dozen ready-made suits in this list of sizes. We're going to make lots of money, Giovanni!" They smiled and toasted with another round of homemade amaretto and panettone.

As the trip neared an end, Giovanni presented Bob with a gift. "The latest Ferragamo shoes, for you, Bob!"

"Ferragamo shoes, how the hell? He only works with the starlets," Bob laughed with utter appreciation.

"Simple, when you sleep, I steal your shoes for fitting. He make for, I say, Clark Gable. I even show our picture together so he believe me. He very, very happy!" laughed Giovanni.

"Why, you little bugger, you're up to all sorts of tricks! How can I ever thank you?" Bob said earnestly. "You turn every trip into a roaring success."

"Thank me? Why you say this? I tell you, you sava my life; we are now brothers, do you understand?" and the two hugged, friends for life.

"Why you always need to go back through London? Each time you say it's too painful and confusing for you, no Sue, no family, everything. ... Why you don't take ship to America from here? Our company pay for such a good client," Giovanni insisted.

"You're a good friend, Giovanni, and you're right; I have no need to return to London," said Bob, happy for the suggestion and the offer.

Bob boarded the *Andrea Doria* and sailed towards New York City, a place on his list of places to go that he had yet to visit. On July 25, 1956, due to heavy fog, the *Andrea Doria* collided with the east-bound MS *Stockholm*. It was struck in the side, which caused the top heavy ship to immediately start to tilt severely starboard, which rendered half her lifeboats unusable. The shortage of lifeboats resulted in a significant loss of life.

The London Fog had boarded like a stowaway, so Bob's fate rested in the balance.

CHAPTER FOURTEEN

ALL ABOARD

Success is that light you think you see in
the distance that you just have to reach.

CEYLON 1956

PREMA LOOKED FORWARD TO HIS GRANDFATHER VISITING HIM every weekend; it was the only time that he could be a child, and the only time in his young existence that he felt loved. On those visits, Pappy, as old Meedeniya was fondly called, would take the elder boys out for ice cream in a way that never revealed the true purpose of his call.

"Cyril, I thought the boys should do some repair work on the train. The station master inquired whether I knew of someone good with their hands that could sew upholstery in the second-class compartments, so I thought if the boys are free, this would be a good job for them."

"Good, good discipline for them. You're right; be on your way," approved Cyril, happy to be rid of Harri's meddling father and Prema's reckless behavior.

Cyril secretly knew it would be Prema who would do the brunt of the work, as he was the only one good at useless "fixit" jobs. *The others can watch, as far as I'm concerned,* he thought and continued to read the paper and review some briefs over scones and tea.

"Oh, Pappy, more work?" complained Manjula.

"Pappy, I'm not good with my hands," uttered Stephen, concerned about the job described.

It was only Prema who happily went; knowing that he could be on a train was all that occupied his mind. "Could we see how the engine works, Pappy?" asked Prema.

"You see, boys? Now that's a great attitude!" admired Pappy, patting Prema on the head. Prema ducked out of instinct. Sensing this, Pappy took Prema's hand and proudly said, "Come, my dear *Putha,* I'll show you the engine, don't you worry!" He was thrilled at the chance to make the boy happy.

When they arrived at Fort Railway Station, the boys began to roll up their sleeves, preparing themselves for work. What they did not expect was the ability to board the train as passengers and be served hot malu pan (fish buns) and orange barley while looking out the window.

"Really, Pappy, really? We get to ride the train!"

"Yes, boys, you get to ride the train!" exclaimed Pappy.

The train's engine began to screech as it *chug-a-chug-chugged* along the track, until it reached an impressive speed. Prema practically choked himself trying to see the wheels in motion on the track through the window.

"Pappy, I know how it works; I read it in a book about James Watt and how he improved the steam engine! Watt's early engines were powered by the vacuum generated by condensing steam instead of the pressure of expanding steam," and he began going into great detail, describing how the track operated and how the tablet system came to pass. ...

"Actually, it was Robert Stephenson & Co. who invented the Stephenson Rocket in 1824, which has stood as a template for all steam engines to this day!" Prema went on. The other two brothers just listened, Stephen more interested in grabbing another bun and Manjula in the pretty girl who smiled his way from two rows down.

"Oh my goodness, Prema!" laughed Pappy.

"Now can I see the engine room, can I?" exclaimed Prema.

"Yes, child, of course, but I first want to introduce you to someone very important to the Ceylon Railway," and at that moment, a tall man appeared smiling.

"Prema, this is B.D. Rampala, the most respected chief mechanical engineer of our time. His work has improved the standard of the railway tremendously. He's leading the upgrading of major railway stations outside Colombo, and the rebuilding of the track in the Eastern Province to facilitate heavier and faster trains."

"Don't believe a word he said!" kidded B.D. Rampala, extending a hand to his old friend Aloy.

"I say, don't tell that to my grandson," Meedeniya exclaimed, only focusing on Prema.

"You know, son, your grandpa and I go back a lot of years. You should be very proud of him; he's been an upstanding businessman for years. ... I've even learnt a trick or two from him!" Rampala laughed whole heartedly as he extended his brawny hand to the youth.

"Yes, sir, very proud; I love him, I mean, **I respect him** very much, sir!" Prema said, changing the pitch of his voice to sound most convincing.

"Now that's a fine handshake, young man!" Rampala exclaimed, saying nothing of the other two boys, who were equally unimpressed, or perhaps preoccupied with the other distractions on the train.

"Son, as you are now travelling on the Southern Line, or Coast Line, you will be happy to know that this is one of the first steam locomotives ever built and it's called ..."

"The Belmont!" exclaimed Prema, who put up his hand as if in school.

"My goodness, we really do have an enthusiast!" smiled Mr. Rampala. "Come, I'll show you son," said Rampala, putting his hands on Prema's shoulders. "I don't suppose you boys know the name of this train?" he asked patiently, looking in the direction of Manjula and Stephen. But they sat, stunned.

Pappy, unimpressed, looked to Prema. "Go ahead, I know you know!" encouraged Pappy.

"The *Uda Rata Menike!*" said Prema with the most beautiful, sparkling smile.

The day was spent in the engine room, and Prema ended up smelling of coal and smoke, and was dirty from head to foot, but neither Pappy nor he minded, for the joy it gave was miraculous. He also knew the joy it would bring his father. Seeing him look dirty and dishevelled from all the "hard work of the day" would be all that would keep him from another beating.

When the train stopped in Matara, all three boys jumped onto the platform and ran down to the beach, jumping into the welcoming waves along the shoreline, giving a salty spray to everyone who came their way. They threw sand and skipped stones at each approaching wave as Pappy managed to get three Thambili for them to drink.

"Come, boys, let's go. The train is about to leave!" He smiled as they frolicked in the water, reflecting on his own children and how much he enjoyed being with these boys.

My daughters were always so mollycoddled by Maude, I never had a chance. My only son shifted from one private school to the next, and is now residing in London, he thought. How painful the separation was for him, but he knew none so difficult as the days he remained in Kandy, away from Prema.

When the train arrived back at Fort Railway Station, it was 4:00 p.m. and the boys were ravenous. "Now for the finale of the day: Elephant House, Fountain Café!" shouted Pappy happily, the boys hugging and kissing him. As they disembarked the train, onto the wooden platform, Prema's eyes searched for Mr. Rampala, who didn't seem to be present.

"Mr. Rampala went onto Galle, son. He was most impressed with you," Pappy said.

"Oh, Pappy, I wanted to thank him so very much," said Prema, disappointed. Then he managed to catch a glimpse of the train conductor and smiled his broadest smile.

The Fountain Café was a Colombo tradition amongst the gentry, but Elephant House had about 1,800 kade's island-wide, so people of all walks of life managed to enjoy the extremely sucrose tasting cream soda, orange barley, and ginger beers they had to offer.

"What shall it be, boys?" asked Pappy.

"Mixed grill!" they exclaimed, as it was a luxury to have grilled beef, chicken, and sausage. At home it usually was the same menu day in and day out, beef curry, dhal, and rice; or chicken curry, dhal and rice; and sometimes fish curry, dhal, and rice! It seemed the cook knew nothing else, and Mommy had very little time to spice up the menu with so many little ones to care for.

Dessert was always ice cream floats.

"Boys, one blob or two?" asked Pappy.

"Anything. Pappy, anything," Prema said happy, full, and safe. He knew no greater joy than that.

"Two blobs," Manjula shouted, having no problems with asking for what he wanted.

"Manjula, that's rude!" scolded Prema.

"Oh, for heaven's sake, Prema. I asked the question; you all are equally entitled to answer the way you wish! Two blobs all around, vanilla cola floats for us all!" Pappy gave as much as he could, knowing that it was his time that was most precious to them, but most especially Prema. He feared for the child and prayed that he would be all right while he was away. So much trauma for dear Harri and so much trauma for this prince of a boy.

It was a lovely evening; the scent of frangipani filled the garden and the mango trees were laden in fruit. The servants went on ladders to cover the unripe fruit in individual bags, to protect them from the bats hovering above, before the setting of the night sky.

It was an unusually pleasant sight to watch his daughter slowly rocking her baby to sleep in the old cane rocker that her mother had handed over to Harri for moments like this. He quietly approached her, signalling the boys to the back, and handed his daughter some rupees, which she promptly hid in her sari.

"*Thank you Tata!*" Harri held his hand. "Did you have a good time, Tatah?"

"Oh yes, we all did, Prema most especially."

"Thank God," she whispered under her breath, never showing her face.

"Harri, are you alright?"

"Yes, Tatah." She turned and looked into his eyes, exposing her reddened, swollen eyes, "I've made my bed ..." she drifted off and focused entirely on the baby.

He wanted to shout and scream and beat the hell out of Cyril, but there was nothing he could do.

As predicted, Cyril took pleasure in seeing Prema's gruff and dirty appearance, which he purposely preserved for his father to see.

"I hope you did a good job!" he ordered his son.

"Oh yes, Daddy, it was very hard work."

"I want you to wash yourself thoroughly; I don't want

to see one speck on your hands, do you understand?" he shouted, ravenous to taste angers pungent toxin.

The boys cleaned up and robustly entered the room, contented by the day's events, which made him all the more suspicious. Upu rang the dinner bell, signalling that the children's dinner had been served. Like a couple of gluttons, Manjula and Stephen piled into the table, giving no regard to the younger children who needed more attention.

"Boys, show of hands," Cyril said severely. The three boys put out their hands, all seemingly clean, but Prema's white hands reflected like a sign of pure innocence, and he was not to be caught by chafe.

"Uh-huh, I see a spot," Prema's father declared victoriously. "Go back and clean them." Full and contented from the mixed grill, and unwilling to be tortured another night, Prema declared that he was not feeling well and asked to be excused from the table. His father excused him, happy for him not to fatten on his fodder.

Pappy stood in the distance just shaking his head, not wanting to disturb the peace; he sneaked around the back garden and asked Edison to get Prema without making much noise.

Prema joyously came to his grandfather, thinking he had already left. "*Putha*, you know I have to go away now and will not be back for the next two months," said Pappy, saddened at the thought. "How I wish I could take you with me."

"Me too, Pappy." Prema hugged his grandfather.

"I want to tell you another story; it is from Greek mythology. It's the story of Tiresias, the blind seer of Thebes," he began. Prema was attentive. "One day, while Athena bathed in the lake, Tiresias accidentally saw her naked. So angry was Athena that she put a spell on him and struck him blind. Only later did she see that it had been an accident, but it was too late; she was unable to reverse the spell. So in effort to give him something back, she said, 'I have taken away your vision, but I will give you the gift of being able to see into the future.' She gave him the power of soothsaying. As time passed, Tiresias realized that seeing into the future was also a curse, because sometimes he could see someone's terrible fate, but do nothing to change the outcome. To which Tiresias concluded, 'It is but a sorrow to be wise when wisdom profits not.'"

Prema sat perplexed. "What does it mean, Pappy" he inquired meaningfully.

"It means that I wish I could do more for you. Someday I hope you will realize that and know how much I loved you." Tears welled up in the old man's eyes.

"Oh, Pappy," Prema cried, hugging his grandfather with the strength of all his limbs and the sincerity of a lifetime.

In an attempt to give strength to his grandson, he began to discuss the business at hand. "I'll be visiting your Uncle Harry in London, hoping to invest in some war-damaged property, best time to buy, you know, and then I'll meet my lawyer, Mr. Clay. He handles all my contracts with the cloth suppliers and also handles my finances in England. Sterling fellow, trust him with my life."

"I wish you well, Pappy. I will pray for your safe journey and I will pray to Our Lady of Perpetual Hope and St. Joseph for your business success," Prema earnestly said.

It was pointless to ask the child what he wanted, because he was pure as the driven snow, not a selfish bone in his body, which made Pappy love him more. Prema knew that he was loved and favored, but never uttered the words for fear of being presumptuous. The two hugged. Prema watched longingly from the fence as Pappy walked past the araliya trees, and past the old English postbox, case in hand, hat on head, until the night sky became encircled with fruit bats, each honing in on its fruit of favor.

Back at Fort Railway, Meedeniya reluctantly boarded the Bradby Express to Kandy, wishing his grandson would experience a happier tomorrow for the rest of his days. Wistfully, he looked back in search of the boy with the sparkling smile. "Don't worry, Prema, I'll be back soon," he thought out loud.

꿍⊚〜

UPON THE DECK OF the *Egidia*, en route to England, Meedeniya watched the people waiving back from the port. The sheer excitement of a ship in the harbour would arouse crowds from all walks of life, the gentry waiving to relations on board, businessmen arranging shipping documents, dock hands, merchants, and a scattering of outcasts whose awe-filled gazes were so strong that it seemed their hopes attached and transported themselves to a different world for the seconds they stood in her majestic presence.

When only the coconut trees could be seen waiving in the distance, Meedeniya let go his glance and turned in the opposite direction, as if willing the ship's direction forward to England, to where he now had to focus and attempt to leave his worries behind. He gathered his leather case, which held all his worldly possessions he liked to say as if he were Ghandi himself—his books, his Bible, his papers, and his rupees neatly bound and wrapped in brown paper bags—and set sail for England.

After a short walk about deck, he returned to his single cabin, which was very small and rugged and conservative. It had a wash basin and a settee, along with a locker, four drawers, and, of course, bunk beds.

He locked his rupees into the safe that night, along with his pocket watch and monocle, and sorted his files and placed them neatly into the drawers. He was particularly organized, which made him very neat. He brought an empty scrapbook and continued the practice of collecting interesting news articles that he had either read or, in some cases, heard about from other passengers or the crew. The latest news was about the *Andrea Doria*, which sank off the coast of America. A total of 1134 passengers had to abandon ship, and some of them lost their lives. News of this tragedy sent shockwaves across the *Egidia* until the captain ordered the crew to quickly collect the papers before mass hysteria broke out on board. It then became the new rule for the purser to scrutinize the newspaper before passing it out to the guests on board.

Meedeniya read about the new American sensation, Walt Disney, his Mickey Mouse creation, and his theme park, Walt Disney World, which had just opened in Florida in 1955. The photographs and the description sounded so magical, like a child's absolute dream world. He fell asleep in a deck chair of the ship imagining Prema playing in the park and laughing with his brothers and sisters. The look of elation described in the paper appeared on his face, so much so, curious passerby's wondered where his thoughts were. When he awoke, he carefully cut out the article and pasted it into his scrapbook, which he longed to share with his grandchildren.

At tea time, Meedeniya was formerly given an official invitation from the captain of the *Egidia* to join him and his guests at the Captain's Table for dinner at 7:00 p.m. Dress would be formal attire. It was the ship's first night at sea and the captain had already recognized Meedeniya's name on the ship's passenger list. This was generally considered a great form of respect, to which Meedeniya intended to reciprocate the same by attending. Upon delivery of his freshly pressed suit, Meedeniya inspected it to make sure it had been creased correctly. *Perfect as usual,* he thought and proceeded to dress in his undergarments, which consisted of an undershirt that had an array of holes in it. He would wear it and expose it to his wife, Maude, so to prove poverty whenever she asked for money, and then he would say, "Maude, I am a man of very little means; do not ask me for money. Do you not see the holes in my undershirt!"

To which she would roll her eyes and slam the door, knowing full-well he was trying to pull the wool over her eyes.

I wonder why Rohan packed these undershirts; I had new ones, he pondered. *I guess this is Maude sending me her messages of resentment,* he thought with a glint of mischief in his eyes.

He sat on the only chair in the corner of the room and proceeded to pull his socks up and attach them to his sock garters, at which point he slipped his feet, one sock, one garter, and one foot at a time into his tan and crème brogues. As he stood up, he put on his crisply starched white shirt with its detachable collar and proceeded to pull on the pants of his cream China silk suit, which he was careful not to crease.

He was a devotee of the bowtie and took particular pride in tying it, as it required a certain amount of technical skill, which was common knowledge. By virtue of its very presence, the bowtie hinted intellectualism, real or feigned, although Meedeniya claimed he simply loved the challenge. It represented a membership to the gentry, an iconoclasm of an old world classic, and seemed, in itself, to adhere to contrarian points of view. Meedeniya loved broadcasting his individuality by acting as if he was not concerned by what other people thought, when in essence, he knew, as a brown man, he would have to be twice as good to be equal, and therefore, went out of his way to prove it. All the final touches to his ensemble were added, his crème suspenders, multicolored paisley bowtie, a matching puff, and a white rose pinned to his lapel, as he planned to make the most of the company he no doubt would meet.

"Mr. Aloycius Meedeniya, I would like to introduce you to Mr. Joseph Senior, son of the late great W.S. Senior, Bard of Lanka," said Captain Cummings.

"My goodness, what an honour it is to meet you. I had the great privilege of knowing your father back when I was a young man in Galle. He was a great Trinitian, great Vice Principal and educator at Trinity College in Kandy, where I am from. What respect he yielded and what love he had for my country. It was our honour to have known him and for a person such as he to have lived upon our island."

"Oh, that's wonderful. How did you meet my father?" asked Joseph, curious to know more about his most well-respected father.

"When Reverend Senior assumed duties as Vicar of Christ Church, Galle Face in 1916, I came to hear him speak at one of his sermons. He was a most eloquent speaker, so many were drawn to him because of his most distinct, refined, and kind way of speaking."

The waiters appeared, filling crystal glasses with white wine, and water goblets remained full throughout the evening.

"Well, it sounds as if he will be sorely missed," said the captain. The first course was served. "Perlita Caviar d'Aquitaine plated on mother of pearl," announced the maître d with great pride.

"Thank you, maître d," said the captain, raising a glass to toast his guests. "Everyone, welcome to *Egidia*; may she sail through these waters as gracefully as she looks!"

"Here, here," they toasted.

"Please begin, everyone." He gestured for people to begin as he watched Joseph Senior and Meedeniya cross themselves and then, upon the captain's invitation, begin to eat.

"I'm sorry for interrupting; I'm also very interested to learn more about Reverend Senior," said the captain.

"Yes, his missionary work was inspiring. I, along with many other people, donated to his continuous efforts to feed and house the poor," Meedeniya voiced.

"How fascinating," said the captain.

"Might I ask what brought you to Ceylon this trip? I know your father died 10 or 15 years ago," asked Meedeniya.

"Yes, he died 18 years ago," said Joseph solemnly. "It was my father's greatest wish to return to the island that he loved so much, so when he died, surrounded by family and close friends, he asked that his ashes be interned in St. Andrew's Churchyard, Haputale. I wanted to visit his gravesite, just to feel close to him."

"How very touching," the wife of a famed English ship merchant uttered under her breath, as the second course of canaroli rice with langoustine tartare was served.

"He inspired so many. I dedicated my life to African missionary work, and as such, often return to his personal journals, his prayers, his sermons, and his writings to seek his wisdom and his guidance."

The remainder of the meal was spent discussing the beauty of Ceylon, trade opportunities, the state of affairs, imports and exports, trading opportunities, and impending doom in Europe.

Between the Ceylon crab, the roasted vacherin with Mont d'Or cheese, and the Giffard Maraschino zabaglione with berries, there was a good exchange of lighthearted quotes, jokes, and antidotes. Meedeniya raised his glass and gave a further toast to the captain.

"On behalf of the esteemed guests at this table, I would like to thank you, Captain Cummings. We thank the chef for a wonderful and memorable meal, and I thank the guests at this table for very stimulating conversation."

The captain then suggested they serve coffee and tea in the Captain's Lounge, which was most appealing to the men. As the ladies took their leave for an early night, Mrs. Vicheron, who listened intently at the table, began to speak, "Excuse me, gentlemen, before we part for the night, I wonder if Mr. Senior would honour us with a reading of some of his father's work, for we have not had the honour to hear it in France," she said rather charmingly.

Joseph Senior was quite taken a back and looked to Meedeniya for guidance. "What shall I read," said Joseph.

"His work was so beautiful. I'm sure we have his writings on board this ship, but for now, 'The Call of Lanka' is his most beautiful work, if you would do us the honour," suggested Meedeniya.

"I have memorized my father's words. It is one of his greatest works and is strikingly personal. It will be my pleasure to utter my dear father's words." Joseph cleared his throat and stood up with great reverence, as if speaking to him, and he recited the poem.

THE CALL OF LANKA

I climbed o'er the crags of Lanka
And gazed on the golden sea
When out from her ancient places,
Her soul came forth to me;
"Give me a bard," said Lanka,
"A bard of the thing to be."

"My cities are laid in ruins,
Their courts through the jungle spread,
My scepter is long departed
And the stranger Gods instead.
Yet, give me a bard," said Lanka.
"I am living, I am not dead."

"For high in my highland valleys,
And low in my lowland plains,
The pride of the past is pulsing
Hot in a people's veins.
Give me a bard," said Lanka,
"A bard for my joys and pains."

I offer a voice O Lanka,
I, child of an alien Isle;
For my heart has heard thee and kindled,
Mine eyes have seen thee and smiled;
Take, foster mother, and use it,
'Tis but for a little while.

For, surely of thine own children,
Born of thy womb, shall rise
The bard of the moonlit jungle,
The bard of the tropic skies,
Warm from his mother's bosom,
Bright from his mother's eyes.

He shall hymn thee of hoar Sri Pada,
The peak that is lone and tall.
He shall sing with her crags, Dunhinda,
The smoking waterfall.
Whatsoever is fair in Lanka,
He shall know it and love it all.

He shall sing thee of sheer Sigiriya,
Of Minneria's wandering kine;
He shall sing of the lake and the lotus,
He shall sing of the rock-hewn shrine,
Whatsoever is old in Lanka,
Shall live in his Lordly line.

But most shall he sing of Lanka
In the bright new days that come.
When the races all have blended
And the voice of strife is dumb
When we leap to a single bugle,
March to a single drum.

March to a mighty purpose,
One man from shore to shore;
The stranger, becomes a brother,
The task of the tutor o'er,
When the ruined city rises
And the palace gleams once more.

Hark! Bard of the fateful future,
Hark! Bard of the bright to be;
A voice on the verdant mountains,
A voice by the golden sea.
Rise, child of Lanka, and answer
Thy mother hath called to thee.

"By Walter Stanley Senior," he finished.

The women wiped away their tears, as did Meedeniya, who could not help but get caught up in the sincerity of the words. They stood up and clapped, lifted their glasses out of respect, and gathered around Joseph, patting him on the back. He smiled, unable to speak from emotion, which gave way to many tear-filled "thank you's" as he quietly adjourned for the evening. "That was absolutely beautiful," the guests uttered in quiet amazement as the ladies left for the evening.

The men gathered their cigars and pipes and rejoined one another in the comfort of high-back leather studded arm chairs, which drew them into a night of more talk, cognac, and hearty conversation.

The rest of the journey was spent with many evenings like this, interacting with the numerous guests, enjoying one another's company, and forming alliances that would last a lifetime.

It had been a heartfelt journey, and by the end of it, Meedeniya had gone through a gamut of emotion: how to help his grandchildren, how to save his daughter, how to get closer to his son, but in that whirlwind of questions, he knew that he would have to secure a strong financial future to ensure his family would always be taken care of.

From his perspective, money made the world go round, and if he had to go around the world to achieve it, he would.

CHAPTER FIFTEEN

ON THE OTHER SIDE OF THE MOUNTAIN

She dared wonder what lay beyond her childhood mountains, whose remnants lay scattered in the field. ...

HUNGARY 1953-1956

"October 23, 1956, is a day that will live forever in the annals of free men and nations. It was a day of courage, conscience and triumph. No other day since history began has shown more clearly the eternal unquenchability of man's desire to be free, whatever the odds against success, whatever the sacrifice required."

John F. Kennedy, on the first anniversary of the Hungarian Revolution

A S A RESULT OF THE YALTA AGREEMENT BETWEEN ROOSEVELT, Churchill, and Stalin, Hungary had fallen under strict Soviet control. There had been an escalation of Soviet dominance in Hungary. Hungarians who dared defy orders were getting shot on the streets, and as a result, spontaneous outburst of resentment engulfed the hearts of many Hungarians.

All the villages, towns, and cities of Hungary remained overwrought with tension, with citizens' ears glued to the radio, listening to Radio Free Europe and the Voice of America shouting messages of *"rise and shake off your chains"* and *"define or be defined!"* The fear was so great that people were afraid to open their doors in case it was a member of the secret police forcing them to join the Communist regime. Many were so horrified, in fact, that the very threat prevented them from going out to buy food and supplies. This especially was the case in Budapest, which was the centre of business and home to the universities. Unlike in the villages, where smoke houses were filled with bacon and sausage; attics with dry supplies of sugar, flour, beans; and cold rooms with bread, cheese, and baked goods, the city folk were always more dependent on the shops, and therefore were more compromised by the tight grip of Communism.

Despite humanity enduring the heinousness of two world wars, the despicable aftermath of the Holocaust and the atomic bomb, people generally believed that the world would not allow further atrocities to ever happen again, due to the presence of International Human Rights Treaties and the Charter of the United Nations; however, the weapons had hardly fallen silent in May 1945 when the Red Army began what they called the Bolshevization of all those vanquished nations. It was Stalin's belief that is would merely take another three years before he would convert all of Eastern Europe into a Communist bloc.

News of staged trials and executions, life in prisons, and death camps permeated the walls of secret vaults and locked doors, further resonating in the people as a stronger desire to fight. Despite Stalin's estimations, Hungary remained steadfastly unified, which further irritated the Red Army, whose tactics were no less barbaric than those of the Nazis.

It was believed that, due to the powerful and continuous prayers of the people, only a miraculous intervention would enable them to remain united, notwithstanding the re-education campaigns and continuous attempts to undermine national unity.

Erzsike, along with those in her village and those with whom she attended Teacher's College, prayed continuously.

Many crucifixes were erected in pathways, gardens, and fields along roadsides so that they would be reminded that God was always with them. The crucifixes also prevented them from being hoarded and arrested in churches by Red Army soldiers, who often attempted to prevent the propagation and continuation of the Catholic faith.

Rudi became Erzsike's constant companion. While walking to and from college, he would describe what he had seen or what he had heard of the student uprisings in Budapest. Hand in hand, they would stroll along the countryside in silence, as if drinking in the scenery and memorizing the peacefulness of it all out of fear of losing the image altogether. The real-time events and the horrific vividness of the accounts sent shock waves down Erzsike's spine. They needed this quiet time to restore hope in their hearts and purpose in their walk. Occasionally, the distraction of being in love shielded them momentarily, until the sound of bombing blasted any shred of hope once again.

"Erzsike, my friend Janos Hunor is attending Péter Pázmány Catholic University, and he is unable to continue his studies, because the Soviets are blocking the entrances; they are spitting on them and kicking anyone who dares to defy them. Word is, the staff within the building, even some of the professors, are physically digging out an underground exit from the kitchen area, which would enable the students to come and go to classes without arousing suspicion with the guards in front!"

"Where would the entrance be?" asked Erzsike

"A few metres away, in a small park. There is a very large boulder that will hide the entrance. No one would suspect it as it is a common throughway in the park, surrounded by trees, a playground, and a few cafés," confirmed Rudi.

"How very sad to hear of such a struggle, but the courage is so very inspiring; we must never give in to any of this!" declared Erzsike, whose brown eyes blacked with determination.

"Erzsike, you are sounding like Churchill—we must never give in, never give in!" laughed Rudi, attempting to lighten the moment.

"Yes, perhaps Churchill sounds like me!" laughed Erzsike, determined to get the last word.

The two began to run down the street at the sound of a truck nearby. It seemed any sound made them paranoid. Rudi pushed Erzsike off the road and into the cover of long grass, pulling her down to the ground and physically covering her with his body. The sound of the truck grew closer and the distinct sound of Russian soldiers singing became very apparent. Erzsike began to struggle under the protective cover of Rudi. "Erzsike, it's the Russians. Stay still; your coat is red and I must cover you. Be quiet!" he whispered fearfully.

Erzsike was defiant; she would not be fearful, nor would she give in to fear. She retreated to the peaceful state of the image she had just memorized and blocked out the sound of Russian voices. She focused on the smell of Rudi's hair, the square of his jaw, the lines that formed around his eyes every time he smiled. She could feel the beating of his heart next to her breast and the heat of his body. She craved his lips on hers. As if telepathy played a role, he removed his hand from her mouth and looked deep into her eyes. Their souls melted into each other until the two became one. The intensity of this passion was their plea to be free, to laugh, to love, to do anything they wanted, together, without fear. The traditional inhibitions that would normally exist between two young lovers, so inexperienced, would never have allowed this, but the war and the oppression made people defy the rules, all rules, even the rules of the church, if only to be expressed for a few moments in the middle of long grass along a country road that would eventually lead to freedom.

Communist-run government reclaimed the land that had previously belonged to private citizens, who themselves were landholders and, therefore, farmers. The land became entirely government-owned, which meant that all the people had to work the land equally and give all of what they grew to the state. Subsequently, state-owned shops were set up to equally disperse foodstuff to the Hungarians. Most Hungarians made their own bread, but because of the restrictions placed, no one had access to flour, and therefore, the people were unable to make themselves bread.

As Communism spread over the land, people had to succumb to the rules of government. They were therefore obliged to line up for sugar, bread, and salt, a practice that became commonplace. Proud Hungarians were reduced to seeking permission to kill their own pig. Even eggs had to be gathered daily, from which the people were only entitled to 10% of whatever they gave, which meant that families would have to provide at least ten eggs a week, otherwise no eggs. Milk was the same, but whenever Erzsike took on the job, she would adulterate the milk with water. No one had told her to do this, but it was her way of being defiant.

While in line, the people would use this opportunity to share stories and devise plans to defy the Russians. There was word circulating that Russians were now targeting poor village women for food, grabbing their bags in the presence of others to propagate fear, pushing and kicking the women and callously eating their bread and laughing. Attempts to defame and demoralize increased, but the people were equally defiant and prepared for every antidote that was discussed.

One such incidence took place. It had been raining, and about 25 village women stood in a line at the state-owned shops to get supplies. This was after having walked several kilometres, and many of them were elderly. The atmosphere turned into carnage in mere minutes when drunken soldiers drove up to the line, nearly running over the women.

"Here it is, surrounded by some more bloody Hungarians! These ones are too old!" shouted a soldier in a drunken slur. As if pre-rehearsed, the woman at the head of the line stood frozen. The Russian soldier stood near to her and told her. "Go on, get your groceries; spend your forint, go ahead," he said, prodding her on sadistically. "You useless woman!"

The woman at the front of the line signalled the woman next to her. She carefully dropped her home-woven bag and slid it under the counter, at which point an already prepared bag filled to the top with fresh bread and jams was given. "Köszönöm szépen," said the round village woman, "Igen."

Not even a second passed before the soldier grabbed her bag and pushed her to the ground. The others looked on in horror. "Uh, such good fresh bread, too good for you, and jam, rosehip, what jam for you? You're too fat!" The woman remained on the ground, venomous with anger and anxious to strike.

The soldiers took the bag to the truck and proceeded to break the bread and callously spread the rosehip jam thickly over each slice with their fingers. Like slithering dogs, they ate, laughing and taking swigs of their whiskey. About 20 minutes passed before they grew bored with the atmosphere and drove away, first nearly backing over the woman, who was now sitting on the ground.

The women held their breath until the jeep was no longer in sight and then burst into fits of laugher. "Bastards, I hope they liked the shoe polish on their bread!" laughed the women, who were now crying from tears of oppressed joy. "Oh, ladies, what you don't know is that the bread was too hard, so I softened it with a little dog piss and rolled it into cat shit for flavour!"

For a moment even God in Heaven had to laugh, for the clouds moved aside their foreboding expression and let the sun shine through. "Look, a rainbow," said one of the women, pointing it out for the others to witness. It completed the day and brightened their path with renewed vigour all the way back home.

The woman who had been pushed down by the Russian soldier exclaimed, "I feel like marching! Let us march!"

"Yes, let's march; we'll march with piss and vinegar in our steps! Like Büszke Magyars!" They smiled and began doing just that.

The women walked in a crowd of long skirts and aprons with Kalocsa lace designs and homemade woven baskets overflowing with bread, flour, and sugar supplies for the week. As the sun began to set, some of their husbands met them along the pathway home, after a long day on the field, their cows loyally following behind. Only, their husbands heard them from a distance, laughing, singing, and marching. It seemed as though these Hungarians had won the battle, but who would win the war?

After Stalin's death, there was a rise of violence in effort to fulfill his wish that Hungary become part of the Communist bloc. When quiet threats and compromises did not bring about Stalin's desired response, Khrushchev, the new leader of Russia, ordered an unrelenting terror campaign on any Hungarian who defied authority, as this was the height of unbridled dictatorship. Resistance movements and anti-Communist campaigns were instigated from the west and re-education programs were defied, despite thousands being arrested or killed and university students being denied their right to study. The people had endured enough poverty, terror, oppression, and exploitation.

All of this culminated in a revolt for freedom, democracy, and patriotism. One voice unified against all odds, against the almighty strength of the iron fist.

Rudi was part of this rising revolution, which both scared Erzsike and made her proud. When Soviet tanks rolled into Budapest, instead of scaring the people, it merely ignited what became considered one of the most impassioned fights of any nation to maintain their independence. Revolt began to rise in every city of Hungary, in the villages, and on the streets. People came out unafraid, ready to die for what they believed in.

The tanks devastated the city, and piles of bodies began to appear. The grotesque images of tanks actually rolling over countless bodies were symbolic of Russia's iron fist, its determination to dominate no matter what the cost.

"Erzsike, now is the time; for our future together, we must leave. I must help you escape tonight," cried Rudi, out of breath and leaning on her front gate.

"Rudi, what are you saying? Hungary is our home!" she said, desperately trying to deny the reality of the situation.

"You must gather your things and come," urged Rudi. "Meet me behind the cemetery at 9:00 p.m., as it gets dark."

"But, Rudi, my parents? What do I do?" she cried.

"It is a long journey to Austria; can they walk? Do you think they can make the journey?" he asked hurriedly. "I must go, Erzsike. The Soviets have given a false victory to us; they are coming back again, and this time, thousands will die. Do you understand? We are young; we have our whole future before us. ... Your parents will understand!" and in seconds, he kissed her and dropped his grip on her thin arms. "At 9:00 p.m.!"

She watched the love of her life run down her tiny street, past her yellow house with the terracotta clay roof tiles, past her tiny schoolhouse, and past the church. For the first time, she longed to sit and admire her tiny village and take in every square inch of it, but time was against her. Suddenly, the geraniums in the windows were charming and the smell of paprikás in the wind endearing. She wanted to have that cognac with her father she had always promised to have with him, and she wished she had finished making the pillow for her mother, which had the message "I will never let you go" only half-completed in cross-stitch. She wanted to tie herself to her front gate and never let go, but the winds of change were upon her. She looked in the direction of the mountain, the one she longed to know what was on the other side of, and the answer grew near.

She walked into her little house, perhaps for the last time, and touched the walls, crossing herself with every step as if in a trance or a death march. She reached to get a sweater, a blouse, a scarf, an old broken pair of earrings that her father had bought for her, a book of poetry, and her little Bible. She wrapped a loaf of bread and smoked Hungarian sausage and put it into her bag. She did not have the heart to take anything else from the home, for fear of denying her parents of food. No one was home; her father was with her mother at the doctor's, as her arthritis had made her crippled. It would be hours before they would return. It was already 6:30 p.m.

In a bout of absolute guilt and a desperate last ditch attempt to demonstrate her undying love, Erzsike put on the kettle and began cooking. Csirke paprikás, potato stew, and lecsó was all she could find. She set the table and put out cucumber salad and bread. It was too much food, enough for a week, but she knew she would not be home to make the meals; it was the least she could do. She removed the sheets from the bed, washed them, and put them out to dry on the line, then she made the bed with fine linen, just like her mother liked, and she sprinkled rose petals in the bed. She gathered lily of the valley and put it in a vase to make the house smell good.

She combined a week's worth of chores into a few hours, never once thinking that she was leaving, just desperate to complete the chores. The clock seemed unusually fast, and then she heard Rudi in the garden calling for her. She could not breathe and she wanted to die; it was all too much. She grabbed a photograph of her parents and then she saw the cognac. She needed to give her father a signal, some sort of signal that she was all right.

"Erzsike, where are you? Erzsike?" Exclaimed Rudi, who now came closer to the house.

"Coming!" she shouted, physically sick at what she was going to do. She knelt before the crucifix, the one that had endured her childish antics of covering the eyes of Jesus with her scarf whenever she snuck another chocolate off the Christmas tree. *"Dear Jesus, forgive me, forgive me; protect my dearest mother, my dearest father, forgive me. ..."*

"Erzsike!" Rudi called again, and with that, she ran out the door, letting it swing behind her in that familiar way in which it would latch onto the homemade broken lock that had needed to be fixed for years.

Rudi was trying to retrieve something from the cemetery and needed her help to raise the grave stone. "What are you doing, Rudi?" she said, knowing upon first glance that she could never be without him.

"I will lift this stone. There is a coat underneath; you need to pull it out." he said.

"Whose is this?" she started, but she stopped herself. She recognized it; it was the Russian soldier's jacket, the one he had buried months ago. "Why?" said Erzsike.

"I will use it to blend in just in case we get caught." Suddenly, she heard the swing of her house door.

"Erzsike, where are you going?"

Rudi ran towards her.

"I must kiss them goodbye!" she cried.

"No, darling, it's too risky; they will not let you go in time. Don't you see its better this way?."

She struggled from his grip. "No, I must. Papa!" she called.

"Erzsikem, if they see you like this, it will break their hearts. I know you don't want that," Rudi pleaded, patting her head and kissing her. She could hear her father calling until it became a hush.

Within seconds of going into the house, her parents knew something was wrong. Her father had seen it, two glasses of cognac, one glass drunk and one glass overturned. He knew. Erzsike was gone. He walked out of the house and sat on the woodpile with his glass of cognac. As if to fight back the tears, he drank all of it in one long swig, like it was poison, then he smashed the glass against the wall and began to cry into his handkerchief.

Erzsike strained to see her father through the bushes one last time. "Please, Rudi, let me go. I can't, I can't leave them," she cried, physically fighting Rudi off until she fainted into his arms from exhaustion. He carried her away, past the little childhood stones, the boulder that used to be her castle, past her little garden and her playground, into the field, out through the pasture, and onto the platform of the train station.

"Erzsike, Erzsike, talk to me." Rudi lulled her in his arms.

"Papa," she cried. "Mamma," but they were an hour's train ride away from home and an hour closer to freedom.

"Erzsikem, *csillagom*, it is all right; we will be alright, and so will your parents, knowing that you are safe." He gently put her down.

"Oh, Rudi, the pain, my heart is broken; how could I leave them?"

"You are a survivor, Erzsike; you will survive." He put her hand in his as they disembarked the train and continued their journey.

"Erzsike, my other friends studying engineering at Eötvös Loránd University have told me that they are beating men and hanging them upside down on lampposts in the streets. Some are even set on fire! It is horrifying; that is why we have to go. This is happening to the youth of Hungary in the cities. Your parents and mine are safe; they know how to survive, but we are young; we cannot fight anymore," he said, describing the events of the revolution in order to give her strength to move forward.

"I know how terrible it is, I know and I understand" she said, feeling stronger and more focused in the journey. Because they were walking through the forest, they kept silent, for they knew it was heavily guarded by the Russians. At some points they could even hear soldiers talking to one another they were so dangerously close. Then, from behind the trees, came a familiar bird call and they both stopped dead in their tracks. "That's my signal, Erzsike. My friends are hiding over there, just beyond that small house," Rudi exclaimed, relieved to have heard the signal, for he was beginning to lose hope.

They had run about 500 metres when the sound of dogs barking came from behind them. Rudi quickly put on the Russian Jacket and began to resume a normal pace. He held Erzsike roughly by the arm in efforts to show authority over her.

"Who goes there?" shouted a Russian soldier. Rudi, who had mastered a few words in Russian, shouted back in his best accent, "Comrade Dmitri. I'm transporting a prisoner to the holding tank."

"Come, comrade, share a drink with me," said the soldier, unaware of the imposter.

"I would love nothing more," Rudi said in Russian, "but it is the captain's orders; otherwise I will be late, and you know what that means. I will visit en route back, okay?" said Rudi, anxious not to be clearly seen and for Erzsike not to be reviewed by a drunk soldier.

"Dah!" said the soldier, who called away his dogs and went back to his post.

"Say nothing, keep walking. I don't know if he's watching, but as soon as you get past that house, I want you to run," whispered Rudi. Erzsike did exactly what she was told. The others had seen the soldier in the distance and remained hidden. It was only after they walked another 1,000 metres that the two broke away, past the cover of the house, around the trees, through a stream, and then they fell onto the bank of the river.

"Rudi, are you okay," asked Erzsike, frightened.

"I am now," he said.

There was a whistle and then a familiar voice. "Rudi, Rudi?" came through the bushes.

"Ivan, is that you?"

"Yes, it's me," and a tall man with a beard appeared, seemingly, out of nowhere. The two embraced, kissing each other on the cheek and thanking God that both had made it this far.

"Erzsike, this is my dear friend Ivan. You can trust him with your life." The three hugged, and then Rudi and Erzsike followed Ivan to an old farm house where they met other Hungarians who were waiting to make the journey across the forest.

Inside, Erzsike was surprised to see her dear friend Jenny there with a few more girls from her village. "Erzsikem, you made it. I'm so happy you are here," they cried in unison.

At this point the front door opened and a Russian guard stepped in and said, "You are all under arrest. Anyone trying to escape will be shot."

The entire group began to scream. "Rudi, what do we do?" Erzsike clung to his arm.

"We will wait calmly here."

The men of the group began to collect money and jewellery, anything to bribe the guard. The items were collected in Rudi's hat, and they told the women and children to go to the back of the room for protection.

When the guard re-entered, it seemed as though hours had passed. The men immediately pounced on him, offering him money and jewels to let them pass, but all he could see in their behavior were little boys who clung to their mothers' legs for protection. For some reason, the guard appeared very sympathetic and did not take the bribe. Instead, he told a couple of the men to come outside with him. It was there that he instructed them to go straight in the direction of the river, warning them not to deviate from the route, for they would be in Austria within the hour. "I will turn my back on you all;

you must go quickly, because the other guards know of your existence and are coming for the women and children."

Rudi, Ivan, and Janos wanted to hug him, but instead, gave him a look of deep and utter appreciation; after all, they were all just men.

The group was given instructions, and the women and children were told to follow Ivan and Janos in the front, and the rest of the men, including Rudi, would remain guarding them from behind. Amongst those men were political prisoners of war who had made their escape from prison. They could not afford to be found, for these were the Revolutionaries and they were highly sought after by the Russians.

Within an hour they, saw what looked like a mirage, a city whose lights appeared blue, as if a halo of the Virgin Mary was guiding them. "Rudi," Erzsike exclaimed, "look!"

He ran towards her and kissed her. "We've made it, Erzsikem, we've made it!" he said, holding her tight and taking in the sight of freedom.

Shots rang out and Rudi pushed Erzsike forward. "Run, run as fast as you can I'll meet you on the other side," he said, running back to see if any of his fellow Revolutionaries were safe. The women ran with children in their arms, men lifting their wives through the river. Erzsike took charge of a small girl who seemed to have been lost in the shuffle. They reached the other side of the river, but kept running until the threat of capture was behind them.

In the distance two shots rang out. The Russian guard lay in a pool of blood, holding a picture of his little blue-eyed boy, and Rudi, eyes slowly losing focus on the love of his life, watched her reach the safety of the Austrian border. The blood of both men was red, the pain, the sorrow, and the loss intertwined on the same damp cold earth of a Hungarian forest. Now and for eternity, they both belonged to that place and time. For them the war was over.

☙◉❧

DUE TO THE CHAOS that surrounded the night, Erzsike was oblivious to Rudi's fate. Her focus remained steadfast on his words, *Keep going and never look back*. She put the tiny girl on her shoulders and asked her what her name was.

"Beya," she replied. Now that they had reached safety, Erzsike began to quietly sing a lullaby to her, as she was very sad because she could not find her mother.

"Don't worry, Beya, we will take care of each other," assured Erzsike, worried for Rudi's safety.

When they reached the church on the hill, there were several people there to greet them. They spoke very gently in Hungarian and took them safely to the Austrian refugee camp. It was very nicely set up, with a main dining room with lots of food and flowers welcoming them after the long and treacherous journey. Celebrations took place, apricot brandy and pear liquor flowed readily, and snaps were passed around the room. "We're free!" they shouted, laughing and dancing. Her friends, Jenny and Isabella, were hugging her as Beya reunited with her mother, and that was when it hit her. Erzsike had done the unimaginable, she had left Hungary. She dropped to her knees. "What have I done?" she said, and she began to sob uncontrollably.

She was surrounded by people who genuinely cared and carefully carried her to her new room, which she would share with her friends. A small clean room with four bunk beds filled the room, women and children on one floor and the men on the other. "Let her sleep; she must be exhausted," said the nuns who ran the camp.

When she awoke, she asked where Rudi was, but was again told of the division of men and women. Her friends remained holding her hand, gently patting her forehead. They had been informed of Rudi's fate by Ivan, his close friend. "Poor Erzsike, what will she do when she finds out?" cried Jenny.

"She will be devastated," said Isabella, who had watched their love blossom over the past year. A nun and priest were called to her side the next morning to tell Erzsike.

After a long night, Erzsike awoke ready to face the future. She had decided this in her sleep, as she dreamed of getting married to Rudi and starting a family somewhere in the world, anywhere they chose, but upon rising, a nightmare waited to greet her.

"He was mistaken for a Russian because of the jacket he was wearing. It was the Russians who killed him, along with the guard who let us get away to safety. They thought he was a traitor, a Red Coat, and that is why he was shot." Erzsike could not hear the words. She only heard **Rudi is dead**. Her body and mind went numb.

Weeks passed within the camp, each family moving forward with their lives, but Erzsike remained in a deep state of denial. Her friends stood vigil over her, each taking turns. It was Sister Helen who stepped in and read prayers from the Bible, continuously praying over Erzsike until she began to repeat the prayers. Soon Erzsike began to sit up and start refocusing her mind on the Lord. She joined the Legion of Mary and started to do volunteer work, helping others more in need, but fully intending to return to her blessed Magyar land, for she could not imagine life without Rudi and Hungary; it would be too much to ask of herself.

It was during a pilgrimage to Vienna that Erzsike managed to conjure up meaning in her journey by proudly carrying the Hungarian flag. She walked between the priest, who carried the crucifix, and Sister Maria, who held the Blessed Sacrament over a five-kilometre journey through the country, into the city, and into the church. The weight of her reality became daunting as she approached the stairs of St. Stephen Basilica. Her tears began to flow and her heart became so filled with regret and sadness that she prostrated herself before the Sacred Heart of Jesus and begged that she die on the church steps before the altar.

She could not be consoled. She ran out of the church and found herself on the street, not knowing which way to go. A bus sat at the corner with the name *Sumeg* written on the sign on the top. *Hungary!* she shouted in her mind, and ran into the bus, which was filled with older people. "Young lady, can I help you?" asked the bus driver.

"Are you going to Hungary?"

"Yes, we leave in twenty minutes," said the driver. At which point an elderly couple, older than her parents, asked to speak to her quietly outside the bus. She followed them out of respect.

"Do not go back to Hungary," they said to her. "It is not safe for you,"

"I don't care," said Erzsike. "I simply cannot breathe. I have to go back"

"I know the pain is great for all of us, but for you, you will never be allowed to go home, even if you pass through the border crossing; they will rape and torture you," they pleaded to the young girl.

"I don't care, I must," she exclaimed and tried to re-enter the bus, but the doors were closed. "Please open the door," she cried, but there was no response. She banged the doors, desperately trying to pry them open. The priest and Sister Maria watched from a distance.

"Please, dear, now is not the time. Go back to Hungary in a few years, but not now. We speak like this for and on behalf of your parents. They would want us to protect you. It is our duty as Hungarians; we love you and want you safe." The husband slipped some dollars into Erzsike's pocket. "Go, my dear!" they pleaded, and painfully got back onto the bus. Sister Maria now stood firmly by her side, patting her head as the bus drove away towards what would now be her past.

She would have to move forward. If she could not go back, if obstacles remained in her way, then she would have to go past them, past to the other side of the mountain, to the other side of the ocean, to a distant land, as far away as possible so that her ability to run home would be impossible.

At the camp, Erzsike resigned herself to her fate. She opened the book of poetry by Ferenc Kölcsey, which had remained clenched in her hands since she arrived, to the poem "*Szózat.*" She began to hum the first stanza, "*Hazádnak rendületlenül, légy híve, óh magyar ...*" To your homeland be faithful steadfastly, O Hungarian ...

She looked at the map and bravely chose the farthest destination.

She would immigrate to Canada.

CHAPTER SIXTEEN

AS FATE WOULD HAVE IT

Every journey has a fork in the road; life's
purpose is predicated by which path you chose.

CANADA 1957

BOB WAS THANKFUL TO HIT DRY LAND AFTER BEING EVACUATED from the *Andrea Doria*. They landed as emergency ships, medical attendants, and ambulances swamped the port. Over 1,600 of the people who had been aboard were crammed into half the number of life rafts than they should have been. It seemed to be a repeat of the *Titanic*, and headlines in the papers were quick to draw that comparison.

At the Funeral Mass for the victims of the ill-fated ship, Bob stood silently, recounting the events of that unfortunate day and marveling at how just 47 people lost their lives. The hysteria and pandemonium aboard the deck of the ship was reminiscent of the war. Bob was quick to fall back into leadership mode by organizing the emergency evacuation of the ship and directing people to safety.

As fate would have it, it seemed his luck for escaping disaster remained with him, but he was not sure whether he wanted to test that theory again anytime soon. He believed this was God warning him to settle down, and he took the warning to heart.

When he returned home, after the funeral and subsequent trip through New York, he drove to his parents' home in London, Ontario. On approach to his old family home, thoughts of his childhood antics and his desperate need to rebel struck him as he drove up the laneway. Despite his anger towards his father's iron fist, he understood now, what pressure he must have been under to perform on behalf of King and country. As he opened the front door to the house, his parents sat in their respective chairs, each doing what they did habitually, his father reading a book and his mother making one craft or the other. As he went to kiss his dear and aged mother, he found that the earnest sympathy and protectiveness he always had towards her had melted into a quiet respect, for she remained by his side, stoic, inwardly patriotic, and very predictable. Bob's perspective of life had changed dramatically since his war days, since losing the love of Susan and a life spent with her, and now this latest incident. Despite the inquiries from both his parents about what had just happened, they remained neutral to his heroics and near-death experiences. Perhaps this was due to the times, or their inability to truly express emotion, based on the notion of always being in control and keeping a *stiff upper lip*. There was never really any fanfare, but his mother did always manage to have a twinkle in her eyes, though it grew dimmer as the years progressed. He waited on her hand and foot, for the missing years, when he was overseas, were all he thought of. On the worst days of the war, he would sit in the trenches, drifting off to the thought of his mother playing piano, throwing a ball to his beloved cocker spaniel, and eating peanut butter sandwiches. He would often write about how he missed peanut butter, so whenever he arrived home, his mother would make sure there was plenty in stock.

Bob informed them over a rather quiet dinner of his plans to move to the nation's capital to begin a new business in menswear, with the latest fashions out of Europe. His father was not impressed, and his mother remained inexpressive, as usual. This always irked him, but he managed to keep his irritation well intact; the war had taught him that.

Perhaps coming from this background, he became drawn to a life of mischief and humor; it was all he could do to escape his reality as a child and, later, the realities of war. His personality served him well in life and would continue to do so in the future. As for his parents, he had given up searching for approval long ago.

The business was an instant hit for Bob, for there were no other shops anywhere in the city, nor in the country for that matter, that offered the European styles, the quality and the finesse of Italian Cerruti fashions and Zegna fabrics. Giovanni had been right; whenever he visited Bob's shop in Canada over the years, Bob made sure to show him just how grateful he was. The location of his shop in Ottawa was perfectly thought out, as it was a government town and the center of Canadian politics. His clientele were international ambassadors, politicians, and young and rising stars like Pierre Elliot Trudeau, who was joining politics and becoming known as the person to watch in the future.

It was the era for big flashy cars and Bob's physic suited the long wheel base of the Lincoln. He looked like a movie star driving down the parkway in his '61 Lincoln, which was a flashy turquoise blue. His presence dictated respect and his charisma lured many into his web of charm, so much so that he found himself the center of attention no matter where he was. Such was the case at the grand Château Laurier Hotel, where Yousuf Karsh, the world-renown Armenian portrait photographer, had a studio off the main lobby. This illustrious hotel stood proudly next to the parliament buildings in downtown Ottawa.

Only the most recognized, powerful, and notoriously wealthy people came especially to have their portrait taken by Karsh, and as such, Bob would schedule appointments at high tea almost every day so as to meet people, socialize, and pro-mote his business. In many ways it was a reenactment of his life in Europe, where he would be seen networking in and out of the best establishments, where only high society frequented.

Much to Bob's chagrin, life felt transient, as he desper-ately searched for more meaning within. The realization that he was not getting any younger, coupled with the type of people he was associating with, caused him to second-guess himself quite frequently. There seemed to be a revolving door to his morality, in which, quite often, even names became irrelevant. Alcohol began to blur the harshness of this void and the days seemed to blend into one another without much distinction.

He was still strong, as was his will. Whenever he found himself on this downward spiral, he would self-medicate with television evangelists, binge eating, and good deeds. It was during one such period of awareness that he was in his office overlooking the busy street. In the distance he could see a very beautiful young woman lovingly holding her baby and a bag of groceries and attempting to make her way across the street. Instinctively, Bob stood up and ran across the street to save what looked to be an imminent disaster. "Please, let me help you," Bob said to the stunning young woman, who just smiled and said "tank you" in broken English. "May I ask, what is your name?" Bob asked, but she did not under-stand and, to his surprise, went down the stairs into the basement apartment of the same office building in which his shop resided.

He was absolutely smitten by the image of this young lady, who encapsulated motherhood, kindness, and beauty. Her eyes were haunting, and the adorable little boy with the cherubic cheeks captured his heart. He waited for what seemed an eternity outside the apartment until someone came out. The landlord of the building came up the stairs. "Eddy?"

"Hi, Bob, how are you? See business is going well," Eddy said.

"Yes, going very well," Bob said, wanting to cut to the chase. "Eddy, I couldn't help but notice a beautiful young girl and baby went into that apartment."

"Bob, she's young, she doesn't speak English that well, and she's a mother," said Eddy protectively.

"That's obvious. Who is she?" said Bob urgently.

"She has been working as a maid for a few of the office buildings we own," said Eddy.

"But she was holding a little boy?" said Bob, most concerned.

"Doesn't always happen; the child was not well and they wouldn't take him at daycare, so I said if she could handle her child and work today, that would be fine, as long as the job got done," Eddy said, like a priest.

"You're all heart, Eddy!" Bob said sarcastically. "I would really like to meet her, Eddy. Can you arrange it?" said Bob.

"Sure, anything is possible. After her shift shall I bring her to your office?" said Eddy, anxious to get on with work.

"Please, I'll be in the office the rest of the day," and with that, Bob walked up to entrance to his office, deep in thought, as if he had been thunderstruck.

Bob found himself actually nervous, tidying his office, putting cushions on the chairs, removing them, and then readjusting pictures, pens, and his tie, then combing his hair and smoothing his mustache. *What the hell is wrong with me?* Bob thought when he heard the sound of Eddy's voice.

"Bob, still in?"

"Yes, Eddy, come on up," responded Bob, trying to look absorbed in his paper work.

He shook Eddy's hand, and standing not far behind him, was the beautiful angel he had helped earlier in the day. Sensing Bob's tension, Eddy quickly introduced the two. "Robert Cross, I would like you to meet Erzsike, Erzsike Puha." Bob looked tenderly into her sad brown eyes and extended his hand to hers, whereupon he bent down and kissed her hand.

Erzsike, who was carrying her little son, Rudi, was taken by surprise, as it had been a very long time since any man had kissed her hand. *The first since she arrived in Canada a year and half ago*, she thought, still uncomfortable to be in such a seemingly cold society.

"Erzsike, what a pretty name; what does it mean?" Bob asked, but she looked a bit confused.

Eddy was quick to answer the question, feeling like he was a third wheel. "It means Elizabeth," said Eddy.

"Oh, and what is your son's name?" said Bob and again Eddy answered.

"It's Rudi."

To which Bob said, under his breath, "So, Eddy, are YOU free for dinner?"

Realizing that this was his cue to leave, Eddy looked at Erzsike and said, "I'll be outside in case you need me," and then begrudgingly left.

"Please, won't you sit down?" said Bob, offering her a seat.

She smiled and sat with her son in her lap. "May I help you?" she said.

"Yes, I would like to know, where are you from?" This, according to her limited experience, seemed to be a very popular question amongst Canadians.

"I am from Hungary," Erzsike said. "I leave my Hungary during Revolution."

"I see, that must have been very difficult for you. Did you come with your parents?" Bob asked, not realizing that it would stir up deep-rooted emotion.

"No ... I come alone," she said and then patted her son's head. "He was with me, but not born when I come."

Bob had enough sense not to go any further with the questions, but he wanted to know everything about her and offered her little boy a candy. "Chocolate?" Bob said, but was met with an instant "no tank you," although Bob couldn't help but notice that she seemed quite enticed by the candies. "Please, I insist," said Bob, once again making her feel welcome, but at the same time confused. She took one for her son, unwrapped it and carefully gave him half at a time. Wanting to do more, Bob took a handful and put it into the little boy's hand; it barely fit and flooded to the floor.

"My, my, thank you, enough, thank you!" She readily smiled while feeling slightly uncomfortable. Erzsike attempted to be professional. "Do you want me cleaning office for you?" she asked innocently, unaware of Bob's direction. Without any thought, he agreed, but insisted that she bring her son to work. This seemed strange to her, but also made her very happy, for it would save her two dollars a day for daycare. Every penny helped when she could only earn seven dollars a day.

The initial visit to the office was met with an awkward tension that Erzsike could not pinpoint. In her eyes, Bob was an older, refined gentleman whose English was so proper and eloquent, she wished to be in his company, if only to learn how to pronounce the words. His needs seemed limited to a little cleaning, in which she was treated like a privileged guest rather than an employee. He had even insisted on making her lunch; however, unfortunately for him, his cats played on the kitchen counter earlier in the day. When she saw this, she quietly refused the sandwich for fear of germs.

So as not to give himself away, he gave her $10 at the end of the day, when all she could think of was the fact that she had only worked half a day and therefore would only get half-a-day's pay. After receiving this generous pay, she was happy to oblige. The next time, her work was considerably less, and Bob seemed in pain to ask her to do anything. But he knew that she was a highly principled woman and could not justify taking money any other way. As the days progressed, Bob found himself becoming very fond of Rudi and absolutely falling in love with Erzsike.

On her off days, Erzsike worked at other office buildings, which Bob soon came to know. He discovered her routine and would make sure he was parked nearby to drive her to work or to daycare. He would always make out that he was in the neighborhood, but she began to realize that it was no coincidence.

The more attached he became, the more she moved away. One day, Bob gifted her a beautiful new coat, which she could not accept, for if a woman accepted a gift from a man it meant that she was easily bought. This gesture worked against Bob, as she became more occupied with other work.

Winter soon set upon Ottawa, and it was bitter cold just before Christmas. Erzsike had worked ceaselessly since arriving in Canada. Her entire journey by plane to Montreal was a blur, for she willed herself not to feel the pain of what she left behind, and this remained her mindset ever since she arrived. She worked, worked, and worked until she could afford a pair of shoes, a coat, some clothes for Rudi, and, of course, food. It was a very hard life, and on one particular day, it seemed more difficult than ever. Erzsike was determined to have her own Christmas tree to let her little Rudi experience a traditional Christmas, but she had very little money and virtually no one to help her. Determined nonetheless, she ventured out of her small rented-room apartment by foot to find a place that would sell one. As she made her way through the drifting snow and the slippery ice, the sole on her shoe began to come undone. Her feet became numb and Rudi's cheeks swelled from the cold. She tried to take shelter in a shop doorway, but was redirected farther into the brunt of the storm. Another three blocks away, and in the middle of the season's first snow storm, Erzsike walked through the unfamiliar and piercingly cold streets, bought a tree and dragged it, with a broken shoe and frozen feet whilst attempting to carry and shelter her son, for over a mile.

When she finally made her way up the stairs to her small apartment, she dropped the tree in the doorway, gently put Rudi down, and began to cry. Erzsike was at her lowest ebb, feeling very sorry for herself and for the life she was exposing her son to. Rudi was her world, her unexpected joy, a miracle. When she discovered she was with child, she felt like the Virgin Mary and that God had sent her this gift so that she would never forget her lost love. She rocked her baby boy tightly in her arms, under a warm blanket, quietly whimpering into his neck, trying to warm him up from the cold. It was while she was in this state of utter vulnerability that a knock rang out, most unexpectedly, making her quickly wipe away her tears and answer the door. It was Bob, who was smiling ear to ear when she opened the door. "Hello, Erzsike, how are you and your little Rudi?"

To which she opened the door and let him in. "We are fine," she said proudly. "May I fix you cup of tea?" she said.

"Thank you," said Bob who started to play with Rudi. "I came to tell you that I will be leaving for London, Canada today and I just wanted to stop by to wish you a Merry Christmas," said Bob, smiling. Then he noticed the small tree defrosting in the room. "Oh, please let me help you set up this tree," Bob said attentively.

"Oh no, it is okay, I do soon," Erzsike said protectively.

"Well, at least let me get you a stand for the tree, otherwise it will have to lean against the wall and may fall on Rudi," Bob said with concern, quickly putting on his coat. "I'll be back in a minute, Erzsike, I know where to get a tree stand." By the time Erzsike made the tea, Bob had returned with a box full of bobbles, trinkets, and chocolates. He pulled out a tree stand and proceeded to lift the tree into the stand, securing the base with three screws that were part of the stand. Rudi began to smile and Erzsike could not help but feel absolute joy and relief from his help.

"Vhat is in box; I cannot ..." said Erzsike being very formal again.

"No, Erzsike, it was free; it came with the stand. It is a Christmas tradition, and you must accept," Bob said insistently, smiling and handing her an envelope. She began to say no, but Bob gently put a finger over her mouth in order to lull her. "It is a card. This is very normal here in Canada," he said, desperate to win favor in her eyes. Then, once he finished the tea, he said thank you and attempted to wish Erzsike a Merry Christmas by leaning in to peck her cheek. Sensing awkwardness, Bob turned towards Rudi, picked him up, gave him a big kiss on the cheek, and bid his farewell.

After he had left, Erzsike opened the envelope which

read, *This is for you to buy your son a little something from me for Christmas. Merry Christmas! Affectionately, Bob*, and there was a twenty-dollar note tucked into the envelope. She was so relieved and so moved by the gesture that she allowed herself to think and to feel again, after almost two years.

What began as a Christmas holiday in London with his parents turned out to be a very short-lived visit, because while there, he could think of nothing else but going back to Ottawa. When he did return, he ran up the stairs to her rented apartment, knocked on the door, only to see clearly what his path had led him to; it was the most wonderful Christmas gift of all, a beautiful readymade family right before his eyes.

INDEED, ERZSIKE'S FIRST YEAR in Canada was not spent loving the country, but rather spent discovering and despising the differences in culture, or the lack thereof. To her, there seemed to be no traditions, which isolated her further. Upon entering the country, there were many who tried to make her feel at home, which she was very grateful for, but the fact remained that she was from a foreign land. Large Hungarian communities were established in Montreal and many like her flourished, having the ability to maintain their culture while still integrating, but Erzsike never did anything the way others did. She was alone, she had no family, and the pain of separation was too extreme; therefore, in order to survive, she felt the need to disassociate herself from anything Hungarian. She had decided that she wanted to leave Montreal and go to the capital of the country, believing that this would be the hub of all activity.

Ottawa was, seemingly, smaller than Montreal. The size of the downtown core had all the makings of what she associated with a capital, for the parliament buildings stood proudly in the center and, to her astonishment, were accessible to the public. Being able to walk around the government buildings without security screamed freedom to her very soul and allowed her to drop her defenses and her aversion to her new home dramatically.

Soon, she became familiar with places like the Byward Market, which felt like home, but on a larger scale, where she could see familiar things and approach them with relative ease.

When Bob proposed to her, it sounded more like a business proposal to her than a statement of undying affection, which made her initial reaction appear rather understated. For Bob, this was quite normal, based on his relationships with women, and therefore, emotional love and public displays were not something he either expected or was familiar with. In his mind, he believed that she didn't truly understand what he was asking and was prepared to be patient with her; however, the more he watched her struggle in life, the more in love he became and the more protective he was of her son.

Finally, it was emotion that moved him to act on his feelings. Bob pulled her close and gently caressed her face, slowly outlining the strands of willowy locks falling over her brow. "Elizabeth, Erzsike, I want you to be the mother of my children. For the rest of my life, I want to make those sad brown eyes happy. Please be my wife, marry me, move in with me?"

She blushed, feeling most uncomfortable, but the more she looked at him, the more she could see the clarity of his intentions. The idea of having someone care and provide for her and Rudi, after such a difficult two years battling to survive, sounded like a dream. When she realized that she, too, could give back to Bob what he so eloquently stated, she was able to say yes. "Yes, I, we will marry you!" she said, smiling, and at that moment they kissed, breaking down the walls of difference and embarking upon a journey that would forever intertwine them.

The relationship began on an unequal keel, as the two were so very different. There was an eighteen-year age difference, and, with that generation gap came inequality in education, the arts, society, and, of course, language. It was the psychedelic '60s, and the times were quite outrageous in terms of freedom of speech, expression, and dress. Miniskirts, colored pantyhose, social drinking, smoking, and dancing were the rage, but all very strange in comparison to Hungary.

Erzsike felt like hiding whenever the opportunity to socialize arose, because her understanding of English became nil when alcohol was added to the dialect. Soon, there was a whole level of wit she neither understood nor appreciated. This would often result in her getting hurt, which in turn, would irritate Bob, ultimately leading to him drinking more. She found herself unable to speak the way others spoke, laugh the way others laughed, or drink the way others drank, so in order to fit in, Erzsike began to smoke, and smoking became her crutch in tense situations. It was very stylish at the time, and therefore, she felt she had finally broken into the who's who as far as social norms and expectations were concerned.

As much as Erzsike fought off feelings of depression and alienation, these feelings were deeply rooted, to the point where she took nothing for granted. One morning, Bob read the paper with a constant running commentary on the articles. He read:

"Jacques Cousteau has discovered another species of fish

in his explorations! Lorne Greene will be the next narrator of Greene's New Wilderness. He'll be hosting those great nature documentaries. Boy, would I love to go to Africa ... see the wild elephants, the lions; what an experience that would be," said Bob in a most wistful frame of mind.

"Who would you take?" asked Erzsike, feeling highly threatened.

Bob coolly sipped his coffee and glanced back at the paper. "I would take Charlotte Whitton, no doubt," he said and took the final bite of his toast. "Anymore peanut butter there?" asked Bob, teasingly.

To which Erzsike abruptly slammed it on the table and flew off claiming to be busy. "Have a good day" she uttered in a most hurt voice.

"You too, dear" Bob reciprocated, then he put on his hat and left.

At nightfall, Bob returned, as close to sober as the day permitted and in a, seemingly, more tender and sensitive mood.

"Good evening, dear, how was your day?" The tension in his Erzsike's voice was clearly apparent, so he called her down to his study as he wanted to talk to her.

"Yes, Bob, vhat is it? Do you vant some coffee?" she asked.

"No, dear, just sit. I want to talk to you. This morning you asked me a silly question, to which I gave a silly answer, and then I realized that you really do not understand."

"Vhat are you talking about?" said Erzsike, not knowing what was silly about the words they exchanged earlier that day.

"You asked me who would I take to Africa if I went. That was a silly question, as obviously, I would take you, my wife!" he exclaimed to her surprise.

"That is not vhat you said this morning; you said some voman, Charlotte Vhitton!.

At which point Bob pulled out the paper from his briefcase and opened to the third page. "Can you read the heading, Erzsike? It says Charlotte Whitton, new mayor of Ottawa, to be sworn in today!"

"So then vhy would you say that to me?" Erzsike asked in utter confusion.

"I said it to make a point. You are a beautiful woman, which is why I married you. You do not need to be insecure. Insecure women are unappealing; you need to be strong and secure. I suggest if you want to become a part of society, you should first start with reading the paper and getting to know the world around you, then no one can make you feel insecure about yourself. I know that you can do it. You are better than those women you try to befriend. You must now grow to become the secure woman you were meant to be, and you don't need a man to be that!" said Bob in a most unusual pep talk that sent Erzsike into such a state of shock, that from that day forward, she worked on becoming the strong woman she once was and wanted to become again.

Despite this rare bit of advice given to her by her often absent husband, the differences remained throughout the years, for even during the day, in her own social circles, small tea parties that she would organize with the ladies in the neighborhood out of an earnest desire to be a part, she would end up intimidating others, who believed store-bought cookies and coffee in a mug was culture.

Erzsike's efforts seemed extreme to others, for whenever she had a tea party she would iron and starch tablecloths and napkins, bake nut pastries and apple pies all night, and make fresh tea served in china teapots and served with small shots of apricot brandy. This was always very much appreciated, but never reciprocated, due to the gulf of indifference from the other women on the crescent. Often she found herself omitted from what was clearly a gathering down the street, which initially hurt her, but eventually toughened her to this new society. She tried to stop caring, and when she did, she blossomed.

Her life became about her home and her three children, whom she danced attendance on morning, noon, and night. She taught them little things about Hungary, sang nursery rhymes, taught them how to speak, and cooked Hungarian food whenever Bob went out of town, which was at least once a month. The pain and separation from Hungary lessened the more she was able to share that intimate part of herself with her children. During these times, Erzsike would literally let her hair hang down, and only then would her children see another side to her very complex character.

As Rudi grew up, he began showing signs of jealousy towards his sister, Beya, whom Erzsike doted on because she was very shy, and Erzsike wanted her to grow up to be a strong woman. Something that had served her well and, in turn, would do the same for Beya. Little did she know that Beya's life would be far different from her own, and the characteristics of her basic personality would become acclimatized to the environment in which she grew up in, quite opposite to the life Erzsike had had in Hungary.

Each child took on a role in the family. Rudi was the eldest and, as such, endured more discipline than Beya or Alan, a situation that resulted in sibling rivalry. Rudi tried to dominate his siblings by virtue of his sheer size and age. Perhaps because Rudi had his parents to himself for the first five years of his life, the first two, solely with his mother, the thought of sharing them with another sibling caused deep-seated resentment. Whatever the case, Erzsike would not hear of it and found herself screaming at him whenever she sighted potentially jealous behavior. Quite often she would catch herself, realizing that her shouting was like an echo of her own mother. Rudi was a true Hungarian in every respect. In fact, he only knew how to speak Hungarian until the age of three. Both he and his mother had to learn English in order to make their new family work. Perhaps knowing who his father was, Erzsike would look to him as not only an extension of herself but her link to Hungary. She made sure he and his siblings knew about Hungary, but there was something about Rudi and his strong work ethic and serious-ness that reminded Erzsike of the old country. Rudi was very emotional, which often surfaced, but came out in different ways throughout the years, under the veil of manhood.

Beya was her first child with Bob. Her role was that of caregiver. She was the little mother of the household, often cooking and cleaning and attempting to do anything and everything to please her mother, and more so whenever she felt her mother, whom she adored, was not properly doted on by her father. Perhaps Beya's concept of romantic love came from the television, but what she witnessed was a very loving mother who devoted her entire being to family, but seemed to get little in return from her husband, who was either physically or mentally absent. She observed her mother swallowing disappointment like required medication. Even as a child, Beya knew that her Mother deserved more.

As far as her father was concerned, Beya could do no wrong, as he was easily satiated by the many savory treats and goodies she would make for her father whenever he had one of those "hankerings" he would often allude to. The hankering for peanut butter remained through his life and seemed to be passed onto to Beya, who, as an adult, was con-vinced there must be a gene with a propensity for peanuts or something of that nature! She would see her father come down the stairs every morning, immaculately dressed, polished, and businesslike, while her mother was in her housecoat, happily dancing attendance on him, with a breakfast that was always very large and piping hot and in perfect timing with his arrival at the table.

From the eyes of a child, this was marriage; husband is taken care of and then goes to work, while mother makes the house a home and takes care of all the domestic needs within the household. Mornings were always the happiest times, because the entire family would be together before work and school, and the conversation was light and happy. Everyone had to eat correctly, no picking, no sniffling, no using hands, but once those rules had been established, it was a relatively relaxed and happy atmosphere, which Beya and the others would try to hold on to, for fear of it changing by nightfall.

The events of the day brought her father home a changed man, which Beya blamed on work or the people at work, but the fact was, her father was an alcoholic, which made his behavior switch from a very kind, happy, and congenial person to one who seemed rash, curt, and unleashed. Although they never spoke much about his behavior, it was an unwritten rule never to have alcohol in the house, and if there was, it had to be hidden. Discussions with friends pertaining to their father's behavior were not allowed. Everything was rather hush-hush, and Beya, in particular, was encouraged to confide in her mother whenever she felt upset, for Erzsike knew that society was very judgmental and unforgiving, and she did not want her daughter or her sons to be labeled because of their father's poor choices.

Beya grew up to be a charming beauty, whose greatest difficulty was remaining mad at people long enough to hold a grudge. This worried Erzsike, who often felt the instinctive need to fight many of Beya's battles. That was all she knew, and the older Erzsike became, the more inclined she was to innuendo, but Beya operated on a very different premise and carried other forms of ammunition to make it through life.

Alan was the youngest son in the family. He was the most mischievous and very undisciplined, but none of that mattered, because he had a personality that made everyone laugh and forget any shortcomings he might have displayed. Everything about him was like his father, in looks and in habit, and he, perhaps, would have remained mischievous throughout his life if he had not been failed in grade eight for incomplete homework. Like the war was to his father, failing school was the shock he needed to push him forward into a life of academia and away from a life of mischief.

Bob and Erzsike's marriage continued, although strained for many years. Bob gave into temptations on many occasions, which was a force of habit at that point. Often he would say, with preempted regret, how sorry he was that he would not live to see his children grow up. This fatalistic attitude did not arise from the war, but rather from his father, who, on his 63 birthday, simply died after dinner, while drinking his night cap. This was typical of his father, completing everything possible in the day before dying. How terribly efficient!

Initially, this fear of dying was voiced by Bob when he himself approached the age of 63 and became painfully aware of time. One day he walked into the house, saw his young curly-headed son, Alan, and said, "Poor bugger, too bad his father won't be around when he gets to high school!" When Erzsike heard this, she cried for three days; such was the manipulation of an alcoholic on his family. As time passed, she realized that she would have to start relying on herself, once again, and soon Erzsike was converted to Elizabeth. She worked intensely on learning English, often reading entire shelves of books within weeks. The first set of novels she ever read in English were written by Charles Dickens. With every unknown word, out came the dictionary, until soon, her understanding, her vocabulary, and her ease with reading the most advanced and sophisticated English gave her a lifetime love of literature.

When she altered her name to Elizabeth, it broke down barriers to the world around her. It was further butchered to the offshoots "Betty" and "Liz," which used to drive her crazy, but seemed to make her more approachable to those around her. Still, her personality would not bend completely from the proud person she always was, as she was often heard correcting people with *"my name is Elizabeth,"* said in her thick accent, which in time, was soon sought after, respected, and no longer shunned.

Ultimately, Elizabeth grew older, wiser, smarter, and more content with herself, whereas Bob began a steady decline as he aged. He was still operating a successful business, but his views became softer as Elizabeth's became more pronounced. Somewhere along the way, Bob stopped learning and growing, but she continued, enabling and empowering herself in ways that would ultimately lead her to a successful career outside the home. It was time.

The lack of connection between the couple resulted in Elizabeth living her dreams vicariously through her dearest Beya. She enrolled Beya in music lessons, singing lessons, dance, ballet, and figure skating, giving her all the opportunities she never had. When Beya became a young lady,

Erzsike decided, because of her height, she would be best suited for modeling.

Beya encountered great success in modeling during her teens, and quickly rose to become one of Canada's top models, winning pageants and becoming quite well-known in her field. She was very naive and sensitive to the hypocrisy that existed around her, which caused her to stray from vanity. Unable to separate her conscience from business opportunities, she followed her head and her heart by searching for a life that she thought more respectable and, ultimately, more meaningful. Her search for acceptance became her search for a life with meaning,

Upon reflection, Bob and Elizabeth were an unusual couple, each from opposing cultures and generations. They were like Lucille Ball and Desi Arnaz, only reversed in gender. When their children were growing up, they couldn't help but admire how one parent's strength was often what the other needed to stay in the marriage. They were comical at times, lovable all the time, and, ultimately, each destructive to the other's life, for a number of reasons, all of which were the culmination of varying journeys and how they aligned in the end.

CHAPTER SEVENTEEN
MAVERICK

"Chance favors the connected mind."

-*Where Good Ideas Come From: The Natural History of Innovation* by Steven Johnson

ENGLAND 1960

ALOYSIUS MEEDENIYA WAS AN EXCEPTIONALLY BRILLIANT SELF-made man whose business savvy and far-thinking mentality enabled his family to lead very comfortable lives for many generations to come. There would, however, only be one with whom his influence was indelibly etched into the very framework of what and who he became, and that person was none other than his grandson, Prema.

Pappy's very presence served as a life raft for Prema's journey through stormy waters. A protective calm was instilled by the very sight of Pappy and the indelible feeling of being loved. This was of profound significance to Prema during his formative years, as his grandfather was the only positive force he had in his life, besides, of course, religion. Prema was empowered by this love and further guided by Pappy's advice, which he doled out because he was asked to and not because of arrogance. In fact, Prema watched every move his grandfather made, every thought he had, and every habit he formed, because he wanted to be just like him. He idolized his grandfather and made a point of committing absolutely everything taught to him or observed to memory, an action that would serve him well.

During Pappy's various trips abroad, which would each take between two and a half to three months, Prema would feel such utter despair that only prayer and an active imagi-nation allowed him to survive his torment.

Pappy's old scrapbooks remained in Prema's safe custody and were visited when he was under his bed, the safe haven where he slept, if the word safe could possibly be used. An overall sense of danger would be a more accurate way of describing the nature of Prema's world, and as he grew, he came to realize that it was his similarity to his mother's side of the family that was the key thing that irritated his father and, therefore, set him off. Harriet's side of the family was highly intelligent, in a cunning way, which differed from the righteous ways of the other. No matter the case, it was Pappy's influence and genetics that continued the line. Sadly, none of his children ever admitted to the good of their inheritance, but insisted on criticizing him for his supposed shortcomings.

The most outspoken complaint about Pappy was that he was cheap. To Prema, though, he was frugal. It was, perhaps, a matter of perspective; however, from whichever way one looked at it, Pappy was truly a unique character, and his frugality, or cheapness, seemed a subject for debate among his posterity.

As a young man of 24, Pappy's first occupation was that of town guard, which meant he was given a bungalow to live in while performing his duties. The bungalow was an intolerable mess, dingy, damp, and broken-down from it being overused and under-kept by all the previous owners.

Despite his faults, he did have standards, and therefore, regardless of his efforts to make due, he found himself intolerant of the situation he was in. The job was fine, as it brought him respectability and an ample amount of time to meet people, initiate deals on the side, and seize opportunities when they would arise, but his bungalow, at the end of the day, simply would not do.

Knowing that no money would ever be doled out to

improve his living quarters, unless it was his own, Aloysius decided to take matters into his own hands. He began to circulate a rumor that his mother was not well and that he did not know how long she would last. One Friday morning, making full use of the audience at the platform, Aloysius decided to speak with great worry and concern over the fate of his mother, garnering sympathy from all sides. Unbeknown to them, he was hatching a plot that would see him owning a new house by the end of the month. That evening, he packed all his personal items into his suitcase, piled his furniture into the center of the bungalow, doused it with alcohol, and set it alight. Before the flames could be seen, he and his suitcase were aboard a train back to Kandy. The next morning, the papers read "Bungalow burns down, Town Guard's body not found." The investigation was still on when Meedeniya returned, only to be regaled as the luckiest person on earth. The fire was deemed an accident, due to electrical wiring problems, and the bungalow was rebuilt, with Meedeniya put in charge of planning and construction. He made sure the house had all the amenities that he would enjoy, and the house was built in one month, ready for its first new tenant.

The city was happy, and he was happy, but it did not stop there, for while building the house, he made sure that, in the night, half the building supplies were put on one of the cargo carriages of the train and sent to Kandy under an alias. The division of supplies began immediately upon receipt of the goods, which were divided by him personally, driven to an abandoned site, and left until the next pick up took place. In an effort to appear honest and upright, Aloysius gave the matter of inventory to a junior employee, who, undoubtedly, was to be held accountable for any shortcomings. However, by the time word went out that an inordinate amount of wood, brick, and cement were used for just one house, all the numbers matched and the city felt that they had been cheated when supplies were en route to the house, rather than after their arrival!

Aloysius proceeded to build a house on part of a small plot of land he owned, and when he finished, he sold it at a huge profit and began investing in and then selling real estate. This line of business made him a force to be reckoned with, as he always had additional cash, and this soon led him to becoming a money lender. He lent to poor people, and when they could not pay him back, he would take possession of their houses. It is said that at the time of his death, he owned over 250 homes around the Kandy, Colombo, and Haputale districts.

There had been many a night when Cyril would get into disputes over the legality of what Aloysius Meedeniya was doing, but he was also a strong-willed man and was not easily coerced into anything, let alone guilt. Aloysius believed that what he was doing was charitable, as whenever he took possession of people's homes, it was only at the time of their death. He never made anyone homeless; in fact, they received his money and the ability to pay him back, either interest-free or not, and then when they finished with their house, if the loan had not been paid back, the house became his. "I'm better than the bank," he would state proudly, to which Cyril would scoff and Harriet would secretly derive strength from her father's fearlessness. Prema, also referred to as "eyes and ears of the world," would be somewhere off hiding in a corner, eavesdropping, admiring his grandfather, and vowing to be just like him when he grew older.

Once a year, Cyril made the supreme effort of driving the

family to Meedeniya's mansion in Kandy, and other times, to his country home on Kitulgala River, where the children would take river baths, laugh, and play. It was the only time in which there was freedom. Sometimes, if they were lucky, Cyril would take Harriet back to Colombo with the five little ones and leave the three older boys with their grandparents.

These were the most glorious days of Prema's marred childhood. Days were spent absorbing the peaceful atmosphere, the smell of the garden, the sound of the rushing river, the chirping birds, and laughter, which was a delicacy to the boy's ears. Laughter seemed to keep Pappy forever youthful, for he reveled in his grandchildren's mischief and seemed to look forward to their arrival as much as they did.

Prema idolized him and could never sleep for fear of missing something interesting or utterly charming about the place or Pappy. So every morning before sunrise, Prema made sure to meet Pappy on the veranda, where he would start his day with an egg flip, which consisted of a farm-fresh egg flipped into hot Sri Lankan coffee, mixed with condensed milk, and whisked to a steamy froth.

This concoction was heaven to Prema and simply a must for Pappy. The servants were quite familiar with this procedure and had mastered the art to perfection.

The next thing on the agenda was reading the paper, which was delivered early morning, promptly at 6:00 a.m., by the paperboy, who drove his bicycle, leaned it against the gate, and handed the paper respectfully to Pappy. It seemed only he received this specialized delivery service, Prema had observed, and when he asked Pappy why, there was, inevitably, a proper explanation. "You see, Prema, I have been a loyal customer of the *Daily News* for years. They are guaranteed of my loyalty, so long as I receive my paper in pristine

FAR AWAY, I LAND

condition. There are valuable articles in those papers and they should not go to waste." And with that, Pappy's eyes were distracted by something in the paper; *Dr. Martin Luther King Jr.—I Have a Dream Speech—An Inspiration—1963*, which he read, highly engrossed.

"I see a pattern, Prema. The human spirit is strong and it is resilient, and it will fight back," he said, trying to get a message across to Prema. "Generations of people have gone through atrocities of war, of prejudice; finally, they just stop and say no, I can't anymore, I won't anymore. I learnt so much from our dear friend Ghandi, when he visited us in Ceylon, you were too young at the time."

"I remember Mommy telling me about him, Pappy; he stayed in your guestroom and refused to sleep on the bed because it was too nice, and he ended up sleeping on the floor!" said Prema.

"Yes, and he was from absolute nobility, and yet he believed in equality. He believed his role was to lead by example and teach the oppressed to rise up in an overwhelmingly non-violent movement that would give the British no choice. He led the people into victory and won back the independence of India in 1947, and with that, our own independence in Ceylon two years later. There are so many examples of human endurance and resistance, Prema. Now another great leader rises up in America, Dr. Martin Luther King, fighting for the rights of the colored man in America. I'll read you part of the speech."

Prema listened intently as Pappy read, and as he heard the words, a seed was planted and he too began to dream.

After Pappy read every article that was of great interest to him, he put a small tick in pencil next to it. Then, after he was finished, he handed the paper to the servant and it was promptly ironed and sent over to his best friend, Harry Solomon's, house, whereupon Harry would send his copy of *The Island*, which was in relatively good shape, over to Pappy. Pappy would go through the same procedure, and at the end of the day, when both papers were back in his possession, they were ironed once again, whereupon the articles that had a tick next to them were carefully cut out and given to Pappy, who painstakingly pasted them into a scrapbook that was labeled and dated accordingly: *INTERESTING NEWS ARTICLES JANUARY-JUNE 1963*, and so on.

This was a procedure Pappy felt was most important to perform, for he thought it was his duty to keep abreast of situations both local and worldwide. As the patriarch of the family, it was also his duty to advise others of this information and make sure that they would be able to recite it whenever called upon to do so. Unfortunately for him, despite his best efforts, there was, again, only one who thought this procedure worthwhile, and that, of course, was Prema. This was why Prema took great care to keep the scrapbooks both in hand and in mind, as best he could, and often recited news articles at whim to assure his grandfather his efforts had not been in vain.

This regurgitation of information was not limited to news articles; it also included conversations (other people's) and radio ads, like, "*London Transport use Daganite, Rolls-Royce use Daganite, Viscount and Comet Airliners use Daganite, your car deserves Daganite, 18 months guaranteed. Sole distributers, Walker and Gray.*"

Prema repeated these ads to adults continuously, amusing some and irritating most. "Pappy, do you want to know about soap?"

In a girl's voice Prema would say, "*Rani presents Miss Ceylon 1962, Miss Yvonne de Rosario. I have always used Rani's sandalwood soap. I am very pleased with Rani and I can truthfully say that Rani does wonders to the complexion."*

Then in a loud narrator voice: "**Rani, the Queen of Soap, the Soap of Beauty Queens**."

His timing and his elocution were superb and were regarded as a great source of entertainment by Pappy, but most others either stifled the poor boy or abused him further for his efforts. To most, the bad appeared to outweigh the good, but for Prema, if there was hope of even the slightest positive reaction from Pappy, or anyone for that matter, the glory of that recognition or praise was worth all the beatings combined.

When Prema was old enough to know the senselessness of his upbringing, he thought that if he had his life to do over again, he would wish to have a father like Pappy. There had been many heated arguments where Pappy had insisted on adopting Prema and caring for him in Kandy so that the child would be spared the wrath of Cyril's anger, but society and what it thought played a big role, and therefore, it never came to pass.

Between the ages of twelve and sixteen, Prema's beatings increased to every single day. In fact, the predictability seemed as normal to his father as taking a shower or eating. The only thing unpredictable about them was what would set them off and how severe they would be. Pappy's advice guided him part of the way, but it was his faith and his own instincts that helped him survive.

The church had been his refuge, where he would gaze at Our Lady of Perpetual Help, whose sad eyes showed her yearning to protect him. He could imagine the warmth of her arms around him, patting his head and mending all his wounds. It was on one such occasion, when Prema knelt longingly at the foot of the Virgin Mary's shrine, that Father

O'Hare appeared and instantly recognized the frail silhouette of the young boy.

"Prema, is that you?" asked Father O'Hare, who came from behind the statue of St. Joseph and into the light.

"Yes, Father, it's me," uttered Prema, afraid to make eye contact.

But the priest could see the black and blue of his eye and the rip on his shirt.

"Dear God in Heaven," Father O'Hare said, mournful of the tragedy that knelt before him. "Come here, sweet boy," he said, ever mindful of the situation. Prema stood up and slowly walked towards the priest, who sat on the pew waiting for him.

"Please sit, Prema. I want to talk with you," he said quietly.

"Yes, Father," Prema said obediently.

"Prema, I have now been witness to your father's abuse, leveled towards you on more occasions than I care to remember. I want you to know that no matter what you could have possibly done to provoke this supposed 'discipline,' as it was referred, nothing would warrant what you have had to endure. Do you understand?" Father O'Hare said in a most loving voice.

"I think so," said Prema.

"What I mean is, you do not deserve to get treated this way. You are not a bad boy; you are a very good boy, and the person who is doing this to you is very, very sick."

Although Prema knew he wasn't bad, he had never thought of his father as sick, just angry, very angry. "Does he have a disease?" said Prema, confused but somewhat relieved that there was a reason for his father's anger.

"Well, Prema, you must pray hard and you must keep yourself out of harm's way. God gave you intelligence and great faith. You need to know that you have to stay away from your father as much as you possibly can. Okay?"

"Do you think that would make him less angry?" asked Prema.

"I really can't speak for your father; only a doctor could help him with the anger that causes him to abuse you, but I do know that it is my duty to protect you. I think it would be a good idea if you kept a journal, Prema. A daily account of what you are enduring at home. If you write down what is happening to you, perhaps you will see a pattern, perhaps you will realize that you don't deserve to be beaten, and perhaps it will stand witness to your life until you are strong enough to stand on your own two feet."

Prema sat deep in thought, unaware that Father O'Hare had left him alone on the pew to consider his destiny. It was the first time Prema had thought about his own plight, his life, or his future; up until then, his main concern was simply to survive.

The smell of something savory cooking permeated the church and Prema's stomach began to churn.

"Prema, come join me for dinner," called Father O'Hare from the door behind the altar, to which Prema happily accepted.

"Thank you, Father," said the very hungry child, who, at the end of dinner, was given the journal that would change his life.

The concept of keeping journals had, of course, been introduced to him by Pappy, and therefore, was not a difficult discipline to adopt. He wrote at school, under his bed, inside culverts on the roadside, in trees, anywhere that he could find privacy and peace in which to write.

When his brothers grew suspicious of what he was writing, Prema soon found a hiding place inside the chimney to protect his journal. Initially, it was therapeutic for Prema, but in time, his journal became his best friend when Pappy was not in the country, for it was the best listener and confidant he could ever wish for. In it he outlined the day's events, what would bring about conflict within the home, and what would bring about abuse from his father.

His writing channeled a creativity in him that had little to do with writing and more to do with inventing. His journal began with words and then became drawings, first of wildlife and people's faces, usually angry and vicious. Then they turned into more schematic drawings of gadgets and boxes, houses with trapdoors, unusual locks, secret openings, and levers. Out of pure necessity and a sense of desperation, an inventive mind was born, which in the years to come blossomed into pure genius.

Although Pappy was inventive, this remained largely in terms of business, creative accounting, and making deals. He knew a good opportunity when he saw one, and therefore, seized it as and when it happened. Such was the case for his latest trips to England, when the government of Ceylon supported textile mills and power loom and handloom centers, and began to import raw materials to produce yarn, raw fabrics, and finished fabrics in an effort to promote the textile industry.

On a prior trip to England, Meedeniya discovered companies like James Taylor would sell more conservative colored raw material, like grey, blue, white, black, and green, to their local market, leaving the brightly colored raw materials unsold. Colors like red, pink, fuchsia, yellow, and orange were marked as rejected stock lots and, therefore, sold at hugely discounted rates. Meedeniya, a far-thinking man who'd never before dabbled in the textile business, seized the opportunity and bought the entire stock lot of rejected colors, which were, in fact, the most popular in Ceylon. He sailed back to Ceylon as the sole agent for James Taylor, with a brochure with the original prices, and sold it to the government and the private sector, making sometimes 80% profit on every sale.

This was a most lucrative business, and over time, Meedeniya required a lawyer to manage his funds in England, where he kept most of his profit for future investment. The man hired for this task was Mr. Clay. Mr. Clay prided himself on only having his clients' best interests at heart. He managed his clients' funds and carried out Meedeniya's instructions to the letter, often advising him against land acquisitions without thorough due diligence taking place.

Whenever Meedeniya sailed home, he was secure in the knowledge that he was well-taken-care-of and shared his utter satisfaction with his beloved grandson whenever they would meet.

"That Mr. Clay is a good man, a good man, I tell you; saved me from buying that old bank in Knightsbridge. Nearly lost a good chunk, but he insisted on the title deeds and discovered the broker was a rogue!" said Pappy.

"What happened, Pappy?" said Prema, now an adolescent and keenly aware of the need to make money.

"Well, since the war, there are many bomb-damaged sites in London. Many of the title deed owners are dead, so you will often find brokers masquerading as the title deed owners and trying to sell you something they cannot. Anyway, I did manage to buy several pieces of good real estate while I was there, asked your Uncle Harry to do the needful things. I have asked Mr. Clay to transfer the funds to him once all the proper documentation is provided."

"Does that mean you have homes in England, Pappy," said Prema, most impressed.

"Why yes, it does, and someday I will bring you there to show you myself. Would you like that, Prema?"

"Oh yes, Pappy. I'm so glad you're back home." Prema hugged a now frailer Pappy, who seemed to be getting shorter.

"You're blossoming into a fine young man, so handsome, Prema. You're like a prince!" These compliments were rare and confusing to Prema, whose existence on the planet seemed to be purely for the wrath of his father and those who came under his influence.

"Pappy, the boys tease me at school; they call me Parrot Nose. How can I be like a prince?" Prema asked innocently.

"Parrot Nose! Why, they're jealous! Prema, remember this: you have a nose like a Roman senator!"

These words reached him on a level that no other encouragement ever had. He derived so much confidence from this that whenever he looked in the mirror, he would say to himself, "You have a nose like a Roman senator." To which he would put it up in the air and stand even straighter, further accentuating his lanky figure.

This new-found self-image was a godsend to Prema, who, until that point, had only observed, admired, or feared others' confidence; now he began to build his own. Pappy, sensing this unearthed strength, filled his head with as many stories as possible to support his theory of survival in life.

"I was on a train due for Kandy, sitting in the first-class cabin long before I could ever afford to. As usual, I was immaculately dressed: China silk suit, top hat, brogue shoes, and monocle, and reading *A Book on British Jurisprudence.*"

"Isn't that law, Pappy; you read about the law? I thought only my father did that." said Prema, highly intrigued.

"Of course I was reading that book, or rather, glancing through the book," said Pappy.

"Why pretending?" asked Prema.

"I was pretending to read this much respected book to appear scholarly, which I am; however, in the eyes of the British, I am just a native. So I wanted to appear just as learned as the British by consulting one of their most prized books. I would sit with legs cocked up, book in hand, and monocle positioned, and would order a shot of the finest King George V Scotch whiskey. This would always provoke attention, because most of the British who travelled in that first class compartment could barely afford that brand of Scotch themselves, so they became envious. On one such occasion, a British diplomat became so infuriated by my arrogant disposition, that he came to my compartment, opened the window, and threw my hat out of the train saying, *'you don't belong in the first class cabin!'*"

"What did you do, Pappy; did you leave?" asked Prema, who was now on the edge of his seat.

"Heavens, no. I looked at him through my monocle, unaffected by his actions, and stared him down. I said nothing. About an hour later, I went to his cabin to find him asleep. I took his shoes, opened the window and threw them out. When he awoke, he came storming to my cabin, infuriated, *'Where are my shoes?'* he shouted, to which I calmly said, 'They went looking for my hat!' Then the train reached its destination and I disembarked!"

"Oh, Pappy," Prema said, laughing, "you're quite a guy, Pappy! I wish someday to be just like you!"

"You will be, dear boy, and much, much more," said Pappy, who hugged his grandson, never realizing the impact of his influence.

"Prema, I want you to wear this Miraculous Medal. It will protect you throughout your life.

"Thank you, Pappy, is this what makes you so successful?" asked Prema.

"I think so, Prema; hard work, a prayerful life, and a little extra help from St. Anthony. ... You see, that's St. Anthony on the other side of your medal," he said lovingly.

"St. Anthony?" Prema asked, holding his medal and sitting at the foot of the verandah, near his grandfather, who was sitting on the cane chair overlooking the garden.

"St. Anthony—Saint of Miracles. If you pray to him, miracles happen," Pappy said pensively. "Well, it's that time again." He stood up, walked into the house, said his goodbyes to the family, avoiding Cyril like the plague, and then came back out to Prema. "Goodbye, son, take good care of yourself, and thank you for keeping those scrapbooks so carefully for me."

"You're welcome, Pappy. They are very important to us, to me," he said, correcting himself. Pappy kissed Prema's forehead, put on his hat, and left with his usual confidant stride, refusing to be any bother to his daughter's already complicated life.

"Oh, Pappy, I'm sure Sedaris could drive you to the station," said Prema pleadingly, sensing his grandfather's age.

"Oh no, Prema, I can outrun that old car. Besides, the walk will do me good!"

As he watched Pappy walk away, he saw him turn around and start walking back. Prema ran to him. "Why, Pappy?"

"Here, son, I want you to say this prayer whenever you need St. Anthony's help." Pappy handed him a small prayer card with the following inscription:

O holy St. Anthony, gentlest of saints, your love for God and charity for His creatures made you worthy, when on earth, to possess miraculous powers. Miracles waited on your word, which you were ever ready to speak for those in trouble or anxiety. Encouraged by this thought, I implore of you to obtain for me (request). The answer to my prayer may require a miracle. Even so, you are the Saint of Miracles. O gentle and loving St. Anthony, whose heart was ever full of human sympathy, whisper my petition into the ears of the sweet Infant Jesus, who loved to be folded in your arms, and the gratitude of my heart will ever be yours.

Amen. (Say 13 Paters, Aves, and Glorias)

"I will, Pappy, I will, and thank you," he called after him.

From that day on, that prayer never left his pocket, and it proved quite miraculous after all.

CHAPTER EIGHTEEN

ST. ANTHONY

The glory of God is said to increase by the
intercession of a saint.

WHEN THE FOCAL POINT OF HIS DAY BECAME MAKING journal entries about his abuse, Prema would often sit and reflect, gradually getting angrier as time elapsed. Since the age of 12, he had been writing what was intended to be his account of trauma. Upon review, he soon realized that there was an entry for every day. Four years of constant abuse and many more years unaccounted for. Father O' Hare had been right; it was important to write it down, because only then was Prema able to see the pattern, the triggers, and the disgrace. Perhaps this was the reason why Prema refused to submit to this evil or cow down to submission. The more he was hit, the more obstinate he grew, and this pleased his grandfather, because he knew that Prema would survive. In a world of prejudice and hate, Prema would thrive.

The abuse gradually gathered strength. After all, there was an entire childhood to destroy, so Cyril was patient in that regard. After a gamut of physical abuse, Cyril knew that as Prema grew older, it was his mind he needed to control, so the abuse centered on mental torment, the kind that made a person question his sanity.

It was Saturday morning on the weekend Cyril had promised the entire family that he would take them to the zoo. It was not particularly expensive, nor was it far, but it was an effort for an attorney of such prominence, if only in his head. All the children were extremely excited, none more so than Prema, who decided to take it upon himself to create a zoo made of colored construction paper so that he could describe the animals they would see and talk about animal behavior, the lion's roar, the monkey's screeching, the elephant's trumpet.

He went into painstaking efforts creating a merry-go-round that actually turned, using a series of paper clips, tooth picks, and pencils. Prema loved to tell these stories to the children, out of love for his siblings. He desperately tried to make up for the unhappiness that permeated the house whenever the sound of slapping or crying occurred. He learnt to bravely conceal his tears and his cries of pain for the sake of the whole, but his mother could not, so he bore the burden of abuse as well as the burden of guilt on his shoulders.

On this particular morning, none of the children were too interested in their breakfasts because of the excitement of going and, therefore, left half-eaten plates at the table. Their father bellowed, and this served to terrorize the children. "I want every crumb eaten, otherwise I won't take you all to the zoo." The children, half-trembling, tried to eat, but simply could not because of fear that his abuse would funnel their way. The girls wet themselves and the middle son hid behind the cupboard.

"Don't worry, *aiya*, I'll eat it," assured Prema, slowly taking the food and eating it himself to free them of this unnecessary hassle. Prema's mother kept signaling her son with her eyes, warning him of his father's distance, for she could not actually say anything for fear of any number of repercussions.

One by one, the children stood up and showed their father their empty plates, and then they were excused from the table, running to each other in the yard, unable to conceal their anticipation of the trip.

Slowly, slowly, six of children stood up and were told to

wait outside. Then Harriet stood up with the baby and she, too, made her way to the garden, but Prema remained seated. He knew the day would not be complete without some sort of altercation, so he remained silent in his seat.

"Do you think your father is an idiot?" Cyril said angrily.

"No, father, I do not" said Prema, rather confused.

"Do you think I didn't see you eating all the little ones' food?" he leered at him, as if staring at the most disgusting thing he had ever seen. Prema remained silent and entrapped.

"You will stay home and clean the dishes after fattening on my fodder, and I will take the servant to the zoo, because you're not worth taking, you disrespectful scoundrel!" He shouted to be heard by the children in the front.

"No, Daddy, Prema made a beautiful zoo for us; he taught us about the lions and the panthers and the giraffe. He's the one who should go, Daddy," a few innocent mouths dared to speak.

"Shall I cancel the entire trip then?" Cyril asked slyly, as he jetted towards the group of them in the garden.

The younger children began shouting, "NO!" sensing the danger of their father and realizing the seriousness of the threat.

"Alright, then. Sedaris, start the engine; we're going to spend a happy day at the zoo!" Cyril shouted like Saint Nick himself.

The family piled into the Morris Minor and drove away, some doused in guilt and others oblivious. Prema watched from the verandah, stunned with the disillusionment of absolute betrayal. The hurt ached to his very core and was more painful than any beating he could have encountered. He sat on the wooden floor in an utter state of shock and gazed at an army of ants taking away the carcass of a cockroach to feast on.

Suddenly, like an electric shock, the complexity of the

situation hit him. All the broken promises and abuse that led up to that day had been meant, by his father's demented mind, to have this effect, to incite this particularly desired torture. Prema's shock turned into boiling rage as he stamped on the ants, freed the cockroach, and ran to the kitchen, smashing every dish in the sink and smiling with delight. *You bastard!* he thought, determined from that day on to get the hell out of the cesspit in which he lived.

When the family returned, Prema, who had decided to beat his father at his own game, had made dinner for everyone. He had left the food out and gone to bed; after all, he didn't want to fatten on his father's fodder. He went under his bed and played with the animals at the zoo, knowing that one day he would go to the zoo, to the jungle, even to Africa, without anyone's permission. This would be his destiny. He recited St. Anthony's prayer and drifted off to sleep to the sound of crying wolf and roaring tiger.

The children, trying to be sensitive to the fact that their brother did not go to the zoo, tried to downplay the day's events, but it was Prema who insisted that they tell every detail. Cyril sat on his chair by the radio, overhearing the children speak so excitedly about the animals, but to his utter irritation, every time the children spoke of an animal, it was Prema who gave them even more information than they learnt the previous day.

"Prema, how did you know? You didn't even go," said his younger siblings.

"Why, you forgot about my zoo, Prema's Zoo!" said Prema.

"But that's not real, Prema," they began to laugh.

"Oh, yes. In fact, last night a hyena bit me. Do you see? See my hand." He showed his hand to a very naive bunch of siblings.

"What, did he really?" said Pavani, clinging to the sleeve of her sister.

"Yes, and in order to free myself, I had to make the sound of a lion, and only then did it release me."

"Oh, Prema, tell us more," they squealed, highly entertained.

"The hyena had a horrible laugh, rather sadistic, and laughing when really all it meant was evil," Prema said, really describing his father, who was growing angry.

"Prema, stop that nonsense, you jealous swine, trying to outwit the children. I know what you're up to!" he threatened. "Now, all of you come, it's time!" At which point, he turned on the radio for their weekly treat: *Sunday Half Hour*. They all gathered, deriving great pleasure from the privilege of hearing the radio, though Prema was all too aware of the fact that most households had the radio on almost all day, every day; but he didn't want to spoil the fun, and he came and sat as well.

"*Ladies and Gentlemen, Sunday Half Hour: Some folks enjoy, some merely come, but as for me, I come forth to sing ... Sunday Half Hour, presented by Lyle Godridge. Now we shall sing. Ave Maria ...*"

They hummed along, the father thinking he was Harry Belafonte himself, and attempted to tap their feet to music best suited for a funeral, but as soon as Ponds Hit Parade, presented by Tim Horshington, came on, the radio was turned off, eliminating all life from their home for another week.

This, however, was to be an unusual week for the family, as Uncle Ram had sent postcards from England stating that he and his wife would be arriving shortly, and the date circled on the calendar was that day. It was such a big thing that the entire family, and extended family, cousins, etc., climbed into their selective cars to drive to the airport and greet them. The journey was a day trip, and all had made sandwiches and packed drinks for the trip. The crowded car, the overheated bodies, and the excitement made some of them carsick, which ultimately spoiled the thought of picnics and the like, but still, they toiled on, Prema in his own world, as he had gone down this path before and thought it ridiculous then, and this time even more so.

Somehow, his father ultimately tried to deliver some sort of "life lesson" to the children when he spoke respectfully about Uncle Ram and how he came to travel on a plane. "This is what happens when you achieve something," Cyril said.

Unfortunately for Prema, his mouth moved faster than his filter and he uttered, "Anyone can buy a ticket if he has money." His mother couldn't help but grin in whole-hearted agreement with her son, but Cyril insisted on making Prema kneel when they finally arrived at the airport, but the crowds gathered, and even Cyril forgot the punishment, and Prema scattered off with the rest of the children.

Actually, Uncle Ram, or so he was called, was not a blood relative, but rather a close friend of Cyril's, as they had schooled together as children. The term "uncle" was given to almost anyone senior to themselves. So the moment a friend walked into the house, the children were made to kiss them on both cheeks and say "Hello Uncle or Hello Aunty," depending on the gender of the person. Prema hated this procedure, as the kiss on both cheeks was moreover a motion to kiss without actual connection. In many cases the kiss became more like a sniff into the ear, for those who liked to exaggerate the gesture. Either way, Prema thought it to be unnatural and felt it a ridiculous custom.

As it happened, Pappy was in Colombo on that Saturday and decided to go along to the airport for the sheer pleasure of being nearer his grandchildren. His aim was to remove Prema from harm's way by taking him and the older boys in his car. But as it happened, his car because chauffeur to the maid, the food and drink supplies, and two of the younger sisters.

While eating short eats and cutlets, Prema remembered the postcard from Uncle Ram in his pocket. It was a picture of Piccadilly Circus. The picture happened to have a picture of a famous London postbox, which Uncle Ram had carefully circled and said, "Guess where this was posted."

So Prema asked Pappy, "Doesn't Uncle Ram live in High Wycombe? Don't they have postboxes in High Wycombe?"

"Yes, *Putha*," said Pappy.

"Then why did he go all the way to Piccadilly Circus just to mail this letter?"

"You're right, *Putha*," said Pappy, entertained by the way Prema thought.

So as Uncle Ram made his way towards Pappy, Prema stuck his head in between and began questioning him. "Aren't there post offices in High Wycombe?"

"Of course there are. There's one on every street corner!"

At this point, Prema pulled out the postcard and began questioning Uncle Ram's logic for posting from Piccadilly Circus. The questions became almost like an interrogation, and soon, Uncle Ram became very uncomfortable, for others began questioning the same. Fearful of losing his importance, he walked up towards the seats in the gallery, as if to separate himself by way of height, and began to make an announcement.

"Thank you all for coming to greet us at the airport. It has been a wonderful homecoming and we have many stories to tell," at which point many of the poorer relations began asking about England and how he came to live there.

"It is a rare honor to be asked to become a loyal subject

of the Queen, but Rosalie and I accepted." He pulled out his passport and began to read, with all eyes upon him:

"*Her Britannic Majesty's Principal Secretary to the United Kingdom and the Colonies requests and requires in the name of Her Majesty all those whom it may concern to allow the bearer* (THAT'S ME) *to pass freely without let or hindrance and to afford the bearer such assistance and protection as maybe necessary.*" The crowd began clapping, and both Pappy and Prema just remained in the background rolling their eyes.

"Pappy, doesn't everyone have the same passport?"

"Yes, of course ... and as usual, you are wise beyond your years!" Pappy laughed, patting his grandson, proud that he understood the hypocrisy of it all.

Prema was wise beyond his years, because he spent most of his time outside his home, unable to safely live there during his father's waking hours. He was forbidden to eat the food or stay there after a while. Although it was probably the best for all concerned, it was terribly sad for Prema, who walked the streets like a street urchin, trying to find food and shelter along the way. If not for the kindness of strangers, he may well have never survived.

During a period of deep depression, feeling hungry and very abandoned, Prema awoke to the sound of dock men shouting directions, guiding a Greek vessel safely to harbor. Once docked, hundreds of men started unloading boxes from the ship and loading more crates back on board. The ship was to remain docked overnight and then set sail in the morning. It was at that moment that Prema seized the opportunity and decided to get on board the ship when no one was looking.

He nestled himself inside a life raft and fell asleep, happy for the first time in years. This great escape began with a feeling of euphoria and ended with the nausea that came with the sway of the ocean beneath his head.

"I did it, I made it, I'm going to Greece!" Prema exclaimed to himself!

But as fate would have it, a sailor walking near the lifeboat heard the sound of the child's voice and soon that same life raft became his voyage back to shore. He cried and pleaded, but they would not play a part in his getaway, disbelieving that any child could ever be treated as he described. The authorities took possession of the boy when he reached the shore and they accompanied him home.

To his horror, the port authorities, too, were in utter disbelief and decided to tell his story to none other than his father, who answered the door to these officials. "I'm sorry, he did what?" commanded Cyril to the authorities.

"I'm afraid we found him as a stowaway on the Greek vessel. Can you tell us why your son would want to run away, sir?"

To which slyness appeared once again on Cyril's face and he invited the two authorities inside. "Please pardon me. You both must be hungry; a drink to start while I have the servants serve us dinner?"

"Oh no, sir, we couldn't trouble you" they said.

"I insist," Cyril said, at which point his finest brandy was served to the two men, along with a tray of String Hoppers, beef curry, and seeni sambol.

Cyril set the stage, including time to caress the heads of his children, kissing each of them good night; even going to the extent of kissing his wife's hand and thanking her for being such a good wife.

Prema watched this in utter horror, for he never knew just how diabolical his father could be until that moment. He could have received an Oscar for his performance, but Cyril knew he was being judged and his reputation would be on the line, thanks to Prema, so he was determined to make a liar of his son. By the time the two officers left, they had forgotten why they came, thanked Cyril profusely, and left under the light of the moon, which was now half-covered by clouds.

"Storm's looming; best be going as soon as possible. Thank you, kind sir," they both wished Cyril and left.

Once out of range, Cyril grabbed his son by the neck, literally strangling him as he carried him out to the yard.

"You will kneel here all night, arms extended. Do you understand? If you move, I will kill you!" Prema did what he was told, because he knew his father would kill him otherwise. The storm set in with thunder and lightning, and torrential rain poured down, beating him over and over again, making him fall to his face many times, only for him to struggle back to his knees.

His mother, cried at the sight, "*Dear Jesus, help him, Mother Mary help him,*" but even that was stopped.

"Harriet, where are you? Get in here!" It was time for her wifely duties and all she could do was wince at the thought.

By morning, Prema's body was deeply entrenched in the mud of the earth and frozen stiff. His arms were straddled and all that carried him through that night of terror was the thought of Jesus on the cross. "*I give myself to you my Lord,*" Prema prayed over and over again, sometimes being just feet away from being electrocuted and only wishing to be dead by morning.

It was the servants, Edison in particular, who couldn't take it, and Edison stood outside with Prema, holding an umbrella as best he could, but the impending threat of the master was just too severe. Once he received permission to remove Prema from the lawn, Edison ran out to him, "Dear

God, that is what he prays to. What God lets this happen, that a father should be so evil?" Edison said angrily as he massaged the boy's arms and removed his wet clothing.

"Try to eat, child," Edison said, trying to put a piece of bread in his mouth.

"You must escape this, dear *Putha*. I will help you, if it's that last thing I do, I will help you," he muttered as he frantically tried to revive the boy.

Prema's mother appeared in the servant's quarters. "How is he?" she asked, afraid to enter for fear of the worst, or worse still, being called by her husband.

Edison, trying to be civil, managed to answer without sarcasm. "He has a high fever, he's in shock, and he is very malnourished and weak."

She couldn't stand back anymore. The wall of fear disappeared and the arms of a mother reached out. She put his head close to her womb and caressed him for the first time.

"Oh, Prema, what can I do? I cannot forsake seven others for you. You must stay as far away from him as possible."

But Prema did not hear the words, just the sound of love as he tried desperately to memorize the smell of her clothes and the touch of her hands on him, which penetrated through the cold flesh and cramped muscles of his skinny frame.

She quickly handed Edison a large plate of rice and chicken. "Please, take this and try to feed him. I will be back later to check on him. Keep him out of sight," she said.

The sound of her voice and the touch of her hand on his head renewed his faith in life, and he began to come round, eating the rice Edison fed him, one mouthful at a time. As the weeks and months progressed, Edison took it upon himself to teach Prema the art of retribution and survival, until he had the strength to stand up to his abuser once and for all.

"*Putha,* you are a good boy. You are the only reason I stay here, to watch out for you. I have to teach you how to outwit your father; he needs to be taught a lesson."

So lesson number one was house security. Edison believed it to be most appropriate because Cyril prided himself at being well-connected, the Head of the Police Commission, he was king of his castle and could do anything he wanted. Or could he?

"Let's do a surprise attack, Prema. We're going to pelt stones at the house and drive him crazy," Edison said, which marked the beginning of a month-long attack on the house. The stone pelting began always during Cyril's dinner, to irritate him the most. First, one stone was pelted to hit a window in the front of the house to cause a disturbance, then, once he was out of his seat to investigate, a stone came from another direction in the very room in which he sat.

Cyril sent out the dogs, but of course, they didn't catch the criminals because the criminals lived there. He looked all around the house himself, calling out the servants, and asking where Prema was, but Prema was innocently sitting and reading his books.

The next night, in the same pattern, stones were pelted, dinner disturbed, again an investigation, and nothing. The next night, Cyril waited, postponed his dinner till after the predicted attack time and nothing. Once he sat, "bang," glass shattered. They repeated the pattern. The first two nights, they started the attack at the same time, then the next night, a different time, then nothing the next night. Edison vowed, "We won't stop pelting until he stops hitting you!"

"Well, I guess our house will look like a bomb-damaged site before too long!" Prema laughed, wondering if this was more an exercise for Edison to seek revenge than for him, for after a while it grew tiresome, until Edison finally bombarded the house about 10 times, shattering every window in the front of the house.

That night, Prema, in order to protect Edison, who he knew had gone too far, ran out of the house and started shouting, "Daddy, Daddy, I saw the guy; he ran that way," he said and pointed in the opposite direction of the one Edison escaped in. After that night, 20 security guards were plastered around the house and the neighborhood, and the pelting stopped like magic.

"Funny how it all stopped," Edison laughed.

"I was praying to St. Anthony to protect you," said Prema.

"This saint must be pretty powerful. Perhaps he will have the power to make you escape being locked up!"

"What do you mean Edison?" Prema asked.

"I mean, every weekend you get locked up in your father's office when they go out to their parties."

"Yes," said Prema curiously.

"Well, I want to show you how to unscrew the grills on the windows so that you can escape and do whatever you want while they're gone!.."

So, quietly, the two ventured into Cyril's office and the tricks of the trade were presented to Prema, who quickly maneuvered himself, stealthily, in and out of the house whenever he was locked in. He began to look forward to being locked up just to act like a cat burglar and get away with defying his father. After a while he began to resent his brothers and sisters, who added to his plight by constantly telling on him and complaining.

Finally, he thought, *I'm going to make them a little crazy. They keep calling me* Pissu, *well, they're the ones who are crazy. I'll show them.* Prema thought, and finally it came to him, *St. Anthony!*

As usual, the night began with being locked in the office, being told to kneel, and kneeling as if at this point he was actually going to listen. Then all the children were kissed goodnight and told to go to bed by 8:00 p.m. There was always about a 15 minute lull, and then all hell broke loose, with the children creating havoc around the house, laughing and screaming, them along with the servants. It seemed like a normal household and a necessary release for them all, save for Prema.

This used to make him happy, just to hear them happy, that is, until the older ones began to stand in front of the office door and tease Prema.

"So, you're a dirty rotten scoundrel; can't behave; poor Prema," they shouted that night, but there was no response. Instead, the door remained steadfastly triple-locked and silent. This aroused suspicions among the children.

"Prema, are you in there? Prema, are you all right?" they asked, but there was silence. The room became so silent that each of them tucked their ears to the door, "It's quiet. I can't hear anything when you talk!" Manjula said.

Then, suddenly, from across the room, Prema came out with his arms in front of him like a zombie. "Hello, Hello!" shouted Prema, pretending to be sleep walking.

"Oh my God, Prema!" shouted Stephen, and the girls screamed, "How can it be? You're locked inside."

"St. Anthony, St. Anthony let me out, St. Anthony let me out!" Prema repeated in a ghostly voice.

Manisha started screaming and crossing herself. "Dear Jesus, forgive us for making fun of Prema; we didn't mean it!"

"You all will have to pay for the evil you have done to me, St. Anthony said," Prema howled down the hall, knowing that his parents would be home any second. He quickly returned around the back, refastened the screws on the grills and knelt down the moment he heard the front door shut.

"Daddy, Daddy, Prema, it's Prema. St. Anthony let him out, St. Anthony let him out!" they screamed, horrified at the implications.

"What on earth are you saying? That's impossible; he's locked inside, cannot possibly escape," he said while rechecking the locks that remained firmly locked.

Then he unlocked the door and found Prema kneeling. "Get up. Now, what on earth have you been doing terrorizing these children?"

"How can I terrorize them? They have been cruel to me, mocking me through the doorway. I have remained here; where else could I have gone?" Prema looked perplexed, and Edison smirked in the background.

Failing to see any logic in the possibility of the story of an escape, he berated them and sent them all off to bed immediately. "That goes for you!" he shouted at Prema.

"No food again?" he mumbled as he made his way to bed.

His father heard him and actually felt sorry for him. It was true he had been hard on him, and this time he appeared innocent. "Edison, get Prema a fish bun and tea and then lights off."

Edison, shocked but delighted in giving Prema food, quickly made him a huge plate of rice with beef curry and a fish bun and delivered it to him, which he would have done whether his father had wished it or not. The two had each other's backs and one never did with if the other was without.

"Thank you, Edison. I was starving!" Prema said, and quickly ate the plate of rice.

"They delivered ginger beer and strawberry jam to the

house, so I was able to nick a few jars for us and put it in our hiding place in the chimney," Edison exclaimed.

"Oh, good, I'll get some bread and we'll eat it after they've gone!" said Prema. "I need to sleep now because I have O levels to write tomorrow and I've studied as much as I possibly can."

Prema was still recuperating from being kept out all night during the storm and still went in and out of fever. His body was frail and had been so badly beaten that he felt as if he was 90 years old from all the stiffness he suffered through.

That morning, he actually slept in, so when Edison checked on him he had fever. "Prema, don't you have exams today?"

"Oh no, what time is it?" he said frantically.

"It's 9:00 a.m.!"

"I'll get your uniform," Edison assisted.

Prema dressed and hurriedly ran to school, bothered that no one cared to check on him. His father was well-informed of the exams and, in fact, tutored Manjula through English to make sure he would do well, then he gave him a good breakfast and personally drove him to school. So while he was wishing him luck on his exams, he saw Prema running through the courtyard of St. Benedict's.

He angrily charged into the school after Prema, determined to send him into the exams with an angry sermon, but instead, he found Prema running back out of the exam hall, back through the court yard, and, seemingly, back home.

When the instructor came out, he said, "He forgot his student I.D. card at home; won't be a second I'm told." He smiled comfortingly at his father.

But that was enough to set Cyril off, as the previous week's concession towards his son now acted against him in this innocent misdemeanor of forgetting his I.D. card for the exam. Cyril was determined to fuel his rage. He hurried into his car and went after Prema. When he saw Prema, he ran him off the road into the ditch with the car. His small body was strewn by the force, causing him to hit his head against a pipe and bruise the parts still left uninjured. Like a madman, Cyril got out of the car took a rock and bashed Prema's fingers until they bled. "That will teach you to be so irresponsible!"

Prema sat dazed in the ditch, fingers bloody and swollen, body battered, his fever high. ... He simply could not believe the hate, or why he was always singled out. He had nowhere to go and nowhere to hide. From somewhere inside his soul, he managed to ferret out strength and decided to proceed with the exam, despite all the obstacles. He walked slowly back to school, but the pain in his entire body was so great that he began to experience dizzy spells.

When he made it to the exam hall, the exams had already begun. The invigilator saw Prema, shirt dirty and torn, face swollen, hands bleeding. He sat Prema in the back of the room and put cold compresses on his head and hands.

"I can't watch this, you poor, poor child. Don't worry, I will write the test for you," he said, and with that news, Prema blacked out and dropped to the floor. He was put in the nurse's office and tended to and given pain medication, and once again, Father O'Hare came to pray over him.

"Oh, Prema, I don't know what to tell you. The Lord may be testing you now, but I assure you he loves you more than the whole lot of them. I know it doesn't seem like it now, but you will be blessed in life, you will be."

When Father O'Hare knew Prema's father would not be home, he sent for Harriet, through the driver, so he could talk in confidence with her about her son.

"Mrs. Alvis, I'm sorry to bother you, but we are most concerned about the welfare of your son. You are obliged, as his mother, to protect him, and if you can't, then you must seek help from those can help you. Do you understand how dangerous this is? He will kill your son if you let it happen!"

To which she shook her head in shame and quietly left the room. She made a trunk call to her father, "Papa, please come. It's urgent. Prema needs you," was all she said as she resigned herself to whatever fate that lay ahead and put down the receiver.

Prema was the world to Pappy, so on receipt of such a call, he hurriedly gathered his things and set out the door for the train station. He put on his old glasses, that he bought for just ten rupees at an estate sale, and made his way across the busy intersection.

Brakes screeched and horns blew, and then there was a hard knock as Pappy lay in the middle of traffic, unconscious.

Prema jerked awake, as if from a nightmare, and sensed that something was very wrong. "Don't worry, son; you will be all right now," assured Father O'Hare, but Prema had a bad feeling and insisted on getting up. "No, son, you will have to rest. Your Grandfather is en route."

Sadly, the only direction Pappy was going to was the hospital, and it wasn't until nightfall that Harriet received a phone call from the hospital that her father was in critical condition.

Her world came crashing down, and soon, Prema's world and his hope, too, ceased to exist. Only a miracle could save them.

The next morning, the family was told that Pappy had come too in the middle of the night when the priest came to give him Last Rites, and he asked, "How's the stock market?" but sadly, shortly thereafter, he died in his sleep.

For some reason, maybe because it all happened so fast,

neither Prema nor the other children had been informed of the accident, but when he rose the next morning, he did so with the uncanny knowledge that his grandfather had died. It took him two seconds to confirm this when he saw his Mother's face.

At that moment, he knew he was on his own, and that he would have to culminate all the strength of Pappy's wisdom to carry on. Somehow, he would make Pappy proud, and he believed Pappy would be with him in spirit, permanently. He could not cry; he had to think and he had to plan his next move. He didn't dare show emotion, for it would expose his vulnerability, and that was too personal. He would not be robbed of his grief, nor would he be humiliated by people who proved to be his enemies; this would never happen again.

At the funeral, Prema slowly touched Pappy's hands for the last time and prayed for his soul, gently kissing his forehead without anyone's knowledge. He whispered in his ear that he would not let him down and promised to make him proud. It was important for Prema to tell him this, like a secret pact that went beyond life itself.

Life did continue and Prema carried on, through the beatings, the torment, and being locked up. In the month that followed Pappy's death, Prema did not subscribe to his usual antics for he was in deep thought. Instead of attempts to escape from the office, he soon found himself going through files on his father's desk. Cyril was the executor of Pappy's estate, and so he had to individually go through all Meedeniya's assets to sort out a legal remedy to his estate.

Prema looked through the number of homes Pappy owned through the years and thought about the stories he used to tell. How he built his fortune and the way he lent money to those in need or invested money in property when he made it.

Prema sat on his father's office chair and just thought. He could hear his siblings through the door, asking whether St. Anthony would let him out those nights, but all this prompted him to do was reach for the Prayer to St. Anthony Pappy had given him.

As he read it over and over again, he felt the need to go through the files individually. As he turned the pages, a small piece of paper fell out with the name of Mr. Clay, his lawyer, at 1065 Bryanston Mews, Earls Court, London, United Kingdom, and underneath this was a banking slip that showed two thousand pounds in an a bank account under Aloysius Meedeniya.

"Pappy, is this what you wanted me to find?" he asked under his breath. "St. Anthony, have I found what I think I have found?" he said as he slowly folded the paper that contained this life-altering information. He slipped it into his pants and waited deep in thought until his parents arrived home.

St. Anthony had delivered his first miracle to Prema, a message from Pappy, his way out, a new-found hope, a new direction, a new country, and a new life.

CHAPTER NINETEEN
FREEDOM

... is the ability to breath, without fear.

For almost two months, every day, Prema waited nervously outside his gate for the postman to arrive, sometimes hiding in the bushes so as not to be spotted by a soul and then springing out when he saw the man.

"Prema, you have to stop doing that. You will give this old man a heart attack," exclaimed Mr. Gunaratne.

"Anything?" Prema asked hopefully.

"As a matter of fact …" he said cautiously as he reached inside his bag and pulled out a letter stamped "Air Mail" and with stamps of Her Majesty the Queen upon it.

"Oh, thank you, thank you, thank you!" Prema exclaimed.

"You're welcome, and thank you for the extra 50 rupees. Every little bit helps this poor man," said the postman, not wanting to intrude on what appeared to be of topmost importance to the young man.

> *"Dear Mr. Meedeniya, I'm in receipt of your instructions and have enclosed a ticket for your grandson on Air Ceylon, leaving in December, as per your request. Please have him call me upon his arrival and I will arrange to give him some funds. I look forward to meeting the apple of your eye in the very near future. Yours Most Sincerely, Mr. Clay, Barrister at Law."*

Prema sat in the bushes, stunned. *It worked, it actually worked*, he repeated in his head over and over again. "Pappy, thank you, I'm going to make you proud," he said, looking up to heaven, as that could be the only place possible for one such as he.

Prema had two months before he left, and he had a lot to organize, now that he had a ticket and the promise of funding when he arrived. He only hoped that by the time he arrived, Mr. Clay would not yet have been informed of Pappy's death, so that he wouldn't link the timing of the typed letter from Prema as being fraudulent, which, of course, it was. In Prema's mind, it was justified and motivated by every school of thought his grandfather taught him, as he knew that this was exactly what his grandfather wanted for him.

His friend, Tony Offen's, father worked for the airlines, so Prema decided to ask him what was required of a person in order to travel, "Mr. Offen, sir, if one were to travel to Germany, for instance, what would one have to have besides a ticket?" Prema asked coyly.

"Well, son, one would have to have a passport and, of course, money," he said nonchalantly.

"Oh my God! I mean, where are passports issued?" Prema asked frantically.

"The Department of Immigration & Emigration located at No. 41, Ananda Rajakaruna Mawatha, Colombo 10. Does your father need a passport?" he suddenly asked.

"My father, no, of course not; he has one from the war days. Uh, I was just wondering, for a project at school" said Prema, thinking his recovery was smooth.

"I see," said Mr. Offen, sensing there was more to this story, but knowing how to remain impartial.

"Well, Prema, if you need any help at all, I will be happy to help you, just between you and me. I'm a professional; this is what I do," Mr. Offen said, patting Prema on the shoulder.

"Thank you, sir." Prema felt somewhat relieved.

"Prema, perhaps you would like a passport application?"

"Pardon me?" asked Prema, distracted.

"A passport application, it's what you have to fill in when you get a passport, along with a photograph of yourself. Here, take one, I have plenty," he said, handing the application to Prema on a hunch.

"Thank you, sir," Prema said, taking the form and walking out of his office. He removed the prayer of St. Anthony from his pocket and gently kissed it, knowing another intercession had taken place.

Prema read through the application over and over again. *If under 18, must be signed by a guarantor and at least two people known to you for five years.* Who could he go to; he needed this to be private. First things first, he needed to get a passport photo. Prema wandered past St. Theresa's on Thimbirigasyaya Road, the banana *kade,* and the milk bar. Near the Hopper Hut, Mr. Thomian had a small photographic studio where he sold Kodak film. Prema had sought refuge at his shop over the years, often doing voluntary work for him. It is there that Prema learnt how to process film, and it was also there that he felt great solace and comfort, a shelter from the storm of life. Mr. Thomian and his wife would feed Prema as and when they saw him, knowing all too well of the horrible conditions in which he lived.

"Uncle, I, uh, I need a passport picture," Prema stuttered, not sure if he should be revealing this to him. Mr. Thomian looked at him hard, reading the thoughts in the boy's mind.

"I'm so happy for you. Is that all you need?" he inquired.

"Well, Uncle, I may also need a you to sign as my guarantor, if that's not too much trouble."

"Certainly, Prema, it's not too much trouble at all," and

FAR AWAY, I LAND

with that, the process began. Prema kept all his files inside a plastic bag and tied it carefully into a neat package that he hid inside the chimney. He could not trust a soul with this information, not even Edison, who had been with him through his most trying days. On the day he presented his passport application, the passport officer was quite suspicious of the boy.

"Where are your parents? This is usually done by your parents," said the officer.

"My father is overseas and has asked me to proceed as usual. Is there a problem? My father said there would not be problem if I had all the correct signatures, and the signatures are there!" Prema said sternly, trying to assert himself in a way he was unaccustomed to.

This surprised the officer into submission, as she knew her questions were unprofessional and she was just being nosy, a seemingly national trait. "Everything is in order, Prema. Where are the 500 rupees for the fee?"

Prema had slowly collected the money over a month and knew if he had been caught with this type of money, he would have been shot by his father, but again, it was money he found scattered amongst his grandfather's effects, and he knew it was his destiny.

"Son, you are twenty cents short," the passport officer said.

"Twenty cents?" uttered Prema, as if it was a million rupees. He was sure he had collected it all. "I had the money. I mean, it was there this morning; it must have fallen. I, I really need this passport," Prema pleaded.

Sensing his desperation, the officer went into her purse and deposited the money into Prema's small pile of coins.

"Oh look, it was there all along," she said, smiling at the boy.

"Thank you, Madame." Prema smiled, wondering how strangers could be more loving than family.

"Your passport will be ready in two weeks. Would you like us to mail it to you to save you the trip?" she asked.

"Oh no, I'll be here and pick it up in person." He smiled ear to ear.

From that day forward, nothing could bring Prema's spirits down, not even his father. He would endure anything until that day would come. In the meantime, Mr. Offen began questioning Prema.

"The form I signed as guarantor, it was only for school, wasn't it? I mean, you're not actually going to Germany," he asked, suddenly thinking about the implications should this boy run away.

"Germany?" Prema exclaimed. "How on earth could I afford to go anywhere?" Prema laughed, reassuring him that there was no underlying motive to obtaining his signature and relieving him of all responsibility.

Secretly, Mr. Offen wished Prema was leaving that place, for he knew his background and felt the boy had so much potential. To be abused the way he was, was most unfair.

The tension built in the weeks that passed, until that one glorious day in which Prema obtained his passport: Premalal Franklin Alvis—Citizen of Sri Lanka. The same passport officer that accepted his application form gave his passport.

"Now you have to get your visa," she announced, plummeting Prema's heart to the ground.

"For what?" Prema said.

"I would have thought your father would have told you. All citizens of Sri Lanka have to have a tourist visa when travelling abroad," she said.

"Yes, of course. I mean, I thought it would be issued with

the passport," Prema said quickly recovering. He was so close to his goal.

"I will take you to the visa officer. He will interview you and ask you the reason for your trip. After all, so many Sri Lankans travel and never come back. That wouldn't be you, now would it?"

"Never come back, I wouldn't dream of it!" Prema exclaimed, saying exactly the opposite of what he felt.

The visa officer was an elderly fellow who seemed more concerned about how close the clock was to lunch hour than the answers Prema provided.

"Purpose of trip?" he asked.

"I will be visiting a family friend upon my father's instructions," Prema said coolly.

"Length of stay?"

"I will be staying two weeks," he said without wincing.

"Do you plan on extending your trip?"

"I am told it's very cold in England at this time of year. I think I will be back sooner rather than later," Prema answered. "Besides, my dear family is here. How could I leave them?" he said for effect.

"Right, then. I will submit your passport, and your visa will be issued within one week. Mail or pick up?"

"Pick up," Prema said, getting up and pointing to the clock. "Lunch time!" Prema said, coaxing the officer.

"Yes, you're right, lunch time, finally!" at which point the officer quickly filled out the form, asked Prema to sign, and had left the room before Prema turned around.

"Thank God for good cooks," Prema uttered with a smile.

Prema kept his passport with its official tourist visa stamp and his ticket well-protected and tucked deep within the crevasses of the chimney, checking it sometimes four times a day, until the day came that was to be his great escape. He wandered around the neighborhood, pensively observing everything. He watched his siblings playing on the yard and prayed for his mother to find peace once he was gone.

In his distracted mindset, he did not see his father enter the house, nor did he respond as did all the others. He remained in the backyard. He heard the ranting of his father, complaining about everything from his work to the servants, then the state of the house, and then he slapped his wife. Prema instinctively ran into the house and stood in front of his mother.

"What are you doing?" his father shouted. "This is not your business."

"It is my business. She is my mother; don't touch her again!" Prema shouted for the first time in his life. Then his father went to the study and brought out his gun and began beating Prema with the butt of the gun. One, two, three slams, until like a phoenix from the ashes, Prema rose up, grabbed the gun, and hit his father across the shoulder, sending him flying across the floor.

"Don't you ever touch me or my mother again, you bastard!" Prema kissed his mother's brow and ran out of the house, not caring if his father was dead.

He could hear all sorts of screaming from the house, but he had done what he needed to do. Later that same night, he snuck back through the back gate, climbed up the chimney, pulled out his passport and ticket, and was on his way. Suddenly, he went back, entered the servant's room and whispered into Edison's ear.

"I'm leaving and won't be back for a very long time."

"I'll come with you then," he said loyally.

Prema stood and stared longingly at his beloved companion and protector. "Where I'm going, you will not be able to follow, but you will always be in my prayers," Prema said, tightly hugging his dear servant and friend for the last time.

"You have been more than a brother to me," Prema said.

"And you to me," Edison said.

"I have nothing to give you and you have given me so much," Prema said with tears welled up in his eyes.

"Prema, you must listen to me. Knowing that you are escaping all this is the greatest gift you can give me. I want you to show the world the prince you really are."

Prema reached into his homemade cloth bag, which he had sewn together especially for this trip, and pulled out his well-used red and purple sling shot.

"Remember this from our stoning days?"

"How can I forget? It took us two weeks to carve it. See your initials, I carved them right there," Edison said, pointing to the center of the handle. "I didn't want anyone else to claim ownership."

"I want you to have it," Prema said, needing to give his most loyal ally something that meant a lot to him.

Edison sadly took it and said, "I'll keep it safely until ..." but then he stopped short and said, "I'll keep it safe." He was filled with great joy and relief for Prema, but his concern for Prema never ceased.

He gazed in the direction of his *Sudu* prince and prayed for the first time in his life. It would not be the last.

The two young men left the house that night, one traveling south and the other toward the north, to the airport and beyond.

❧

PERHAPS IT WAS PURE and utter elation that kept Prema from

feeling fear and sadness, or perhaps it was not realizing the gravity of the situation, but there he was, a few days short of 17, on a plane for the first time in his life, and headed to a country he'd never been to, with one pound taped to the inside of his shoe for safekeeping. The fact that he thought to carry a seeni sambol bun and a banana was far thinking, for he had no plans whatsoever, just a great sense of relief and overriding joy that stemmed from freedom.

The stewardesses were most curious about this gangling young man with the infectious smile. "Where are your parents?" asked one.

"In London, of course!" Prema said in a confident voice. "They are waiting for me when I arrive!"

"Really, what does your father do?" Prema thought carefully before he spoke, fearing that they would turn the plane around if they knew how he came to be there.

"He's a lawyer, on assignment, a ... high profile criminal case."

"Really, would I know about it?"

"Can't say, even I don't know the details other than that. In fact, I'm not sure whether I should have told you, you know attorney-client confidentiality being what it is."

"Yes, yes, of course. I'm sorry, sir. What can I get you to drink?"

Sir, drink ... Where am I, he thought, reveling at being referred to as sir. "What are you serving?" Prema asked carefully, thinking about his grandfather on the train.

"We have apple juice, orange juice, cola, and ginger ale, ... coffee and tea," the stewardess said with a smile on her face.

"How much would that be?" Prema asked, pretending to have money.

"It's complimentary, sir," she said, "... no charge," she continued, to make herself clearer.

"Do you have ginger beer?" he asked, thinking that was quite an elite thing to drink.

"As a matter of fact, we don't usually carry it, but I think we do have some. Just a moment," she said, and when she returned, she handed him a whole tin of ginger beer, a packet of peanuts, and a packet of cookies.

"Thank you," he said, thrilled at his luck. It was his first time on a plane and the first time he was ever given a whole can of ginger beer. *This was heaven*, he thought. He carefully slipped the peanuts and the cookies into his bag, and when another stewardess passed, he asked for another, saying that he dropped his on the floor.

"Of course, no problems, back in a moment." She smiled, and when she returned, she handed him three of everything, peanuts, cookies, and chips.

"I thought you would enjoy these for the flight," she said with a smile.

For the trip? he thought, *this is enough food for a whole week.* He smiled to himself, feeling secure in the knowledge that he could survive at the other end for some time.

He gazed out the window and was able to see the engine and how the wing of the plane adjusted itself, like a bird. He was fascinated by everything, how the seat moved up and down, the safety belt, the overhead compartments, the safety devices that were supposed to drop down in case of emergency, the washrooms, and the film projectors. Unbeknown to him, the captain was watching the young boy looking so intently at every component of the plane. "Hello, young man. I'm the captain; would you like to see the cockpit?" Prema was taken aback.

"If you're the captain, sir, then who is flying the plane?" asked Prema, startled.

"Well, let's take a look," he said humorously as he put his hand on the boy's shoulder and escorted him through the serving station into the cockpit itself.

The lights, buttons, switches, and large gear shift overwhelmed him and put him in a state of shock. It was enough for him to be given the opportunity to see everything, but further adding to his shock was the polite manner of the captain. Not only did he explain how the cockpit operated, but Prema was allowed to ask as many questions as he wanted. Prema wasn't sure if this would cost him money, but he was willing to wash plates for a month for it. When landing time approached, Prema was sent back to his seat, but not without being given a small pin to commemorate his first Air Ceylon journey to London.

"Thank you, Captain, sir. It was a great honor for me to see the inside workings of your fine plane."

"It was an absolute pleasure, young man, an absolute pleasure," the captain said as they exchanged glances.

The flying time was over in ten hours, but the excitement during that time was like a flash in the dark. Prema wanted to relive the moments again and again, just to acclimatize himself to how the world really behaved. He gathered his small bag, now filled with the riches of air travel, including a pillow and a blanket, which he thought might come in handy wherever he found a place to sleep.

The stewardesses escorted Prema off the plane, but fear seized him once more when he saw the unfamiliar setting and a policeman in uniform.

"How did they find out about me so fast?" He panicked as he made a beeline to the washrooms.

"Prema, are you all right?" called one of the stewardesses.

"Yes, thank you so much. I see my parents, goodbye!" he

exclaimed, not realizing he would have to go through customs before he could have ever seen his parents, or anyone for that matter.

He remained in the washroom for a good 30 minutes, but when no one came to capture him, he peered out and checked whether it was safe for him to leave. He made eye contact with a few people and they did not appear to be after him, so he soon he found himself walking in the same direction and same pace as others from his plane. He recognized one old man who was in a wheelchair.

He was on my plane; I better follow him, he thought as he walked alongside the old man.

His behavior caught the eye of the man and he asked, "First time to London?."

"Yes, as a matter of fact, it is," said Prema, still uneasy.

"Don't worry, I'll pretend I'm your grandfather and escort you out; just follow me," With this, Prema clung tightly to his picture of the Perpetual Heart of Mary and followed the lead of the old man.

Prema walked through customs alongside the old man, so when the customs officers looked, they could only assume he was accompanied by the man. Prema's heart skipped a beat when the customs officer asked him, "How long do you plan to stay in England, young man?"

Prema answered, as if pre-rehearsed, "Only two weeks, sir. It is much too cold for me!" The customs officer stamped his passport and handed it back to him. As Prema reunited with the old man in the wheelchair, he walked past the stern-looking customs officers, who seemed to be looking firmly in his direction. The fear was so daunting that he was thankful for the support of the wheelchair as he felt his knees going weak at sight of them.

Holy Mary Mother of God, pray for me, protect me, save me from being caught. Prema prayed so intently in his head that he was sure his thoughts could be heard.

Once past the doors and into the sight of families happily greeting passengers in the arrival hall, Prema made a mad dash into the crowd, leaving nothing to chance. He stayed low and as inconspicuous as a tall, gawky Asian boy could be in a crowd of pink-skinned Englishmen.

He seemed to instinctively know where to go as the set up in the arrivals hall was similar to the airport at home. He knew he was free at that point, based on his many undesirable trips to the airport with his family back home. He saw the exit doors and ran towards them. Putting his whole weight on the door, he thrust it open and was hit with the sharp sting of cold. The initial shock of it set him back, but soon he was taking in deep breaths and rubbing his hands together with glee. *It's a bit like Nuwara Eliya in the morning, cool and crisp,* he thought. He remembered Pappy telling him that Nuwara Eliya was often referred to as Little England because of the weather, and now he understood why.

Countless taxis pulled up the curb, dropping off passengers and picking up others. He noted the exchange of money and knew the one pound coin he had taped in his shoe wasn't going to take him very far. Mr. Clay lived in Leeds and that would entail more thinking as to how he was going to make contact with him, without letting on how poor he actually was. He needed a plan, one which he could control. If Mr. Clay had picked him up, then Prema could not control the situation in so far as making Mr. Clay leave. No, he had to think of a way to personally get to Leeds, meet Mr. Clay, take the money, and run.

He was glad he had taken the cabin blanket, but at the

same time, knew that in this weather, it would hardly protect him from this type of cold. After all, he was now a veteran at living on the streets. *Oh yes, Uncle Harry's address and phone number, let me find it*, he suddenly remembered, and began to scrimmage through his bag.

The problem of wasting his only pound on a phone call plagued him, but if he didn't, he was not sure what he would do or where he would go.

What if I call and Uncle isn't home and then I lose my money as well? he pondered, sitting beside the public phone stalls that lined the wall nearest the exit gates. He watched people indiscriminately putting in handfuls of coins to make their calls. He watched as they smiled and laughed on the phone, and he also noticed how they checked something at the bottom of the phone once they hung up. One man took his change out, then another, and then another.

As he neared the phone, he could see "coin return" written at the bottom. *Oh, so maybe not all people are checking this*, he thought, and low and behold, an angry woman hung up the phone, yelled in the direction of the phone, which was no longer connected, and then stormed off. Prema slowly edged his way towards the phone, pretending to look at the phone book, and there in the coin return were two five pence coins. *"Thank you, Mother Mary,"* Prema said, smiling, and he immediately pulled them out, re-deposited them, and began to dial his uncle's number.

It took three nerve-racking rings before a stately English voice answered the phone. "Good morning, may I help you?" said the voice, most formal and so unlike any greeting he had ever heard before.

"Good morning," Prema said in a most insecure tone, "I

would like to speak with Mr. Meedeniya, my Uncle Harry, please."

"Pardon me, young man, and whom did you say was calling?" uttered the intimidating man on the other end.

"Yes, sir, my name is Premalal Alvis and you?" A trick Prema had learnt from Pappy. "Whenever someone asks you a personal question, ask it back," Pappy had said.

"Well, I'm Douglas, Mr. Meedeniya's butler, and you are his nephew I presume?"

"Yes," said Prema, paranoid that he would continue speaking so slowly and lead to him running out of time on the phone. "Yes, is he home? I'm calling from the airport and I'm at a payphone."

"Of course, I will seek instruction from Mr. Meedeniya quickly," and with that, he left the phone, all the while, Prema recited the rosary, literally begging God to keep the phone connected. As if God were on the line as well, Douglas returned.

"Young man, which arrival terminal are you located at?"

"I'm at Air Ceylon!" said Prema, happy to have relayed the message.

"Right then, I will come to meet you. Judging by the time of the day, I shall be no more than one hour," said Douglas in a more sympathetic tone.

"Oh, thank you, and how will I know it is you?" asked Prema.

"I will hold a plaque with your name on it and ..." then the line went dead.

Thank you, God, Prema prayed, smiling blissfully. He went about people watching, and carefully eating his packet of peanuts, one at a time, so as not to waste them too quickly. *After all, I don't know what I'll be met with when I meet my uncle,*

*but surely, if he's Pappy's son, he will be at least half as wonderful
and kind as he was.*

Prema was suddenly struck with grief at the loss of his
grandfather. He clung to the miraculous medal that was given
to him by Pappy and began to silently weep. He didn't notice
anyone or the time, which seemed to pass by so quickly, and
he was interrupted by a stoic voice. "Excuse me, sir, are you
Premalal?" said the familiar voice. Prema jumped to his feet
upon seeing the man holding the plaque.

"Oh yes, I'm so sorry, I didn't … I wasn't standing outside, I'm so sorry!" exclaimed Prema.

"My goodness, one would hardly expect you to wait
outside in that cold!" reassured Douglas, who stood at an
impressive height and looked like he should have a butler.

"Where is your baggage, sir" inquired Douglas, to which
Prema held up his makeshift sack.

"I see. … Come with me, young man," he said as he led
Prema out to the car park. There were countless automobiles,
so many more than he had seen in a lifetime. Prema was
a great car enthusiast, because Pappy had exposed him to
the various papers and magazines he collected on his travels,
and knew almost every make and model. This impressed
Douglas, who confirmed each one as Prema rhymed off the
names. As they came around the lot, there, on the far right,
was the most heavenly machine Prema had ever placed his
eyes on.

"Oh my God!" exclaimed Prema. "A Rolls-Royce!"

"Yes, sir, that it is," Douglas said as he put his hands on
the rear seat door and proceeded to open it for Prema.

"Oh my God, it's my uncle's Rolls-Royce?"

"Yes, yes, now get in before you catch your death of cold!"
exclaimed Douglas, who was becoming agitated by the boy's

lack of decorum, as Prema had begun to fixate on the silver lady in the front.

"May I?" asked Prema, whose finger rested on the lady.

"Yes, if you will, but carefully," guided Douglas. Prema pushed ever so slightly upon the silver lady emblem as it automatically lowered into the bonnet of the car.

"Never in all my dreams ... May I please sit in the front with you?" begged Prema, who was coming across as a child more than the young man he looked.

"The front seat is usually for the driver only," announced Douglas.

"I know, but I really would love to see the control panel and the gears. ... I won't touch, just look." Prema pleaded his case as only he knew how.

"All right, then, but please don't touch ANYTHING. Your uncle would be most displeased."

Prema was unaffected by the stern words, as he was used to far worse and, in fact, thought Douglas was most polite. Prema entered the car with utter reverence and began rhyming off what everything was and how it was developed.

"*Rolls-Royce, the world's best car, quintessential luxury ...*" Prema began to voice the adverts, not realizing that he had a most attentive audience.

He has a good mind, thought Douglas, *Must be a gene in the family*, he thought as he glided down the highway, oblivious of the envious glances that came their way.

As the Rolls came to a halt, only then did Prema raise his eyes beyond the interior of the car to take in the landscape. They were at a petrol station nearer to their destination and Douglas inquired whether Prema would like to come in to the corner store for a beverage. Parched, Prema left the car and gingerly closed the door. He entered the store and once again was mesmerized with all that he saw: candies in jars, in wraps, in rolls, in packets, hanging on the walls, and there were soda machines, like he had read about, swirling some chocolaty concoction around in the glass top of the dispenser and sending it down a funnel to become a thick, heavenly drink.

"Me thinks the boy ought to have a choc-malt, otherwise his eyes 'r' going to pop straight out of his head, don't ya know!"

"I believe you're right," Douglas said. "Premalal, would you care to have one?" he asked as he reached for his wallet.

Standing in utter disbelief at the luxuries that had been unveiled to him, he just nodded. He felt dazed, partly from jetlag, but mostly from shock.

"Thank you so much, sir." Prema smiled, warming the hearts of both men in the shop. As he sipped the luscious thick chocolate milk, its texture reminded him of a wood apple. The flesh used to be put into a blender and made into a drink back home. He suddenly felt cold at the thought of home, as upon remembering the taste of the wood apple, he felt the sting of a slap from his father, who had ripped the drink from his hand after his mother had so lovingly prepared it for him. Prema had then been sent to the corner to kneel.

"What's the matter, son? Is it not to your liking?" asked the store clerk.

"Oh, yes. I'm sorry, why do you ask?" Prema asked, puzzled then realizing that he had been daydreaming.

"Ya just looked so sad for a bit!" said the elderly clerk.

Upset that he had exposed the true workings of his heart, Prema was quick to survey the shelf to pretend he was looking at something else. "Oh no, I was just looking at that candy. I've never seen it before," Prema said, pointing to a purple foil packet.

"Oh, that'll be Fry's Turkish Delight. Fine choice, me boy. Ye know Turkish delight! Kinda rose water jelly, coated in dark chocolate." said the clerk.

"Sounds good. How much is it?" Prema asked as he went to his shoe to remove the note in an effort to show he was no one to feel sorry for.

"That'll be five pence," said the clerk, but upon seeing the boy remove his shoe for the pound note, immediately said, "but today is your lucky day, as it comes free with every chocolate malt purchase!"

Prema smiled and took the candy, unsure if it had been the truth, but too poor to argue. "Thank you so much, sir!" Prema said when exiting the store.

What a polite young man. There's something different about him, compared to today's youth, that's for sure, the clerk pondered as the door closed, ringing the chime upon closure.

Prema carefully tucked the chocolate bar deep in his sack and planned to savor it once he knew he didn't have to rely on it for sustenance. The wrapper would remain with him for years to come and would always bring a smile to his face upon the sight of its aubergine-colored foil.

The drive to Uncle Harry's from there was short, and Prema wondered why Douglas had made the stop so close to home. After all, there had been enough petrol in the tank.

"It wasn't that far," Prema said as they neared a stop.

"Yes, it is my duty to make sure the tank is full at all times, as we are never sure when Sir wants to be taken somewhere," said Douglas, as if to demonstrate how important Prema's uncle was.

"I see," said Prema, seeing all too well the type of character he was about to meet.

CHAPTER TWENTY
PEDE CLAUDO

"Retribution comes slowly but surely ..."

CEYLON

I N THE WEEKS AND MONTHS THAT FOLLOWED PREMA'S DISAPPEAR-ance, Cyril spent the time in deep in reflection, wondering what had gone so terribly wrong with his life. He never remembered being as miserable as he was, and nothing, neither family nor career, brought him joy.

Harriet savored the quiet within the home, spending all of her time tending to the needs of the children, knowing, upon the joyous receipt of a postcard sent from England, that Prema was safe from his father and out of danger. It felt like there was a stalemate within the home, as Cyril no longer had someone to beat or someone to blame, as both Prema and Pappy were gone.

Occasionally, Harriet wandered into the study to ask whether Cyril wanted tea, but she would back away so as not to be seen when she saw him stroking the burgundy silk ribbon that now held his tattered Bible together.

I almost wish he would go to her and relieve us of this empty shell I am left with for a husband, Harriet thought, knowing full well that Cyril still pined for the one he left behind after the war.

Once, from the corner of his eye, Cyril caught the reflection of his wife's brightly colored sari exiting the room and was plagued with guilt. *Poor woman, it was never her fault*, he thought. *I chose this life; I chose to do what was right. I never wanted to disappoint my parents, so I returned to marry a Singhalese wife from a good family, but at what cost? Dear sweet Helen, how I loved her, her ivory skin, her curly blond hair, her pale pink lips. We should have been together, but I was too much of a coward.* "Damn this society and damn this life," he shouted, without realizing he was speaking aloud.

"Yes, Cyril? Can I get you something, anything?" Harriet reentered the room.

"No, Harri. I'm just going through your father's estate, and am still perplexed as to how Prema managed to get to England," said Cyril.

"Well, Prema was always a very industrious personality," she said, knowing with no doubt her father had something to do with it.

"Industrious! Industrious! … Funny, I never saw him that way," Cyril said, perplexed and looking back through his books.

"You never saw him as anything," she dared to whisper upon leaving the room.

And so the days, nights, and months continued in this way. Harriet was free to sleep as near to her children as she liked, as she was no longer called upon to do her wifely duties, much to her great relief. Manjula was now the planter his father wanted him to be. Not a gentlemen planter, just a planter, as his Judas traits continued as the years went on, sadly, all stemming from his father's initial encouragement to snitch. Stephen often went missing for days, and when word got out that he was frequenting bars and brothels, he was kicked out of the house by his father.

The house was half-empty and never the same again. The younger children believed for many years that their brother was dead, and because of that, they surmised that Edison left that same night because he ultimately knew the truth.

༄༅༄

CANADA

ROBERT, SLOWING DOWN IN his retirement, reflected upon his life and his poor caretaking of it. He thought back to the days of his childhood and his rebellious nature, which led him to think about the war effort. Surprisingly, as much as they were hellish times, those were the days he relished the most.

"Dinner time, Dad," Beya sweetly called down to her father. It was Sunday and a family dinner together was the norm, as no one had time during the week. Rudi had moved out. Beya was in her final year of high school, Alan was in his junior year, and Elizabeth was now the Area Supervisor of a chain of stores. Only on Sundays did she actually sit down for a relaxing family meal. She still insisted on preparing this meal, although Beya filled in for her during the week.

"Ah, roast beef and mashed potatoes, my favorite," Rudi exclaimed as he bulldozed his way to the table, causing the usual sibling rivalry.

"Wait for mother, Rudi," Beya exclaimed.

"You know this, Rudi," Robert said, saddened by the rift between him and his mother, which was one of the reasons he had moved out.

"Yes, I know. I'm just hungry."

"Why, can't cook to save your life?" joked young Alan, the apple of his father's eye.

"That's enough," said Robert with an ever-present twinkle in his eye.

"Start eating!" called Elizabeth from the kitchen. "I'm just heating the gravy." Robert carved the roast, always marveling at how well Elizabeth made the roast taste. Unbeknown to him, she stuffed the roast with garlic and carefully removed all evidence before serving it.

"You know, my mother was English and she could never cook her traditional roast beef like this," Robert said, smiling at Elizabeth.

"Yes, you always say that, but you still haven't realized the British don't know how to cook!." The dinner continued like this, back and forth, with everyone telling how their weeks went. There was some laughter, and the dinner ended with a "thank you" from Robert, whereupon each child followed with the same.

That night, the dessert was made by Beya, who was heavily into new recipes and new ways of cooking. "Tonight, I made chocolate mousse," Beya exclaimed, proudly setting it down before her father. Robert's eyes fixated on the chocolate pudding as the rest of the family hungrily devoured Beya's dessert.

"Dad, what's wrong? Don't you like it?" asked Beya.

In an uncharacteristic bout of furry that lasted as long as the sentence, Robert exclaimed, "I DON'T EAT CHOCO-LATE PUDDING!" and then he left the table.

The family sat there, stunned. Beya motioned to go after her father, but then the doorbell rang, and it was male caller who'd come to take Beya to the movies.

"Mother, what was that?"

"Don't vorry, darling, I'll take care of it. Have a good time," Elizabeth said, knowing all too well that the wounds of the past didn't always heal.

CHAPTER TWENTY-ONE

THE KEY

In life, each one of us must find our way ...

LONDON

PREMA WAS ALMOST THANKFUL FOR THE DIFFICULT CHILD-
hood he had once suffered, for it gave him the advantage of being extremely street-smart and savvy, which
was why he was not shocked when, upon entering his uncle's
house, he was told to use the tradesman entrance. Nor was
he shocked to be given only an old mattress to sleep on in a
very cold and damp basement. This, after all, was a luxury.
The scraps he was given from his uncle's lavish parties,
catered to by Harrods and served by Lyn, his uncle's maid,
were also well appreciated, as there was more in one night
than he usually ate in a week back home.

There was no room to feel sorry for himself, for he was
genuinely thankful. Thankful that, upon his uncle learning
he loved cars, he was instructed to wash and polish the Rolls-
Royce every day that he was home, no matter the weather,
for Prema absolutely adored his uncle's Rolls, which was
traded in every year for a new one, regardless of condition.

Prema was being sent to a public school in the country to
complete his A levels, all paid for by his uncle, who, despite
how miserly he was, did not believe that a boy should be
without an education. He did this more out of revenge to
Cyril than love for his sister, for he always thought Cyril was a
self-righteous bastard, a trait he himself emulated to a fine art.

Prema was happy as he became a more trustworthy
part of the household, vacuuming, dusting, fixing things,

polishing shoes, etc. Prema lessened the work for Lyn, which caused her to feel guilty and sneak him extra servings whenever the master was not looking.

The fact was that his uncle could have been looking, but oftentimes was too drunk to have noticed. After notorious nights out at the Playboy club or his bridge nights out with the rich and famous, such as Omar Sharif, he came back with Douglas, absolutely drunk, unable to walk to his room. On one such night, Douglas was unable to carry Harry alone and called down to the basement for Prema's assistance.

It was that night that Prema discovered how unmethodical his uncle could be whenever he came home drunk, despite his brilliance as a surgeon.

Once they lowered his uncle onto the bed, Douglas and Prema proceeded to remove his shoes, his pants, and his shirt, and to dress him in his nightdress. While Prema was hanging his uncle's pants, a wad of money fell to the thickly piled carpet, within Prema's sight but not Douglas'. Carefully scrutinizing the situation, Prema quickly nudged the money into the closet and dropped a towel over it to cover it till morning. He would wait till morning.

As first light gleamed through the exposed part of the window Prema had scratched open when he first moved in, he pressed his ears against the door leading to the upstairs section of the house and waited with bated breath to see if there were any outbursts like those he had been so accustomed to hearing as a child. When 10:00 a.m. came and passed, Prema knew that he would be expected to start his chores and meekly entered the house.

"I thought you had slept in, Prema," Lyn said. "I didn't want to disturb you. I know about last night; Douglas told me you helped him with Sir."

"Yes, Madame, but not for long, I mean, it was no problem," said Prema.

"Here's some porridge, then. Now, you better eat up. Sir has a whole list of chores that need to be done today, and I'll be out for most of the day to do the shopping with Douglas. Here's the list. I suggest you get his room done first, as if he gets home early, you don't want to be in his way!" Lyn kindly suggested with a smile. Then she gathered her list and bags and called to Douglas to be on their way.

Prema looked at the list: polish all 20 pairs of shoes, including the brown brogues; change the sheets; vacuum the bedroom, including the curtains and furniture; wash and polish the Rolls.

"No problem," Prema happily said to himself, joyous at the thought of being left alone to do the chores.

Prema ran up the stairs and shot into the closet, and there the wad of money remained, untouched and unnoticed. *I must hide it again*, he thought, *this time in his room, for on another day, he might realize it was missing.* Prema searched and decided under his Uncle's bed would be the most logical.

When he returned to the closet, he began to gather the shoes to take down and polish, only, he discovered a safe hidden behind the shirts. It was slightly ajar, and when he looked inside, he saw wads and wads of money.

Oh my God, thought Prema, *I can't believe it; look at the amount of notes, and in different currencies. It's a gold mine!* Instinctively, Prema thought it was a trap. He quickly went downstairs to bolt the doors, and on the way up again, thought to wear a pair of chauffeur's gloves.

He began checking the lock. Part of the security of the safe was a combination lock, and the other part was a key. The combination part of the safe had been taped. This had clearly been done on purpose so that his uncle could bypass this part of the procedure and just use a key. Prema had no doubt this had been done by his uncle, who knew his own weakness for the bottle.

Prema quickly went into the bathroom to get a piece of soap, and then he returned to the safe with it. He put the key into the soap to make a mold, carefully pressing it down to make an impression of both sides of the key in the soap. He wrapped the soap and put it deep into his pocket, remembering to replace the soap in the bathroom with a new bar when he polished the faucet and perfectly cleaned the mirrors. He thought he should close the safe door and lock it, for if it remained open, he would definitely be accused of opening it. *If I do this, the key will remain. What should I do?* he thought. Finally, he realized that the only way this plan would work was if he closed the safe and didn't do his chores in the room. He would leave the room in a mess and lock the door. He looked out the window and saw, in the distance, his uncle walking down the street.

Oh my God, he's coming! Prema began to throw his uncle's dirty clothes back onto the floor, and was about to lock and close the door when he remembered the bathroom. *I cleaned the bathroom! Oh, God, please save me!* he thought as he darted back into the bath; lathered the soap up; spewed water onto the mirrors; left soap scum on the counter, shaving foam on a razor, and wet towels on the floor; and quickly scurried out the door, locking it from the inside and placing the key downstairs in Lyn's pantry, her special hiding place, which she thought was exclusive to her only. As Prema reached the main floor, he looked down and realized he was wearing chauffeur's gloves. *That's right, the car, I was supposed to wash the car!* ...

So Prema belted out into the garage, quickly turning on

the hose to the sound of the front door closing. He knew it was his uncle, and he seemed to be running up the stairs to his room.

"I knew he would remember," Prema said, panicked, and he immersed himself in washing the car; after all, it is what he was supposed to do that day.

"Prema, Prema, where are you?" shouted his uncle.

"Coming, Uncle," Prema replied, giving the all too familiar response.

"What are you doing?" he said suspiciously.

"I'm washing the Rolls; wasn't I supposed to do that, Uncle?" Prema asked coyly.

"Yes, after you cleaned my room!.."

"Yes, Uncle, Lyn gave me the list, but your room door was locked. Can I clean it for you now?" said Prema innocently.

"Yes, and get on with it. How much more time are you going to spend on that car?" Uncle Harry asked abruptly.

"Not a minute more, sir" Prema replied, knowing the car had been unused for two days. He ran back to the garage, dried and buffed the car, and came in to finish his uncle's room.

His uncle remained in the room with a look of relief on his face.

Thought I had left the damn safe open; can't afford to do that again. Thankfully, I locked the room door behind me. At least I haven't lost all sensibility, he pompously pondered as Prema began to clean the bathroom for the second time that day.

"Get on with polishing those shoes, Prema, and keep the door closed. I don't want to inhale all that polish!" he ordered without any consideration of how it would affect Prema.

The thought of being left alone in the closet with the safe made him more hopeful than he'd been in months. *St.*

Anthony, thank you for your powerful intercession, he prayed as he blissfully polished the stockpile of shoes.

From that day forward, he worked like never before. He spent every waking hour carefully filing the soap impression onto a blank. It took him weeks until the day of reckoning came. On yet another Saturday when he was left alone in the house, he walked determinedly into the closet, pushed aside the shirts and nervously put his homemade key into the lock and turned.

All the angels in heaven cried out with joy upon the site of the monumental stacks of money. He fell to his knees and prayed for God's guidance and forgiveness. *Now I can take care of Mommy. After all, Pappy would have wanted it this way*, he thought as he carefully pulled out notes from various piles and shoved them into his pants. He locked the safe, went into the room, looked under the bed, claimed the wad that had been waiting like a gift for him for weeks.

CHAPTER TWENTY-TWO
MUM'S THE WORD

A friend in need is a friend indeed.

LONDON

"TIMOTHY, MEET ME AT THE PUB IN HALF AN HOUR. IT'S AN emergency," Prema exclaimed over the phone.

"Oh, God in Heaven, you got caught!" shouted Timothy.

"No, silly, just come!" The line went dead and the two boys met outside the Barking Dog Pub as Prema grabbed Timothy's coat sleeve and pulled him inside to the table nearest the window.

"What will it be, boys," said the waitress.

"I'll take care of this." Prema smiled. "Two of the largest T-bone steaks you have, two baked potatoes, and two pints of ginger beer!" Prema proudly ordered for his dearest friend in the world, next to Edison.

"No way, you did it, you did it! Oh no, this means we're going straight to hell, we are!" shouted Timothy, now covering his mouth so as not to be heard.

"You see, my friend, what my Pappy taught me was not taught in vain. Besides, Timothy, this is my Pappy's money. He gave this to his son and then my uncle went and cheated the entire family! I'm only taking what is rightfully ours!"

"I can't believe it. How much is there?" Timothy asked as he began to count it. "Three thousand pounds, no less! My God, man, this is enough to buy a house!" Timothy exclaimed.

"I told you this money is owed to my family," Prema said, quickly dismissing it.

"We should go to confession or something," said Timothy, still feeling the guilt.

"The hell with confession; this money is well-earned. If anywhere, we're going to Africa!"

"Africa? Africa? Never in my wildest dreams!"

"Well, it certainly was in mine, and I'm going if it's the last thing I do."

"Why Africa, Prema? What's the allure, besides adventure, of course?"

"When I was growing up, a priest called Father Martins opened *Father Martins' Furnace*, which was an old bomb shelter converted into a small movie house, with movies for 10 cent show. I used to pay 10 cents just for the pleasure of seeing the MGM lion growl at the beginning of every film. The moment the main feature came on, I left because it didn't interest me. Cowboys and Indians and cops and robbers were always the themes; it never was wildlife. This made the sorrow of not going to the zoo as a child that much greater and my determination to go to Africa resolute.

"Everything was always denied, restricted, or used to somehow punish me. I would read about every animal in the zoo, just to piss off my father, who thought he was the only one who could buy the ticket to my dreams. See this cash, Timothy? This was sent to me by my Pappy in heaven. It's a gift, his gift to me, and this is my gift to you. Are you in?"

"You know I am," he sighed. "Boy, do we have lots of planning to do. Hey, it'll be like our graduation gift!" said Timothy.

"One of many," Prema promised, deep in thought. "Now, you know the plan. The money is to be kept at your parents' house, and here, I bought your mom a nice couple of steaks for the weekend and a few groceries for the family."

"Oh, thank you, my dear friend. The guilt is already fading!" said Timothy, who took the money and shoved it into his wallet and then tucked that deep into his pants, finally pulling both his shirt and two sweaters over his pants.

"Aren't you uncomfortable wearing your clothes that way?" asked Prema.

"I'd wear an extra two winter coats if it meant the money would be safer! I'll meet you back here after I do the job. Oh yes, after Economics, if that is okay?" The two nodded and the meeting was over. Prema watched Timothy stealthily make his way out of the pub and across the street to the tube station, as if he was James Bond himself.

∾⊙∾

PREMA'S LIKABLE PERSONALITY ENABLED him to form close ties with everyone he came in contact with. When he went to Harrods to do the weekly shopping for his uncle, the butcher always managed to throw in a dozen more steaks for him, as long as Prema would meet him round the back of the store so the butcher could give him half of the stash that same night. The steaks that he received usually went straight to Timothy's mother, who, in turn, guarded his money with diligence not found even in a bonded warehouse.

Even the tailor made him a suit by double-charging another patron for the cloth, in exchange for a Cartier pen acquired from the pretty girl in the stationary shop, who had given the pen to Prema in exchange for being taken for a ride in a Rolls, past her ex-boyfriend, who had just broken up with her! His connected mind was uncanny at accomplishing more in one gesture than others could do in ten, and he had none other than Pappy to thank for that.

Everyone was happy and no one the wiser, except, of course, Timothy, who was his anchor in all things good and evil.

Timothy was his closest ally and confidant. Whenever Prema was confused by the forward actions of a girl, it was usually Timothy who explained what he thought her intentions were. If Prema came with a story of what a girl had done on a date with another boy, it was Timothy who deemed it right or wrong. He was innocent Prema's moral compass.

Eventually, their youthful curiosity, unknowingly, led then into situations where they ought not to be. This unsuspecting behavior led them into opportunities, doorways, and peep holes, which almost magically appeared during their lives, both on campus and beyond, and they soon quite enjoyed being privy to voyeuristic pleasures.

As they were considered quite naive, friends would flock to them for some sort of moral guidance, like to priests in a confessional, which, again, caused them to be far more knowledgeable than their boyish faces revealed.

Stories of short men with big sticks were at a thunder pitch those days and gossiped about by the very girls who knew the stories verbatim.

"Oh, Prema, it's good I can trust you. So many men are cads, and now look at that one, he's off with another! How will I ever face him again in class?" confided Amy, who was so tall and beautiful both Prema and Timothy had a hard time believing she had done what she had confessed she did.

"How do they do it, I mean, look so angelic and all? They're like wolves in sheep's clothing, I tell you!" Timothy would complain, but Prema had a more plausible explanation.

"He must have made her drunk, or perhaps the devil took over her soul!" Prema would say, unaware of how silly they both sounded.

"Your ears should be ringing, Faddy," said Timothy sarcastically to a man he had Economics with. Faddy Abboud was a an extremely good-looking Lebanese boy, who was all of five-foot four and yet had a following triple his height, if they were to stand shoulder to shoulder, that is!

"What do you mean, my ears should be ringing?" said Faddy defensively.

"Never mind," said Prema, who gave Timothy a stare that could have set his pants on fire.

"Draft outside, that's all," muttered Timothy. The class bell rang and they all exited into the cool autumn air.

❧

PREMA WENT BACK TO the pub, to the booth they referred to as "their office."

"What will it be, love?" asked the waitress.

"Tea please," and with that he pulled out a letter that had just arrived from home.

> *Dearest Premalal,*
>
> *Since you left, nothing is the same. Pappy's death was a huge loss to us, both emotionally and financially. Life is getting more difficult, as there is civil unrest, and this year, I don't even have my cake ingredients to make Christmas cake. I know your father regrets treating you the way he did, and your brothers and sisters miss you. Please come home.*
>
> *Love, Mommy*

I guess I can afford to go home, he thought as he pulled out the wad of cash he had plucked from underneath his uncle's bed and began to count.

❦

PREMA ATTEMPTED MANY TIMES to make a trunk call to Ceylon, but each time it was met with his father hanging up. *Poor Mommy, there is so much I want to give her. Despite him, I must go, I must go*, he thought as he walked through the front lawn of the campus, totally distracted.

"Hi, Prema, what's wrong?" asked Gabrielle, kissing his cheek.

"Oh, it's Mommy. She's finally written asking me to come home. She needs so much and I want to give her everything," he said without disclosing what he was up to with Timothy.

"Then Ceylon it is, let's go! I know how much you admire the cloth in my auntie's shop, so we'll go and select the best pieces for your family!" Gabrielle smiled most lovingly. She was Prema's first girlfriend, and she was extremely well-off, according to Timothy.

"Oh no, what would my parents say of me coming with a girlfriend?" asked Prema like a schoolboy.

"Well, they will have to say, 'nice to meet you,' won't they? Besides, we can stay at the nicest hotel in the city."

"The Galle Face Hotel?" exclaimed Prema. "Are you insane?"

"No, silly, I'm in love!" she winked and ran off to class.

Galle Face Hotel, thought Prema, *from checking garbage cans for food to the Galle Face ... my father's face will fall off. It's perfect ... why not!* he thought victoriously and then ran towards the student travel center to book the trip. *I'm going home!*

CHAPTER TWENTY-THREE

MYOPIA

"It is but sorrow to be wise when wisdom profits not."

-Oedipus the King by Sophocles

B Y THE TIME THE TERM WAS OVER AND PREMA AND GABRIELLE made their flight, two months had passed and all things inferred in the various calls home were now confirmed upon arrival.

"Prema, *Putha*, look at you; you are a man now. Look how handsome you are!" Mommy whispered into Prema's ear as he bent down and kissed her after so many years.

"*Sedaris, coho mada?*" Prema greeted the driver, who had been with them for over 30 years.

"*Sudu Putha, lassanai,*" he said looking at Gabrielle standing beside him.

"Hello, Mrs. Alvis," Gabrielle said, leaning over to shake her hand in an unfamiliar and formal gesture.

"Hello, young lady," Mommy said disapprovingly. Prema, quick to notice this, wrapped his arm around his mother's shoulder.

"Shall we go?"

"Oh, *Puta*, I have so little to offer you. Your father is very, very ill, the children need school books and supplies, and there are no Christmas cake ingredients." Prema said the last part in unison with his mother.

"I know, I know, that is why I came, Mommy. I've brought everything you need. Now we go to the GFH; Sedaris, I think you know the way." Prema directed proudly.

"What, you are not coming home? said Mommy.

"And fatten on his fodder? I don't think so, Mommy, but all are welcome for a meal at the hotel tonight!"

It was an invitation that had not been offered to Harriet since the passing of her father, five years earlier, and one she could not resist. After all, it was her Prema. She smiled, so grateful to God that he grew up so confident and proud.

When Harriet returned home, she quickly ran to the children's rooms and gloriously announced that their brother had returned and that they all were invited to the Galle Face Hotel. Cries of joy filled the house, which aroused Cyril from his study.

"What's this I hear? Prema staying at the GFH, with a woman?."

"He's 22, Cyril; he's a grown man!" she said and quickly exited the room, unable to handle any more negativity from him after all the hurt he had created over the years. This night would be for the love of family and joy. He could join if he wanted, but as for her, nothing was stopping her or the children from going.

Without a word to anyone, Cyril called Sedaris to start the engine. "GFH," he ordered. *This I will stop, if it's the last thing I do.*

As things happened, when Cyril arrived at the hotel, there were glances from the doorman and the manager that implied "we know something you don't know" as the foyer became a buzz with activity. "Yes, sir, may I help you?" asked the front desk manager.

"Yes, my son is a guest in your hotel. Please connect me to his room."

"Certainly, sir, Mr. Alvis is staying in Suite 2310 in the Royal Wing," to which Cyril stood stunned, filled with both pride and jealousy; he chose anger to balance the two conflicting emotions and walked towards the bar where the phone was.

"Here you go, sir, Suite 2310 connecting," he was told and then was handed the phone.

"Hello?" Gabrielle answered the phone.

"Yes, who is this?" inquired Cyril, outraged at the thought of a woman in Prema's room.

"I'm sorry, you are calling me. Who are you is more to the point," she said with her snooty Swiss accent.

"Well, I'm Mr. Alvis, of course!."

Gabrielle paused. She had heard nothing but evil about Prema's father and was witness to the repercussions of his abuse. She was instantly filled with rage. "Good afternoon, sir, how may I help you?"

"You tell that good for nothing ... I mean, you tell my son to come down here right now!" he shouted, to which she put down the phone.

"Who was that?" Prema asked, coming out of the shower.

"Oh, room service. ... I'm parched. I think I'll go down and get a cold drink and meet you up here in a bit, okay?."

Gabrielle checked herself in the mirror, determined to look her absolute best. She decided to put on a more formal jacket over her silk chiffon dress and proceeded down the spiral, red-carpeted staircase that led from their room.

"Could you please direct me to Mr. Alvis?" she asked at the desk. She was brought to the bar, whereupon the doorman pointed to a tall, olive-skinned man with black eyes and grey hair. He seemed to be slightly keeled over on the ledge of the bar, which indicated to her that he was not well. He was definitely Prema's father, she observed; she could see a reflection of Prema in his deportment.

As Gabrielle walked into the room, his eyes were glued to her. It was like seeing Helen all over again. Her ivory skin, wavy blonde hair, and crystal blue eyes ...

"Is that you, Helen?" Cyril stammered, almost in a haze. *How could it be? She's too young.* He quickly shook his head.

"I'm sorry, Mr. Alvis, I'm Gabrielle Pixel," she said assertively and extended her hand.

"Yes, uh, nice to meet you, young lady. Where is Prema?."

"Prema is currently resting. I thought we could meet first, as I want this to be an enjoyable trip for him. After all, he deserves it, don't you think?"

"Deserves a good trip? You've got to be kidding. He deserves nothing after deserting his family and then coming back after so many years and after disgracing us. I'll tell you, he deserves a good kick."

Cyril displayed his wrath towards his son, to which Gabrielle stood up and said, "Mr. Alvis, you poor abusive soul, you have no idea that despite your many efforts to destroy your son, he has grown up to be the most intelligent, kind, and loving soul I could chance to meet. You were blessed with a son like him, but you chose to destroy his life and the rest of the family members' lives as well. God have mercy on your soul," and with that, she exited the room.

That bastard, that awful, awful man. Poor Prema, poor Prema, no wonder the nightmares and the lack of trust. My God, what type of man is that? Gabrielle mumbled to herself, unaware that she was lip talking and had many interested onlookers. She gently smiled and re-entered her and Prema's room.

"Thirst quenched, Gabi?" Prema asked, waking from dozing in the bed.

"Oh, it was quenched all right," she said as she snuggled up beside him.

The evening turned out to be a heartwarming reunion between Prema and his many siblings and his mother, with all of them piling into the hotel room so Prema could unveil the many gifts he'd brought to them.

"Hey, Jeevan, look at you, so tall. Manori, Manisha, Danuka, Manjula, Pavani, Stephen, look at all of you! It's so good to see you again!" The all hugged in a desperate attempt to feel the old bond they had shared, for Prema was their hero, and they all had prayed so much for him in his plight, both as a child and when he left.

"I see all eyes are on the suitcases!" Prema laughed, anxious to distribute everything all at once. "We have brought you all sorts of nice things. Mommy, here are your cake ingredients, just in time for Christmas, no doubt! Jeevan, special pens from England. Manori, Manisha, cloth for your sari's, yards and yards! ..." Then Prema stopped, sensing that Gabrielle was getting irritated at the way he was doling out gifts so quickly. "Wait, let us first go down and eat dinner, and then we will come back later and distribute everything!"

The dinner buffet was a fanfare of Ceylonese specials, hoppers, pittu, string hoppers, curries, roasts, stews, and scrumptious desserts.

"Oh, Prema, it's so wonderful, we're so happy," each said contentedly, looking at Prema with joy-filled eyes.

"Mommy, how's Father?" Prema asked, unaware of the earlier encounter with Gabrielle.

"He is not well, Prema, which is why he remained at home," said Mommy apologetically.

Gabrielle was shocked at the kindness of Prema. He seemed to hold no resentment whatsoever, and that he still inquired about his father seemed like a miracle to her.

"Prema, may we go to your room to freshen up?" asked Manori and Mommy.

"Of course you can. Here are the keys," Prema offered, despite the look of violation on Gabrielle's face.

"It's all very grand for them. They mean no harm," he whispered to Gabrielle, who had remained unnoticed throughout the evening.

"Of course, fine, it's fine," Gabrielle said, reassuring Prema.

By the time Manori and Mommy reappeared, quite a bit of time had elapsed, and suddenly, Mommy announced that the next day was a school day and that they must leave.

"Of course, Mommy," Prema said, "as you wish. I'm also a bit tired, what with jetlag and all," something his mother had never experienced, only heard about from Pappy.

"Goodnight, *Putha!*" She kissed her son proudly while only glaring at Gabrielle. All clamored around Prema to hug and kiss him.

What a wonderful night, Prema thought, feeling strange about retiring to a room in the Galle Face instead of a drain near his home. Gabrielle's heart was warmed as she observed the family he had run from. *Such a pity*, she thought, *they all do love him. If not for that father, all would have turned out quite differently.* Prema and Gabrielle both fell sleepily to the bed.

Prema awoke with the friendly warmth of the sun on his face. Upon rising, Prema noticed that the packages that had been strewn around the luggage the previous night were no longer there.

"Oh my God, we've been robbed!" he exclaimed and quickly called his mother, hoping that there was some sort of explanation.

"Oh, yes, *Putha*, I had Sedaris remove everything and put it into the car. I hope that was all right," she said in a most contented tone.

Taken aback, he withheld his comments and said, "Fine, Mommy, as long as you're happy."

When Gabrielle awoke, he tried to keep her occupied, but soon she went to her luggage, only to find that her personal luggage had been opened. When she opened it, she was aghast to find all the beautiful French lace and expensive silks had literally been cut and chopped.

"Oh my God, who did this to these fine fabrics? Who on earth would do such a thing?"

Prema looked in horror. "I thought they only took the packages. I didn't know they did this, Gabrielle. I'm so sorry," Prema exclaimed, unable to hide his face.

"You mean your Mother actually did this? She actually cut the material? I mean, I bought it all for them. Why did they butcher the material? I was going to give it to them today. I would have given it to them myself last night. Why on earth? I have never seen anything like this, what type of behavior? Where do you come from?" And she stormed out of the room, slamming the door behind her.

Prema walked slowly out of the room and down to the beach to think.

I hate my father; I hate him for turning my mother into a beggar, grabbing and taking for fear of not getting anything at all. Why are things so important to her; wasn't' it enough that I came home? Isn't it enough to know that I didn't die in a drain? he asked himself, wondering what would become of his family, never mind his relationship with Gabrielle.

When he returned to the room, the butchered material was strewn on the bed, and Gabi and her bags were gone. Someone knocked on the door.

"Sir, Ms. Pixel has asked that I give this note to you," the doorman said, passing the note to Prema's hand.

FAR AWAY, I LAND

Dear Prema, I'm sorry. We come from very different backgrounds, and this rift between us will never close. Don't come after me. It's over. Gabrielle."

That answers my question. It's over! Not here 48 hours and already I'm losing one of the best things that has ever happened to me! he thought angrily.

Prema remained in his room for three days with the Do Not Disturb sign on the door. Despite many calls to the room, he did not pick up. Instead, he remained, pensively reviewing his life and the journey he had been on. When room service arrived on the third day, the bellboy had been asked to deliver an urgent message to Prema.

"Sir, I have been asked to tell you that your father is on his death bed. You are urgently requested to come home," and with that, Prema put on his shoes and began to run out the door.

As the taxi neared the house, he began to reminisce.

"Please stop the car. I'd like to walk the rest of the way," he said, slowly exiting the taxi. All of it came rushing back to him, the trees, the smell of the araliya trees and temple flowers, and the all too familiar sound of the "did-she-do-it" bird, as they used to call it when he was a child. He looked at the very drain he was thrust into when run off the road by his father. He was in absolute wonderment as to how he ever survived living on those filthy streets with their rat-infested drains. Only seeing it that day did he know for sure that God had been watching over him and protecting him all the while. He could hear the familiar sound of the creaking gate and the screen door opening and shutting at the side entrance of the house. He heard the sound of tears from his brothers and

• 312 •

sisters and was amazed that they could still conjure up any sorrow for this man, their father.

As Prema walked in the house, it felt surreal, as if he was sleepwalking. Everything seemed so small, so very Singhalese, seeped in culture and tradition. He thought the surroundings were in deep contrast to the occupants, who seemed like shadows of their former selves. He longed to see the comforting smile of Edison, but knew he would never see him again, which filled his mind with more sorrow than the thought of his father dying.

"Mommy, where is Father?" asked Prema.

"Come, *Putha*, he's been asking for you. He's with the priest in his room."

When Father Harott, one of his father's oldest friends, saw Prema, he smiled and stood up to leave Prema alone with his father, whom Prema was no longer afraid of. His father lay motionless, going in and out of consciousness.

"Daddy," he said, not knowing what to say and resorting to what he referred to him as a child.

"Prema? Prema? Is that you?" his father murmured, raising his hand towards Prema. Prema awkwardly took his hand and grasped it for the last time, desperately searching for some morsel of tenderness to hold onto before his father passed away.

"Yes, Daddy, I'm here," he said, being reminded of the demanded response he was always required to give.

"Prema, I hear you have done well for yourself, even a beautiful girlfriend ... I, too, had a girlfriend," he said, tightening his grip in Prema's other hand, "like her." This puzzled Prema, who wondered how his father knew what Gabrielle looked like.

"Prema, the Lord is taking me earlier than I imagined, but

before I go," he said, struggling to breathe, "I need to ask you something. ..." And as Prema leaned over his father's face, his father whispered into his ear his very last words. ... "*Take care of the rest,*" Cyril's hand dropped and his fist remained clenched around a burgundy silk ribbon with the initials H.N. woven into the silk.

Prema could not feel a thing. His horrible childhood came billowing forward as if to crush the memory he had of the ribbon. He tried to hold on to it. He dropped his fathers' hand at the sight of the fabric, which he had heard Mommy cry about many a time. He carefully removed the ribbon from his clenched hand, realizing his mother's suspicions had been correct all along. He took the ribbon and put it into the fold of one of his father's favorite books, out of sight from his mother. *Even in death, he was selfish*, Prema thought. When he left the room, he shook his head as if to say his father was no longer.

The entire family filed into the room, but he could only walk out.

It was clear to Prema that his father knew he had made it somehow, without his help. He chose to interpret his father's last request as his way of telling him that he had faith in him. Prema left with a renewed sense of purpose in his walk, despite knowing that he was probably being myopic.

From an outsider's perspective, it seemed most unfair for his father to have burdened Prema with such a responsibility as taking care of eight souls, but for Prema, it was his father's final and only gift, the gift of respect and a lasting feeling of being needed.

❧◉❧

CYRIL CLOSED HIS EYES with the self-righteous belief that he would meet Helen in heaven; painfully unaware that she had been in purgatory since the day he left her in England. There would be no heaven for either of them.

Prema had entered the house of his youth a young boy, in thought and mind, and he left a man.

A man of honor, for only a man of honor would have continued giving despite all the obstacles that lay before him and the hurt that lay behind.

CHAPTER TWENTY-FOUR

BROWNIAN MOTION

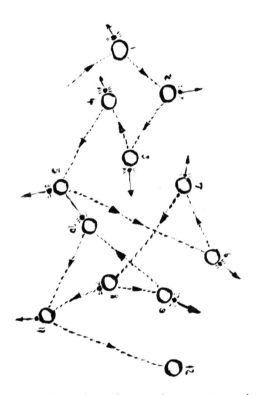

... describes the random scattered dispersal of smoke particles that are moved, as a result of larger air particles, in a random zigzag motion.

Such is fate's hand in our life ...

CANADA

O N THE OTHER SIDE OF THE GLOBE, BEYA DROPPED HER mother off at work and proceeded to the other side of the shopping mall to visit her boyfriend. It wasn't prearranged, but she usually went with her feelings on most things. "Hiya, hunny!" she whispered into her high school sweetheart's ear.

"Hey, what are you doing here?" Camille asked.

"I don't' know, just wanted to see you," Beya said, suddenly feeling unusually sad.

"Hey, we talked earlier this morning; you seemed fine. What's this, tears?" he said, putting his arm around her.

"I'm sorry, hunny. I don't' know where they came from. I suddenly feel very upset and frightened. I don't' know what's come over me," she said and ran out of the shop. Camille ran after her and saw that she was running in the direction of her mother's shop. As Beya reached the entrance, everyone seemed upset and a few were crying.

"Oh God, what's happened? Where's my mother?"

"Beya," Myrna exclaimed, "your mother has passed out and we had to call the ambulance. You better call your father and we'll meet you at the Riverside Hospital." Beya's world crashed.

It was not just that she and her mother were close; it was that they were so close that they could feel everything the other was feeling. Most thought it endearing, but some were spooked by it, as quite often they did the same things without the other knowing, like buying the same ingredients to make a dish that hadn't been made in years or both arriving at the same thought or intention even though just one had begun. Other times, they would start vacuuming and fluffing pillows in the expectation of unanticipated guests arriving, but for some reason, they both just knew. Intuition guided them, giving them a strong sense of knowing before an event occurred. Robert joked about it and said that Beya had some Gypsy blood in her, but on this occasion, all rumor became fact.

For months, Beya had been suffering with migraine headaches, with no understandable cause or explanation. It was a sensation she would wake up with, which always seemed to vary in intensity depending on her mother's state of mind, which went from loving and determined to depressed and weak. Beya could never understand it, but she made it her life's mission to make her mother happy.

She knew that her mother had been stressed with Rudi's upcoming wedding, but she had no idea why, for she liked his bride-to-be and thought he had made a good choice. Something was wrong, but she could not pinpoint what it was.

When they all arrived at the hospital, the doctors met the family to explain the state of their wife and mother. "You see, Mrs. Cross has suffered an emotional breakdown. She is in an extremely weak mental state. I suggest only one person at a time go inside, and only people she trusts." With that, the room cleared and Beya rushed to her mother's side.

"Mamma, Mamma, it's me, Beya," she gently whispered into her mother's ear.

"*Csillagom*, vhat happened? Vhy am I here? I feel so dizzy," she murmured, now on medication.

"You collapsed at the store. They say you are very stressed about something and …"

"Rudi!, Rudi! I must talk to Rudi!" she suddenly exclaimed, which was so odd, as her relationship with her son had diminished so much over the years that they hardly spoke.

"Okay, Mamma, can you tell me what this is about?"

But her mother kept repeating to herself, "Rudi, Rudi!"

"Okay, Mamma, I will call Rudi; hopefully he answers the phone this time. I want you to get some rest. I will get Rudi, don't worry. He'll be here when you wake up." At Beya's reassurance, Elizabeth slowly closed her eyes, though there was still worry on her lips.

Beya tried reaching Rudi on the phone, and when she couldn't, she decided to go searching for him.

"Let's go home, Dad. We'll have to tell Alan, who'll be home from school in an hour. I'll make some dinner, and hopefully one of us will be able to reach Rudi. Any ideas?"

Her father looked perplexed. "I know he was meeting with some of my old clients at the office. He's also been spending a lot of time at the downtown store, now that he's taken over management of the business. I'll give a call to Don and somehow track him down."

All things came together that day. When Beya and her father arrived home, Rudi shot into the driveway like a bat out of hell.

"Rudi, it's all right, mother's fine," Beya said, comforting her brother, believing he had somehow received word and that was the reason he drove so recklessly onto the laneway.

"Yeah, good for her. Where is she?" he shouted.

"What?" exclaimed Beya.

"Where the hell is she?" and before Beya could say another word, he ran into the house. Thinking her father would tell him, she remained outside, looking at her mother's garden and realizing that she should have seen the signs of her coming breakdown sooner. The flowers weren't tended to with her usual flare, the peonies were not cut down and most had faded and fallen to the ground. The dahlias needed water, and the grass needed to be cut.

"What's wrong with me?" exclaimed Beya. "I should have been helping with all this!" she said as she went into the garage and proceeded to get the clippers and unwind the garden hose.

While she was watering the flowers, Rudi came outside with tear-filled eyes and an unusual look of distance in his stare.

"So she wants to talk to you, now, at the Riverside, okay? She'll be fine," Beya said again. But the reply was that of a zombie.

"What, yeah, … it's a little too late for talks," he said as he got into his car and backed out of the laneway. "Rudi, I'm making dinner now, stay!" she said, but Rudi just waved back and sadly drove away.

Beya put down the hose and walked into the house, where she found her father looking guilt-ridden and as pale as death.

"Dad, are you all right. Mother is fine, isn't she?" But her father said nothing. "Why did Rudi look so weird? He said it was too late to talk." But again her father said nothing and walked down to his office.

What Beya didn't know was that Rudi had found out through an old business acquaintance of Robert's that he had been adopted.

Earlier in the day, Rudi was at his father's office when he bumped into an old acquaintance of his father's, who was highly intoxicated and extremely verbose:

"Yeah, Robert was a good man, marrying your mom and bringing you up as his own, a good man indeed," said the intoxicated businessman. "Yeah, I've known your father for around 40 years, now. Good of him, that's for sure!" the man said as Rudi stood stunned at what he heard.

Rudi quickly left the building, feeling the walls cave in on him. Shocked, confused, and angry, Rudi ran into the nearest bar and began to vent. "Give me a whiskey!" he demanded to the bartender and promptly gulped down the drink as if it were poison.

"Adopted, adopted, I always knew it!" shouted Rudi, who had now ordered his second drink "What the hell am I doing? I'm not an alcoholic like my father, because he's not my father!" As he stood up, he grabbed the drink, smashed the glass against the wall, threw a twenty on the counter, and stormed out.

Beya returned to the hospital, not knowing what to say to her mother. I don't' know what's been said or why Rudi said it's too late to talk, but something other than my mother's hospitalization is going on here, Beya fretted as she entered the room.

Her Mother was now sitting up, sipping some water.

"Mamma, how do you feel?" Beya smiled.

"I feel much better, but now you look worried, csillagom. What's wrong?" At that point, all Beya could think was, read my mind so I don't have to tell you about the events at the house. I don't want to worry you. But Elizabeth knew.

"Rudi is not coming, is he?"

Then Robert walked into the room and looked at his wife and said, "He knows." Elizabeth immediately started to cry tears of sorrow.

"What is going on, you two. He knows what?" Beya said frantically.

When the news was told to Beya, she, too, started to cry.

"Why are you crying? Everything is still the same; he's still your brother," cried Elizabeth.

"I know, but it must feel so strange for him to learn about this so late in life. I mean, he must feel alienated," which only caused Elizabeth to cry more.

"Why did you tell him? It wasn't your place; why did you tell him? You know I always wanted to tell him. It was you! You told me I shouldn't; you told me it would only hurt him. This is entirely your fault!" She cried uncontrollably until the nurse came into the room and asked everyone to leave. Robert sat outside the room, crestfallen.

Where the secrets of the past had bound them together; the truth now cut all ties. It would never be the same again, as the repercussions of that day reverberated throughout the family like dust in the wind.

The mood had changed and the roles in the family shifted. Alan, once the comic and rebel, turned more inward and began to study more, choosing a more intellectual path in life, one that was secure and that he could control without fear of confrontation. Young Alan grew up to be an academic, vowing to be more educated than both his parents, thinking that this would be his way of controlling the outcome of his life. Still, his life took turns he was not ready for.

Beya pursued business in order to prevent the family from sinking. Her free spirit became subdued to that of homemaker; eternally trying to mend fences and bring hope back into a very dysfunctional family. Fate linked her with an unlikely match. Together they were strong, and with him, her world changed completely, fulfilling her dreams beyond the borders that she had foreseen. Some say she married early in order to fulfill her need of family when her own seemed to have drifted apart.

Rudi focused his life on business and the pursuit of power and money, any and all things material. In marriage, he chose to become a better son to his in-laws then to his own parents, all stemming from the resentment he harbored towards them. He grew up never realizing that without forgiveness, he would be the one who lost the most.

Robert never got over the guilt of destroying the bond that once existed between mother and son, forever regretting preventing the truth being told to Rudi when he was a child.

Despite bouts of depression, Elizabeth survived through it all, growing older and wiser, no longer justifying her actions to anyone as she remained steadfast in the knowledge that she gave her all to her family.

It was life's natural selection.

CHAPTER TWENTY-FIVE

YESTERDAY'S TOMORROW

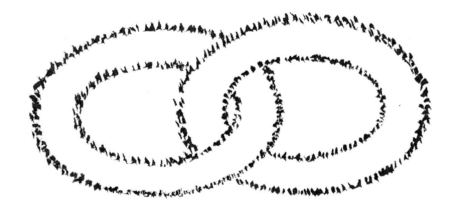

We are inextricably linked to the past,
to our own and all those before ours.

PREMA'S RETURN TO LONDON WAS AN IRONIC CONTRAST TO his initial trip, for now he returned with a link to his past, one which he spent the past few years trying to undo. He had the burden of responsibility on his shoulders and a newfound confidence to direct him.

He could not be flippant with the money obtained by deception from his uncle; after all, he had a family to feed and a mortgage to pay, and he would be damned if his father would judge him in death as well.

Funds obtained were quickly invested into business, where Prema found ways and means to make the most of every opportunity. Prema's need to provide increased his enthusiasm to work at his uncle's, which further antagonized his uncle. The more work he put on Prema's shoulders with no increase in pay, the more it caused him to be suspicious.

Obvious attempts to have Prema work for free and Prema's inability to reveal that he simply could not afford not to have pay led to Prema seeking alternate employment solutions. He began to work on weekends in Newcastle at a spot welding factory. The more he worked there, the more he appreciated the job and all it was teaching him.

He had grown weary of being his uncle's pick-up boy. He could not stand seeing his uncle deteriorate into the drunk he had become and could no longer assist him in his efforts to do so. Even the joy of driving the Rolls to his uncle's various nightclubs grew stale when faced with having to carry his uncle to the car and then upstairs to bed, only to get kicked for his efforts. He thought about dear Pappy and how hard he worked for his family, providing Uncle Harry with all his riches, only for him to waste it in the height of utter selfishness.

This was a brilliant surgeon with more money than he knew what to do with, beautiful nurses at his beck and call, and all he could do was use and abuse them instead of settling down and having a family. *Here my father could only afford to have two children based on his salary and he had eight, and the one who has enough money for eight has none! What a waste!* Prema was morally tormented at the thought.

"Did your uncle change the keys, Prema? I don't see you coming to hide funds anymore," Timothy inquired. "Not that I'm encouraging you to do so, you understand."

"Between working the night shifts at the factory and sending my entire pay home to pay Mommy's mortgage, I don't have the mental energy for the likes of my ungrateful uncle."

"Nor should you, my friend. He's a waste, isn't he? All that money and no decent life to show for it," Timothy said in full agreement of his friend.

The wheels of fate had turned against Uncle Harry. Scotland Yard got wind of his undeclared earnings from the hospital and his thankful patients who rewarded him handsomely. Upon sight of one such agent, Douglas instinctively knew something was very wrong and warded them off at the pass. Plan B was now in play as the entire household set about emptying drawers and the entire contents of the safe. It was ironic that in all this, with all his powerful connections, Uncle Harry could only turn to Prema to be saved.

"I need this to be put in a safe location. Do you know what to do, Prema?" the uncle asked with vulnerability previously unseen.

"I have just the place," Prema assured and quickly left

through the back door servant's entrance. Seconds later, the front door burst open.

Prema made his way onto the tube and exited at the end of the line for fear of being followed. When he was sure no one had followed him, he returned on the tube and exited at Parsons Green station, he turned right and ran down the street to the church and then turned right again and went through the back garden towards a little stone house that stood near the church. Timothy's father was a boiler man and helped with heating the church and the surrounding government buildings. His mother cooked for the priests, who, in turn, provided a small stipend and an ample supply of foodstuffs received from various donations from local grocers and farmers alike. There was a storage room deep in the cellar that kept all these items fresh throughout the year. In the summer and fall, Mrs. Woods also made jams, jellies, sauces, and stewed fruit to be used in the winter. These were also kept in the cellar, and it was there that Prema met Timothy's mother.

"Mrs. Woods, are you downstairs?" called Prema.

"Yes, dear, I'm here storing the eggs!" As he came down the narrow cement stairs, he saw the perfect hiding place under the haystack where she stood storing the freshly laid eggs.

"Good afternoon, Mrs. Woods," Prema said formerly, nervous with what he was about to ask.

"Good afternoon to you too, Prema. Are you hungry; can I get you something eat? You look so tired. Come with me. ..."

"Uh, Madame, I was wondering, would it be possible to store something down here in the cellar?" With a quick glance, Mrs. Woods looked over at the enormous bag he had on his shoulders.

"My Lord, what's your aim, to get it all in one fell swoop? Was anyone following you, lad?" she exclaimed in a worried tone.

"Oh no, it's not what you think it is. I mean, it is, but it's not for me, I mean, it's not just ..." Prema stuttered.

"Better I not know; more convincing that way. ..."

"What about here?" she pointed to the upper shelf.

"How about under the hay?" Prema said, hoping that this day would soon be over.

"It's good if you don't mind the smell," she warned.

"Not at all, it's perfect." Prema quickly relieved himself of the weight on his shoulders and cleverly dispersed it all under the hay.

They went up the stairs to meet Mr. Woods, who greeted him like a long lost son.

"Prema." He smiled, embracing the young man. "I wanted to extend my condolences to you about your father. He was very young, I hear ... quite a tragedy for your mum. We're so sorry to hear it, son, but don't fret. Although I'll never replace your dear old dad, I want you to know you're part of this family, you are, and if you ever need a word with an old feller like me, I'll always be here for you, and don't you forget it."

Prema stood there motionless, knees trembling. Those were the kindest words he had ever heard. As tears welled in his eyes, all he could do was give this dear old man the longest hug of his life.

"There, there, son. Peggy Sue, dish out some of that good beef stew ya made this morning, will you! Now you sit here, close to the fire; it's a cold day and I think young Tim is on his way as well. Good to have the house filled, don't ya know."

The warmth from the hearth was not nearly as warm as the love shown from Timothy's parents. In Prema's heart, they would become the parents he always wished for.

∾⊙∾

LETTER AFTER LETTER CAME in from his mother, month after month, continually filling Prema's head with worries of everything from mortgage payments to wedding dowries for his sisters. He was now the head of the family, whether he liked it or not, and took the burden of responsibility very seriously.

"Here he comes again, every month, unfailingly sending his mother money. What a good boy you are," the lady at the post office always said.

It was nice to receive the acknowledgement, despite it being from the wrong person.

"Here you go, madam, some tea from our tea estates back home," Prema said one day, handing the clerk a packet of tea.

"Tea from your estates! How wonderful and how very kind of you!" declared the employees in the post office, joining the clerk.

"Oh, you are most welcome. In fact, I should have brought more for all of you. Next time I come, I will do just that!" Prema smiled, loving the attention. The gift of the tea, which he had actually bought at the Sri Lankan Tea Board in downtown London, had been intended to defer the pity from his direction.

After all, he was working too hard for people to think he or his family was poor or hard done by, but laterally, he gave because giving provided him with the thanks and the attention he never received as a child. People in London were more civilized and thank you's were doled out as much as the evil eye was back home.

He hurried to the dorm to change for work, as most workers had been called in on this particular occasion, because the boss had an announcement for the workers.

"What do you think it's about?" inquired everyone.

"Don't know; business is good; can't imagine something going wrong?" they speculated.

"People, if I could have your attention. The reason I gathered you all under one roof is that I've decided to close down the business. I'm getting on and variable costs are rising all the time. So this will be the last week of operation, everyone. I'm sorry for this, and thank you all for your service and loyalty."

Some shook his hand and asked if he would change his mind, others angrily stormed out the door. Prema, unclear as to how he was going to survive without the work, desperately searched for solutions to his problems and the owner's.

"Sir, if you don't mind me asking, do you owe money to the bank or do you need a loan?" Prema asked.

"What's it to you, son? Are ye going to lend me the money?" Quick on his feet, Prema said his uncle worked at a bank and that maybe a loan would be possible. This caught the attention of the old man.

"You know, boy, you've been one of my best workers. I know you're depending on this job because of your family, but it's really because of my health. I'm too old for this; I need to live what's left of my life before the Good Lord takes me. If you can find a way to make this business profitable, I'll hand over the keys to run the factory to you, under the condition that you pay me back in one year."

Prema smiled his broadest smile and shook his hand. "It's a deal!" Prema said with a determination that stemmed from deep within his soul.

CHAPTER TWENTY-SIX

OUR DESTINY AWAITS

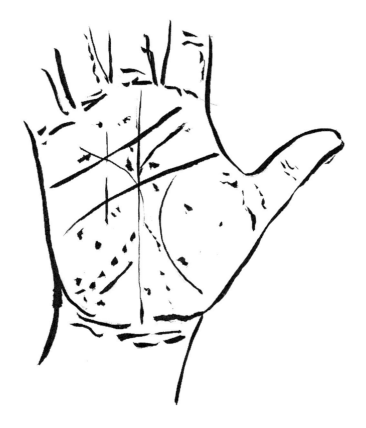

Intuition has a way of sneaking up to you and whispering in your ear, "this was meant to be."

ENGLAND OPENED ITS ARMS TO A BOY AND MADE HIM A MAN. She taught him that if he worked hard, anything was possible. She reinforced this by showing him respect and giving him a mirror so that he could see all that he was and all that he could be.

It's not clear whether he saw the face of Pappy smiling down on him or whether he saw the ghost of his father's rage. What is clear is that Prema was propelled forward, experiencing a journey few would not think possible to either endure or to succeed at.

This journey took him around the world, on his African adventures with a friend who was, in essence, his true soul mate, for they met at a time when Prema needed a friend the most. Together, this bond saw them through school, mischief, relationships, business, and travel to all corners of the globe.

Prema became a sterling-pound millionaire by the time he reached the ripe old age of 24, doing what he did best, seeing opportunity in things people gave up on. He ended up turning the spot welding business into an aluminum extrusion plant which ended up grossing a profit of a million pounds a year. He ended up selling the business outright to Sir Jimmy Goldsmith for a price that brought a smile to Prema's face throughout his life.

He ended up having to lend his uncle money, over and above the funds he had taken, once the tax evasion case was over, as Uncle Harry was ordered to donate his entire earnings to the hospital or face jail time. His life ended suddenly, from one too many cognacs and far too few friends or family.

Prema made a trip to visit Timothy, who was in Her Majesty's Diplomatic Service, in India. He was there on a mission regarding the prevention of the spread of malaria. While visiting, Prema discovered the corrupt way the children were being inoculated, with medical workers splitting one dose between two children, using the same needle, and thereby, spreading the disease rather than preventing it.

This trip helped spawn an idea in Prema, who went on to invent the world's first auto-destruct syringe to help prevent the spread of diseases, such as AIDS, and to prevent doctors from double-dosing and addicts from sharing needles.

The development of this needle brought Prema to Canada, where he had an uncle who offered to introduce him to the necessary patent lawyers to get it filed; their offices were in the nation's capital.

The lawyer's office stood across the street from the courthouse, where university students and business men and women often frequented, in the summer to have lunch out on the lawn, and in the winter to seek shelter between the massive buildings.

Prema, who was temporarily renting a flat downtown, thought of this as a halfway point for his daily walk to work, and he liked to stand leaning up against the massive base of the statues of former prime ministers and sip a cup of tea before going to his next appointments. He was an extremely handsome man, no longer the gawky teenager of yesteryear. He opted for Zegna suits, French cuff shirts, and Italian silk ties, and loathed anything common. These were all things he had in common with Uncle Harry, who only afforded himself the best, a trait, no doubt, passed on to the both of them from Pappy. Prema was quite polished and felt it was working class to sit at picnic tables and eat. He preferred meetings at five star hotels and Michelin starred restaurants. Sipping tea out of a Styrofoam cup was not something he liked doing, and he was attempting, with great difficulty, to ease into a country that seemed to have no culture.

It was culture shock, really, as he went from having nothing, including no self-esteem, to going to a country seeped in culture, ethics, and class systems, and then to Canada, which was different from anything he'd known before. He took the advice his grandfather had given him, which was reiterated by the many bosses who took Prema under their wings and trained him in what was not written in the company brochures. One such boss was a man by the name of Giles Fletcher, who considered it his duty to inform Prema about life, as he grew very fond of him and felt a sense of obligation to Prema. This helpfulness was often aroused by those older than Prema as he grew up, as there seemed to be an air of innocence about him that made people want to help him and, in this case, guide him. One of the greatest bits of advice to Prema was when he said to the then young and impressionable man, "*Son, in this life, you have* to be *twice as good to be equal*, due to the olive color of your skin." Prema took this verbatim and worked ceaselessly. He soon found that he was twice as good as most at most things.

The fact that women were making themselves available to him went unnoticed as he continued on with his interests: church, tennis, and work. These were what made him happy, and as it appeared to bring him balance in his life, he never considered altering his behavior for anyone.

"Prema, I can work late, if you need me to," Brenda said flirtatiously.

"Its six o'clock!" said Prema, restless from staying in one place for so long. "I'm going to play some tennis."

"I play tennis," she continued in her quest.

At that moment, her husband walked in sporting a baseball cap, "Hi, I'm Steve, Brenda's husband," at which point she turned bright red and went to get her purse.

"Goodnight, Brenda, Steve," Prema gestured, also heading for the door, painfully unaware that the secretary had the hots for him.

This was typical Premalal. It could have been any woman; she could have been nude, and he would not have noticed, because he was too immersed in his own world and what he wanted to do.

That was until he met a certain young lady who entered the office to visit a childhood friend, John, who was one of the lawyers at the firm in which Prema was consulting.

"Hey, John, any word from Alison?" Alison was John's sister, who was now living out west.

"She's doing really well. All that reading has led to her to becoming a writer!" he proudly exclaimed.

"Wow, that's fantastic. Any new loves?" she continued.

Then one of the secretaries poked her head through the door and said, "John, you're wanted in the meeting with the patent lawyers."

"Sorry, love, another time?" John kissed his friend on the cheek.

"You know it. Just pass by the house anytime; you know my mother's apple pies are always in stock!"

"That's until Rudi and I attack them!" he laughed. He started to walk away, but bumped into Prema's shoulder.

"I'm sorry, Mr. Alvis, I was just coming to the meeting," John apologized.

"No, no that's fine," Prema stuttered. "I just needed some clarifications," he said, with his eyes glued to Beya.

"Oh," John said, realizing that an introduction was in order, "this is one of my oldest friends, Beya."

"Beya Cross," she said smiling and extending her hand forward.

"Premalal Alvis," he said with a warmth she immediately trusted.

"Very nice to meet you," she continued, not knowing where this was going, based on the intensity with which he stared.

John, picking up on the tension between the two, decided to join in. "Yes, Mr. Alvis is an inventor and businessman extraordinaire! If you don't mind me saying," he said.

"Really, what type of business," Beya inquired, interested.

"Fashion," he said without thinking.

"Fashion?" both John and Beya said in unison.

"Uh, I'm sorry, have to get to that meeting," John said. "I'll leave you two alone." John carried on, not sure what Prema's declaration was all about. *After all, he was consulting with us on getting his invention patented. What fashion would he be referring to?* thought John.

"Yes, as a matter of fact," Prema said, "I've been searching for a representative for a Thai silk evening wear line. Would you know of anyone? I mean, you are clearly fashionable, more so than I've seen here in Ottawa. I'm guessing you might know something about fashion?"

Beya smiled. *How did he know I was a model?* she thought.

"Perhaps we could meet for tea," Prema said. "I don't know your schedule; are you free now?" he added, trying to seize the moment for fear of never seeing her again.

As it was the middle of the day, Beya agreed to have tea with Prema, and by the time high tea at the Four Season's was over, it was 9:00 p.m., and she had divulged as much to him as he had to her. This was Prema's strength, being charming and extricating as much information about someone as possible. It was a strength he picked up during his formative years. His life had taught him to be as resourceful as possible, in order to seize opportunities as they came along. Beya was now his new opportunity.

They walked in strangers and walked out holding hands; it was really that quick. So it did not shock anyone to know that two days later, he proposed, and three weeks after that, they were married!

Everything was fast with Prema. He had an impatience that made him restless and gave him a need to do everything he ever dreamed of right away.

Beya was his sheet anchor. She was a constant in his world, which with her was centered and whole. With this union came the blessings of two children, who brought them both so much joy that they became the center of their universes. Two, he insisted, were more than enough, for he wanted to be able to give then all that he never had.

Therein grew interdependency so strong between the two that nothing worked unless they were together. It was never clear who needed whom more, as Prema demand Beya's whole attention, and she seemed happy to oblige, no matter what direction he deemed fit, which wasn't a bad thing, as he was well-grounded in his faith and his heart was only and always about family.

Although the couple was close, it was not until Prema's deep-rooted need to go back to Ceylon surfaced that their marriage reached a fork in the road; the few good memories of his childhood that he held onto plagued him, and no matter how good his and Beya's life seemed in the West, his soul beckoned for the East.

❧

WHEN PREMA LEFT, HE had every intention of returning. He lovingly kissed the two little ones who sat mesmerized while watching TV.

"Bye, darling, now be good to Mommy and your sister," Prema said, hugging his little blond son, who he called his Meccano set baby. For he used to admire the little boy on the Meccano set box and tell his mother, "I'm going to have a son like that," a statement that was always met with laughter. "How can you have a blonde, blue-eyed son? Have you gone mad?" she would tease, but he believed it deep in his heart and knew God was listening.

"Bye, darling," he said and picked up his baby girl.

"Daddy, where are you going?" she asked innocently.

"I'm going home to see my mommy in Ceylon."

"But, Daddy, isn't there a war there?"

"Yes, darling, but Daddy will be all right."

"Daddy, can you sing that song to me again?"

"Darling, Daddy has to go," Beya said, getting emotional.

"I have time," he smiled and lovingly began to sing:

"When you were a little girl and lived across the street,
We would walk to the candy store, … la-la, la-la, la-la …"

"Oh, Daddy, I love you." She smiled, batting her big brown eyes and pulling him into her spell. "And I love both of you so much!" Prema said. By this time, Beya was sobbing in the background, unable to control her emotions for the family she loved so much.

"I love you infinity," shouted Alex.

"And I love you Bentley," shouted Anastasia, who thought her brother was talking about the make of her grandmother's car and tried to outwit him.

"Okay then, you two go back to watching the movie with Nana," which was short for *Nagy mamma* in Hungarian.

There was audible silence in the car as they drove to the airport, both Prema and Beya wanting to say so much, but instead, saying nothing at all.

All week he had felt a need to give Beya something, anything at all. It was his way of trying to say something and she knew it. She had resigned herself to the fact that he was no longer happy in Canada and she knew he needed to go.

As they held each other in what they wished could be an endless embrace, each telling the other that they loved each other, he tucked a gold charm bracelet into her hand. Before she could react, he was gone.

The charm bracelet was made up of things that brought joy to both of them. He had gone out of his way to make it special. The charms varied from a crucifix to a key to baby booties, a St. Anthony medallion, and a small medallion that looked like the outline of a country, which was inscribed "*Our Destiny Awaits.*" It was the same thing she had written on a picture he had asked for of her just two days after they met. Not knowing why, she had written "*Our Destiny Awaits.*"

The pain of separation was unbearable. Phone calls were never long enough and physical distance created a longing so deep that it resonated into everyone's daily life. It was when her little boy came to her one night and asked, "Who is going to comb my hair?" that Beya fell apart. He was nine years old and yet that was what was plaguing him, the way his father used to comb his hair.

So when everything was settled, Beya followed her heart, packed the children and their dog, Boris, and left for Ceylon.

Erzsike was devastated. Her heart fell when she saw all the suitcases and her darling little grandchildren ready to leave.

"You realize this is my fault," said Erzsike as she stood in the departure hall, holding her daughter's hand.

How is this your fault?" cried Beya.

"Because I was the one who used to sing to you this song as a baby; somehow I always knew. ..."

"What song, Mamma?"

"It's called *In the Misty Moonlight*. I can't remember the words exactly.

In the misty moonlight
far away island
any place is so fine
as long as you'll be mine ...

Anyway, Beya, it seems ironic that that is where you are off to. ..." cried her mother.

Beya hugged her parents tightly, comforted by the fact that they still were together, despite the many upheavals. She tenderly placed her children's hands in hers and led them down the jet way ramp, into the plane, and off to their new life.

CHAPTER TWENTY-SEVEN

FARAWAY ISLAND

The very thing that scares us ends up being
our path to freedom.

WHAT STARTED OUT AS AN ADVENTURE, ENDED UP changing them as individuals and as a couple.

So many things were unveiled about Prema when they began their journey to the East, that not making the move to Ceylon would have resulted in a marriage to a man she would have never really known. An entirely different side of who he was, what he had suppressed, and what he felt slowly surfaced, so that the understanding between them became infinite.

Despite the large age gap, the love between Prema and Beya was intense, quite unbeknown to their children, who assumed that Mommy loved their father more based on her extremely demonstrative and loving ways and his inability to reciprocate.

He was a very intense and complex character whose tumultuous childhood left him with deep-rooted scars. On the surface he exuded charm and confidence, but not too far from the surface was that insecure boy who needed constant reassurance and unending understanding. When things did not go well for Prema, he would lash out with an abusive tongue, one he had inherited, no doubt, from his father. Beya at first shied away from him whenever he entered what she often referred to as his *dark mood*. Over time, however, she learnt what made him tick and what triggered his emotions. For her, not take this into account would have made Beya insensitive and unobservant. She was none of these.

Beya experienced a complete myriad of emotions with

Prema, who was a joy to be with because of his humor, his intelligence, and his wit, but she also understood why he would hide treats in the cupboard without showing anyone, and why he shouted. She knew when he was approachable and when he was not, but most of all, she loved him enough to take the good with the bad and not to expect him to change. Ultimately, she knew that this marriage was the most important thing in her life.

She had made the right decision to marry him, and her father's prediction was right. *"That Prema is an empire builder; if he loses one empire, he'll go on to build another."*

ｃ◎ｃ

"SPUNK!" IT WAS A nickname she had called Prema for years because of his innate ability to bring joy to the most simple and mundane things.

"Do you love me, Spunk?" she lovingly teased.

At which point he would always act Attention Deficit and say, "What, Bubbika?"

"Do you love me?" she would repeat, squeezing his arm.

To which he'd always say, "Nope!" and kiss her forehead with a twinkle in his eye.

Behind closed doors, though, passion ignited between them. All seemingly conservative expressions of affection were always contradicted in private. Beya knew him inside and out. The way he looked at her and the innuendos he alluded to all resulted in this gratifying union, which held them together even when all they could do was fight.

ｃ◎ｃ

THEIR LIVES HAD BEEN full, attempting different businesses

together, losing money, and making money. Experiencing the highs and the lows of a civil war and witnessing the devastation of the tsunami first hand.

When the ferocity of the sea came crashing onto the island that day, the family had been on safari in a jeep, many miles from sea. It was Boxing Day and this was a treat for the whole family, so they all got ready early morning in order to be the first at the park entrance gates.

As Prema was in charge, tardiness was not an option. They began the game drive, but noticed instantly that something was wrong. There were no animals at all, even the birds were not to be seen. The ground trembled and Prema grew quite concerned by the behavior of the animals in the park. It was at this moment that the Tracker's CB radio rang and told them about a huge wave that hit the coast.

"Oh my God, you mean like a tsunami?" asked the children from the backseat.

"Yes, tsunami, that's the word they used. My friend kept saying a Japanese tourist kept yelling it on the beach, trying to get people to run for cover," said the shaken driver.

"Right now we have to get back inland as fast as we can," said Prema, ready to take the wheel. "Sunil, you're too shaken; I'll drive. We must get to Colombo as soon as possible."

The journey back was filled with uncertainty, as many of the roads were flooded and people were running chaotically back and forth across the fields and the streets. Fear gripped everyone, as people, both locals and tourists were scrambling on the road running with no direction and from the fear of the ocean's deadly grasp. Waves crashed on and rolled off the street, carrying with them the debris, tortured bodies, and mangled vehicles in their path. The whole experience was surreal. They sat dazed as the terrorizing scene unfolded before their eyes.

"Oh my God, Prema, we have to do something; we have to help someone. ... I can't watch this," Beya cried, edging towards opening the car door.

"Don't touch your door, Beya. They will force themselves into our vehicle. I'll stop over there," said Prema protectively as he pulled over into the parking lot of a church that sat on a hill. Many people were there clinging to the walls of the church and praying, and others used the height of the land as a vantage point from which to see the ocean's evil hand.

They all got out of the car to view the destruction. "Beya, I want you to stay here with the children. Do not move, do you understand?"

"Daddy where are you going?" cried the children, horrified at the thought of their father leaving.

"Of course I will take care of them, but where are you going?" Beya asked clinging to his arm.

"I know this village, so I won't get lost. I'll take Sunil and search the area for survivors to see what will be required in the rescue efforts before we get back to Colombo."

The children cried, but with hugs and reassuring words, Prema started his decent into the village.

As Prema edged his way towards the coast, memories of his childhood flooded his mind. He had once walked as far as this village from Colombo, for refuge from his father. It seemed so unfathomable that this once calm haven had become a scene of such utter destruction.

He walked through the strewn trees, around disheveled cars, and past flooded huts. Coconuts, slippers, and clothing lay scattered across sand, which was now filled with muddy wells of salty sea water. The smell of dead fish and dead bodies began to permeate the air, until it became so bad survivors began wrapping cloth over their faces to mask the haunting smell of decomposing flesh.

"Dear God, how did this happen? What happened? These thoughts gripped Prema as he approached the area in which he remembered staying one terrible night so many years before. Memorabilia, pictures, pots, and pans were stuck in the sand, as if set up for play, but it was anything but that.

The reality of the situation was overwhelming. Prema's eyes searched the area. He picked up a crying child and tried to console her, and then he found the hand of her mother reaching out from beneath a tree.

"Sunil, over here, help me!" The two men pushed and rocked the trunk until they finally gained enough momentum to push it off the lady. She had been badly injured. Prema gave her mouth to mouth, as she had nearly drowned, but had clung to the tree to keep afloat. She had ultimately been crushed beneath its overbearing weight once the water had receded. Air rescue units were already in the area and police were alerted to airlift yet another victim.

As Prema scanned the area, his eyes tried to make sense of his surroundings, which were now alien to even the most senior residents of the area. He looked for signs of life everywhere. Then, suddenly, his eye caught something slightly familiar, floating in a puddle. Its red and purple colors contrasted against the black murky sand, and he immediately made his way towards the object. As he bent down to see what it was, his heart skipped a beat, for it was his old familiar sling shot, which he had given so lovingly so many years ago to his dearest ally, Edison. Prema pulled it from the mud. He etched his fingers across the engraved initials. P.A., over and over again, as if drawing comfort from the touch. As his fingers outlined the P and the A, he reminisced and found himself in a tsunami of emotion. "Edison, *machan, aiya,*" Prema murmured to himself, realizing the implications of this find.

A hand of comfort rested on his shoulder, and an old man leaned around Prema to help him to his feet. A gasp of utter joy escaped the old man's lips as he extolled a joy that resonated from deep within his soul.

"*Sudu Baba,* is that you? Premalal? You are a *Sudu* Mahathaya now!" he shouted with heaven-sent elation.

"Edison? Edison? Is that you?" Prema exclaimed, and the two men hugged each other, clinging to each other's arms, actually jumping in utter jubilation.

"My Prema, God has been good to you! Look at you, so tall and handsome! How, *Machan?* I heard you made your way to England. What happened to your life? Did you find someone? Do you have children? Oh, how I've prayed for you, my dear friend."

"And I you," said Prema, crying at the sight of his greatest ally.

As the day moved into night, the three men walked towards the car where Prema's family had been anxiously waiting for their return. It was an unusually happy occasion amidst a horrific backdrop. In many ways, it reminded Prema of his childhood, pockets of happiness in a sea of mistreatment and sadness. Edison had never gone back after that day so many years before. Instead, he returned to his village and began working at a hotel. Eventually, he rose up in management and entered local politics.

It was later revealed to Prema that Edison had campaigned for the betterment of the lives of children. He had risen to such a level that he made it possible to set up the first of many centers for abused children. The centers were affectionately named *The Spirit of Prema*.

࿈

AFTER 15 YEARS OF living in Ceylon, Beya had seen and felt it all.

The homes in their area were so close together that people could unintentionally eavesdrop on the lives surrounding their yard.

The highs, the lows, the laughter, and the tears permeated the walls by day and by night. The smells and sounds of karapincha and rampe sizzling its nutty aroma into the air, made everyone ravenous, for not an hour would pass when the members of Beya's family would ask, "What's for dinner?" On lazy evenings, she hoped that they would satiate their imagined hunger by taking an extra breath or two, for one could almost taste the food that was cooking and be able to judge if there was too much or too little of one spice or the other.

The house sat in the middle of this traditional atmosphere, where each morning they awoke to the sound of monk's chanting, followed by the sound of the wailing mosque. They were right in the center of it all, the potpourri of religion and culture that was all so pronounced and once so very unfamiliar to her.

Even the garden looked unfamiliar, from the lush bougainvillea's to the staunch bamboo tree, which stood erect, unwavering, unbendable, just straight. Its branches shot proudly upwards to the warmth of the sunlit sky and seemed to stretch itself towards the Poya moon, providing a place for tree rats to nest and for flying bats, which would encircle the yard, ready to pluck guava and custard apple from the grove, to rest.

Most things were quite foreign to her, as she looked to find the likeness in the differences that she came across.

Eventually, over time, the bougainvillea seemed to need her to quench their thirst and the jasmine seemed to smell sweeter when she commented on its lovely fragrance, but the bamboo tree remained stoic and unaffected by her presence.

The indifference Beya felt towards certain unfamiliar things remained throughout the years, for she was open to anything and everything, so if it didn't make an effort, she put it down to fate and continued with her busy life.

Tremendous change reared its way upon the canvas of the island. Buildings started growing around them, and views were altered, both visually and mentally.

There came over the country a new age of less tradition and more growth. Although predictable, these changes were seamless and happened gradually over time.

Fifteen years had passed and the day came to leave Sri Lanka and return to her roots. Family had been her life, and so it became a natural progression to follow her children, who were now starting their higher education back home.

On the final day of packing, Beya felt very hot and restless and seemed to need to sit down. She was drawn outside to the upper deck of their bedroom, a place where she'd barely had time to sit over the years. A new-found breeze suddenly existed there since the neighbor's house had been torn down.

That neighbor had been an awful old woman who constantly shouted at her servants and who used to pour acid on the bamboo tree, as it blocked her view into their yard, preventing her from eavesdropping.

"Foreigner!" the old woman would screech from inside her window whenever the children splashed too loudly or laughed too joyously while playing and swimming in the pool. Beya shook her head at the thought. Despite the many injuries the bamboo tree endured, it managed to outlive the old woman and every member of that household. It now enjoyed the breeze that ran through its branches like never before.

As Beya sat there, deep in thought, her life in review, she tried to listen to the activities of the people who now lived in the high-rises surrounding their dwarfed and isolated house.

One could still hear the words, but they were the sounds of expatriates with different dialects. The realization that the once foreign Sinhalese had become very comforting to her surprised her, as she fought to hear its familiar sound. It had become a language, a culture, and a tradition that had become her own.

She pondered about the person she once was as she landed in this country and the person she'd become. She wondered if she had made any impact at all on the people or the country during her tenure there. She thought about silly things like her insistence to teach all her children's friends how to say "thank you" after every meal. They always conceded because they said, "Mrs. Alvis is such a good cook, unlike our cooks at home," but she would always take the time to explain why everyone deserved to be thanked, even the hired hand. In the years that followed, she was thanked for the lessons she had taught and for the sincere advice she had offered only because she genuinely cared.

She wondered if she had forsaken her own country for this one and whether it would take her back with love and understanding. Ultimately, she knew that she did it all for the love of a man who deserved to be happy in a land where he was robbed of happiness as a child.

She thought about the voyage her "princess *svuite*" dresser had taken from childhood to adulthood, from Northern Star to Tear Drop Isle; what a story it could tell.

Beya was overcome with emotion at the thought of leaving this land that had played such an intrinsic part of her life. She clung onto every memory, unable to let them go, believing that by selling this house, she would lose them completely. As tears streamed down her face, a deep sense of sorrow filled her heart, and Beya began to write the following words.

GOODBYE SWEET FRIEND, GOODBYE ...

Should the day come when my time here is done ...
And we can no longer be as one ...
I shall not question why,
Why it has come to this goodbye.
I'll pack my bags, stare up at your sky
Wipe my tears and thank God on high,
Ocean breeze will caress my face,
And the sun will bend down to embrace
My soul, this life, will never erase
The incredible memories of my home: this place.

Sweet Ceylon, perhaps you will forget about me,
But in my children you will always be,
Through their veins history runs deep,
A culture, a heritage that will always reap
The rewards of your greatness, they can turn to with pride,
Guiding them through life, like a mother by their side,

So perhaps in some small measure Ceylon
You will know how I feel
By these words written upon this reel ...

As she finished writing these words, she sobbed deeply, from the very depth of her soul. Life without this place overwhelmed her. Upon reflection, she realized that the intertwining journeys of her predecessors had now met her on route. She wiped away her tears, took a deep breath, folded the paper she had written on, and lovingly tucked it into a crevasse in the wall, like a secret covenant.

A breeze from a storm at sea began to rustle the branches in the garden under the poya moon sky. The once stoic bamboo tree suddenly let itself bow down to touch her face. The arid land of unfamiliarity was quenched by the graceful touch of the bamboo leaves that gently pet her brow. In that epiphany moment she awakened to the knowledge that her "secret place," her weeping willow tree from her childhood, had been there all along, protecting Beya and her family throughout the years.

She touched its soft leaves and thanked it. "At ease, my unfamiliar guard, my long lost friend. ..."

In the misty moonlight, this far away island had truly made life come

full circle ...

CPSIA information can be obtained at www.ICGtesting.com
Printed in the USA
LVOW08*0703071214

417434LV00002B/3/P